ANTON'S GRACE

Braxians - Book 1

REGINE ABEL

CONTENTS

READING ORDER

The Braxians series is part of the Veredian Chronicles universe. While this book can be read as standalone with a complete romance arc and no cliffhanger, to fully enjoy the overarching story, it is recommended to read both series in the following order:

1. Escaping Fate, Veredian Chronicles 1
2. Blind Fate, Veredian Chronicles 2
3. Raising Amalia, Veredian Chronicles 3
4. Anton's Grace, Braxians 1
5. Twist of Fate, Veredian Chronicles 4
6. Ravik's Mercy, Braxians 2
7. Hands of Fate, Veredian Chronicles 5
8. Krygor's Hope, Braxians 3
9. Defying Fate, Veredian Chronicles 6
10. Keran's Dawn, Braxians 4

ANTON'S GRACE

Revenge is a patient beast.

Grace is in trouble. Her agent and ex-boyfriend, Marcus, has fled, leaving her stranded on the Venus Hive pleasure barge. His creditors want compensation and with Marcus nowhere to be found, they've decided Grace will do nicely. Desperate for help, she turns to Anton Myers, the wealthy and ruthless owner of the Hive Network. He agrees to help her. The terms: anything he wants for six months.

Anton has waited a long time for this moment. Grace may not remember him, but he hasn't forgotten her. Signing herself over to his every command will not keep her safe. A Braxian never forgets a slight to his honor. And Grace will pay… with interest.

Anton's Grace is a twisted tale of unlikely second chances that will leave you squirming in your seat. Can you stomach the darkness?

This dark romance is not for the faint of heart. It contains explicit scenes of violence and deal with topics such as domestic violence and slavery. Sensitive readers please abstain.

DEDICATION

A special thank you to my beta readers whose feedback has been invaluable in my first venture into the dark romance genre. In particular, much love to Lynn Kline Underwood for holding my hand through my angsts-ridden bouts of self-doubt, and Debra McDuffie for all your help.

Samantha Hanson, you are one amazing lady. The unexpected kindness and support you have shown me went above and beyond. From the bottom of my heart, thank you.

To my family, especially you Mom and Dad, no daughter has been more blessed than I have been. I love you.

PROLOGUE

Anton's Grace is a ***dark romance***. This book contains explicit sexual brutality, dubious consent, and graphic violence that *will* be disturbing to some people. If you are a sensitive reader then this book is NOT for you.

PLEASE HEED THIS WARNING.

While it is recommended to read it as part of the Veredian Chronicles to better understand the Braxians, it is **not required**. You can skip this book and still fully enjoy the rest of the Veredians and the other Braxian books.

Otherwise, welcome to Venus Hive!

CHAPTER 1
GRACE

My mouth was dry, and my heart hammered as I walked up to the sleek reception desk of the Venus Hive headquarters. From the moment I began a serious singing career, I dreamt of entering these walls where the most influential man in the entertainment industry reigned. However, I never imagined it would be to come begging for a handout.

When Marcus and I first arrived on the Venus Hive space station a couple of weeks ago, I believed we had finally hit the big time. The station could hold a city of six million people. Although labeled a pleasure barge, it exclusively catered to entertainment in all its forms. From tribal dance shows to classic or popular concerts, exotic animal racing to casinos, dance clubs to fetish clubs and everything else in-between, Venus Hive had it all. It didn't matter which alien species you belonged to, you were guaranteed to find something entertaining – and I intended to be part of that entertainment. With Marcus as my charismatic agent, we were bound to move in no time from the Commons into the VIP area.

Then things went south.

An attractive redhead sat at the reception desk; her attention focused on her computer. I cast a nervous look at the sexy, but tasteful art pieces covering the white walls. Most of them depicted dancing babes in lingerie or couples of all pairings locked in steamy embraces. I wasn't much into BDSM but one picture of a beautiful naked male being flogged by his gorgeous Domme was especially striking. The artist captured the perfect mix of pain and pleasure on the man's face, as well as his trustful submission to his powerful Domme.

My footsteps were drowned out by the chatter of a small crowd gathered in the hall. Their numbered badges and constant fidgeting indicated they were here to audition. As though sensing my approach, the redhead looked up and greeted me with a polite smile. I wiped my sweaty palms on the colorful print of my dress.

"Welcome to Venus Hive. How may I help you?"

"I–I wish to see Mr. Anton Myers, please," I said, cursing my trembling voice.

"Do you have an appointment, Miss…?"

"Hopper… Grace Hopper," I said. "And no… I'm afraid I don't have an appointment, but it's quite important."

She blinked, her smile becoming strained. "I see. If you're looking for work or wish to audition, please fill a form at one of the terminals over there and—"

"I'm not here for a gig," I interrupted, trying not to sound rude. I glanced at the holographic nameplate on the desk which read 'Dana Brooks.' "Look, Dana… I know you probably get a hundred freaks in here every day wanting a piece of Mr. Myers. I promise you, that's not my case. This is an urgent personal matter." I leaned over the desk, pleading. "My life is *literally* in your hands right now. I only need a few minutes of his time, then I'll leave without a fuss."

Dana leaned back in her chair to assess me. She pursed her lips while giving me a once over. I felt happier than ever to have settled for one of my more modest outfits, consisting of a colorful sarong draped as a halter dress and medium heeled pumps. Had I worn my usual skin-tight, barely-there dresses and fuck-me shoes, Dana would have already turned me out on my ears. With a sigh, she tapped the com system and spoke into the microphone hanging beside her cheek from her earpiece.

"Mr. Myers, there's a Grace Hopper here requesting to see you on an urgent private matter."

I hated my last name. As an infant, my parents abandoned me at the orphanage with only Grace pinned to my clothes. Mr. Carston, the caretaker, thought it amusing to give me the last name Hopper. Then I turned twelve and Carston requesting the presence of his little Hopper took on a completely different meaning. After fleeing the orphanage, I couldn't afford a name change. By the time I could, my name as a singer was established enough that changing it would have harmed my fledgling career more than it was worth. And so it stayed.

Dana listened quietly to Mr. Myers' response, her gaze never leaving mine. My heart pounded into my throat while I awaited the verdict.

Her eyes narrowed. "Yes, Mr. Myers." She ended the com and straightened in her chair. "Well, it seems you have your wish, Ms. Hopper. Mr. Myers will see you immediately. Please proceed to Elevator One, and I will grant you access to the penthouse." She gestured toward the left side of the reception desk.

Relieved, I beamed at her. "Thank you… Thank you very much, Ms. Brooks."

Dana's face softened as she smiled back. "Good luck, Ms. Hopper."

I'm going to need a fuck-ton of it too.

Negotiating wasn't my thing. I didn't know shit about it. Contracts, management, making deals, Marcus always took care of that crap. My strength was performing. Put me on stage, tell me what kind of show you wanted, and I'd rock the house. I loved the eyes of the public on me, making them drool and go wild. That, I could handle. A ruthless business shark like Anton Myers was a completely different challenge. It scared the living daylights out of me.

I swallowed past the lump lodging in my throat every time I thought of Marcus. He was my best friend. My only friend. How could he have abandoned me like this? Nothing made sense. Without him, I felt lost. It was pathetic that at twenty-two, I should be so helpless without someone looking after me.

But now wasn't the time to dwell on my former lover.

I followed the spotless white and chrome hallway beside the reception desk. Five elevators numbered two to eleven stood on each side of the corridor. In the center, at the end of the corridor, Elevator One, framed with luminescent tribal patterns, beckoned me. The doors opened at my approach and closed behind me as soon as I stepped inside. Without any input from me, the car ascended to the penthouse.

The doors opened onto a stern looking middle-aged man. His informally chic attire didn't hide the muscular body underneath. Everything about him screamed former mercenary or space pirate.

"Ms. Hopper, if you would follow me," he said, waving me in.

Without waiting for my response, he started down the hallway left of the sumptuous living area. After knocking on a closed door at the end, he opened it and walked in first.

"Ms. Hopper is here to see you."

"Thank you, William," a deep, gravelly voice said.

As soon as I entered, William walked out, closing the door behind him without giving me a chance to thank him. I swallowed and looked at the massive man sitting behind the desk. Obsidian eyes slowly undressed me before locking with mine. The intensity of his stare felt like a punch in the gut. I averted my eyes, unable to withstand his gaze. A strange smirk stretched his lips. I couldn't tell if it was mocking or pleased.

The air filtering vent whispered above my head while I withstood Mr. Myers' examination. He pointed at a chair. "Have a seat, Ms. Hopper."

Grateful for the opportunity to get off my trembling legs, I obeyed. The empire red leather and mahogany chair was both beautiful and comfortable. Only Anton Myers could afford such extravagant Terran antiques. I crossed my legs demurely and folded my hands on my lap.

Why couldn't this be an audition?

Then I wouldn't be such a nervous wreck. Performing was my life. If the judges didn't like my performance, they only needed to tell me what was wrong, what they wanted, and I'd do it. I liked following orders. It was easy – no need to think, worry or second guess your choices; just do.

"Let me guess, Ms. Hopper; you need help dealing with the… unpleasant situation your agent has left you in." It wasn't a question.

My eyes widened. "How do you—?"

"I make it my business to know what happens on my space station, Ms. Hopper."

"O–Of course, you would." With that one sentence, Anton managed to throw me completely off my already shaky game. "So, you understand my situation?"

Anton leaned back and, with his elbows on the armrests, pressed his fingertips together. "I understand your boyfriend dumped you. He left behind a large debt his creditors expect you to pay on his behalf… immediately."

I tucked a stray strand of hair behind my ear. "He's not my boyfriend," I said in a small voice.

Anton narrowed his eyes. "Since when?"

"A–A while," I said, unnerved by the curtness of his voice. "At least a year."

Anton's brutish face twisted in anger. "Don't fucking lie to me."

Anton Myers was not a handsome man. The hybrid son of a human woman and a Braxian male, he greatly favored his father. A prominent forehead and thick brow ridge gifted him with a permanent scowl. His broad nose was flatter than a human's and his jutting square jaw was wider. Anton's one redeeming facial trait was his mouth; plump, perfectly drawn lips. He wasn't repulsive, but he would never win a beauty contest. And right now, his anger intimidated the hell out of me.

"I'm not lying."

He was out of his chair in an instant, circling the desk to tower over me. I gaped up at him, my blood rushing through my veins. How could I forget how ridiculously tall and large Anton was? I had to lie back in my chair to look up at his face, my ankle brushing against his leg.

"Barely six months ago, I saw you with Marcus Gayle on Lilith Hive. You seemed quite cozy then and he claimed you as his woman."

"I promise, Mr. Myers, we were no longer together then. Marcus said it would stop customers harassing me." I breathed heavily, my pulse racing.

Anton's features lost their angry edge. Tension bled out of him while his eyes roamed like a caress over my body. Leaning down, he rested his large hands on the armrests of my chair, his face inches from mine. My breath caught in my throat. I felt like a rabbit caught in the snares of a predator.

His eyes bore into mine. "Do you know the size of his debt, Ms. Hopper?"

"Ten… Ten million credits."

He snorted. "That was two weeks ago. The loan sharks have a ten percent interest rate per week once you miss your payment date. The debt is now over twelve million credits."

My breath rushed out of me. How was I ever going to repay that? Convincing Anton to front me ten million had already seemed like an unlikely sale, but twelve?

"Assuming I decide to help you out of this predicament," Anton said, his eyes studying every inch of my face, "how do you intend to repay me?"

For the hundredth time since the thugs barged into my hotel room, I kicked myself for bailing on my contract negotiation meetings. It was mind-numbingly boring. With Marcus taking care of me, it had been a non-issue. That also meant I was clueless as to what kind of numbers I brought in.

"I was hoping you'd let me perform for you in one of your venues. You would keep all the proceeds, minus whatever minimum I need for food and lodging. I draw good crowds—"

Anton threw his head back and laughed. Loudly. He straightened, shaking his head at me like I had lost my mind. He sauntered over to his mini-bar. While he poured a couple of drinks, I stared at his back, unable to decide if I felt more confused or offended. I was a good singer with a large following.

"Ms. Hopper, your 'performances' wouldn't generate enough revenue to repay me in ten lifetimes."

I fisted my hands, outraged. "My performances kept Marcus and me living in comfort for years!"

He finished preparing the drinks and prowled towards me, his gait fluid and confident. I reluctantly took the glass he offered, fighting the urge to throw it at his smirking face.

"No, it hasn't," Anton said. He leaned against the edge of his desk, his tight t-shirt stretching over his chest. "You have a decent voice, but what you do on stage isn't singing. You draw crowds because you handle your mic like a stiff cock, and every male in the audience fantasizes it's theirs."

My face heated. Marcus spent a lot of time showing me how to move on stage to arouse my audience. It bothered me at first because it didn't feel so much like singing as it did stripping, but it drew a lot of people. In no time, teasing and flirting with my fans became a turn on. Over the years, Marcus taught me to find a lot of things normal.

"People don't pay for fantasies unless they come true," Anton said. "You attracted crowds that paid very little to see you but paid much more for the extras that your boyfriend provided – mainly illegal recreational drugs and black-market goods."

"But—"

"Don't argue with me," Anton said. "I never talk out of my ass. If you had listened to me when I told you to wake up six months ago, you wouldn't be in this predicament."

Anton downed the contents of his glass in one shot and went back to his mini bar for a refill. The first time I met Anton was on the Lilith Hive pleasure barge where Marcus had managed to book me a few shows. It was one of the seven entertainment space stations of Anton's Hive Network. Back then, although I still hadn't managed to perform in one of the elite venues, we were living large. While looking for Marcus during the grand opening of a new club, I ran into Anton. I had been thrilled to meet the big boss until he started giving me speeches. According to him, I lived an illusion and needed to learn the business of being an artist. Otherwise, sooner or later, I would find myself out in the cold and starving. I dismissed him as a prophet of doom.

Hindsight is a bitch.

"If you won't take my singing as repayment, what else would you accept to help me? I need this."

Anton gave me a cold stare. "You know exactly what the price is. Let's stop playing games, Ms. Hopper and speak terms instead."

Yeah, I had known the price all along. However, if he made the demand rather than me offering, I could accuse him of being a bastard rather than call myself a whore. With a stiff nod, I downed the glass of brandy. It burned going down, and I couldn't hold back a cough.

Can't even handle my damn liquor.

"What are your terms?" I asked, my eyes cast down.

"Six months, anything I want." His sharp tone made it clear there would be no negotiation.

My jaw dropped. "Six months? That's crazy!"

His face hardened. "You're in serious need of a reality check, little girl. The debt is twelve million credits – that's two million a month to spread your legs and do what you're told. Even our highest paid escort doesn't earn that much. Is your pussy made of gold?"

The comment made me flinch. He was right; I hadn't thought this through – I never did. All things considered, this was an extremely generous offer. I just never realized it would be for this long. The problem was, I had dependence issues. While I embraced my sensuality, I found it hard to separate intimacy and emotions. Hence I didn't sleep around. I got too easily attached. Six months was a long time to belong to someone and still look at them as a business arrangement, especially because Anton wasn't a man to become attached to.

Anton downed his second glass and slammed it on the mini bar.

"My offer is non-negotiable. You can take it or leave it. The door is right there," Anton said, pointing at it. "Good luck finding a better offer elsewhere."

I shifted in my chair, knowing there were no better offers. In my desperation, I had knocked on every other door.

"Of course… I–I understand, but… What does 'anything you want' actually mean?"

His eyes roamed over my body again. "Exactly what I said; anything I want."

"I'm not into that BDSM stuff," I said, shrinking into myself.

Instead of the angry outburst I expected, his expression softened. "I doubt you even know what you like, but I intend to find out." Anton walked over and lifted my chin before running his thumb over my lips. His touch was incredibly soft for such large, calloused hands. "You will give me anything I want, Grace, and that includes your obedience at all times, whatever the order, or face punishment. Do we have an agreement?"

The black pools of his eyes never left mine. It was hypnotic. We had an agreement before I even walked in here – I was that desperate. The thugs that broke into my hotel room last night made it clear that if they didn't get their money, they would have fun with me then sell me on the slave market. A pretty slave rarely remained so for long. If they sold me, who knew what kind of twisted pervert would buy me and own me for the rest of my days. At least, Anton was reputed to treat his women well and it would only be for a fixed term contract. Had he been human, I would have come to him first. But from all accounts, Braxian males had a low opinion of women and a twisted definition of what a relationship looked like – not that we would become a couple or anything.

"Yes, Mr. Myers," I said, my shoulders sagging. "We have an agreement."

His smile made me shudder. "Good girl," he whispered.

Anton straightened and leaned once more on the edge of his desk. He took away my empty glass and placed it beside him. "Kiss me," he said.

I got up from my chair, my hands twitching and my stomach fluttering. Anton was an impressive specimen of manhood. What his face lacked in attractiveness, his body more than made up for. The skin-tight black t-shirt molded the muscular outline of his chest. I stood between his parted legs and placed my hands on his waist. The heat coming off his body made my palms tingle. Anton gave me an expressionless look as I leaned forward and pressed my chest to his.

When I brushed my lips against his, a sudden throb between my legs took me by surprise. I hadn't had sex in more time than I cared to admit but didn't expect to be aroused by Anton. This was a relief considering, enjoyment or not, I was his for six months. Then again, power and authority always turned me on. Judging by my current reaction, maybe our arrangement wouldn't be so bad. I pressed my lips harder against his. His lips remained unresponsive, and I pulled back, baffled. He returned my gaze, his face void of emotion.

Oh shit... this is a test.

One I couldn't afford to fail. Switching into audition mode, I felt more in my element. I licked my lips slowly, seductively, while running my hands up his stomach to his chest. Leaning in again, I nipped at his lower lip before sucking on it. My thumbs circled his erect nipples while my tongue teased his lips until they finally parted. I tasted the brandy on his breath. A deep moan rumbled from his chest and triumph swept over me.

Gotcha.

I reveled in the sense of elation that washed over me as it always did when I made my audience go wild. Sinking my fingers in his long black hair, I deepened the kiss. Anton's large hands covered my ass, pressing me against him. I could feel his shaft hardening. The dull throbbing between my legs reminded me once more that it had been too long since I'd had a man. He fisted my hair and pulled my head back, breaking the kiss. His lips followed my jaw line down to my neck. My pulse thundered in my ears, disturbing the otherwise silent room. I shivered when his hand slipped under my sarong, caressing its way up the back of my thigh, over my ass and onto my back. I thought Anton would tear my dress off, but his hand slipped back down. He pulled back, although he kept one arm around me.

"No bra... I approve." His voice was thick with desire. "Lose the thong. From now on, you will not wear underwear unless I specifically tell you otherwise. I want free access to you at all times."

"Yes, Mr. Myers," I whispered, his commanding tone reverberating through me.

He snorted. "Considering you've just had your tongue down my throat, and I'm about to put my cock down yours, I think it's okay for you to call me Anton."

My face heated at his crude comment, and I instinctively licked my lips. The gesture didn't go unnoticed. Anton ran his thumb over my lips, swollen by his kisses.

"I think I'm going to enjoy our time together, Grace."

Anton looked over his shoulder and grabbed a datapad on his desk. He gave it a quick once over before extending it to me.

"This is our official agreement. Read it, sign it, and then I'll have your debt settled."

I took the datapad. Looking down at it in disbelief, the words blurred before me into a jumbled blob. "You already have a contract drawn up?"

"I told you I make it my business to know everything that happens on my space station. So yes, I knew you would come here and that there was a good chance you would accept my offer. Are you having second thoughts?"

I shook my head. "Where do I sign?"

"Didn't I just say read it?" Anton snapped. "Have you learned nothing from your current situation? You can't simply take what you're told on faith. Life isn't just about singing and looking pretty on stage. Read the damn contract so you know what you're committing to. How do you know I haven't changed its duration to a lifetime of indentured service?"

I felt hot and cold at the same time. He shouldn't have needed to tell me that. I was stupid and lazy when it came to this stuff. That's why I relied on Marcus. It was embarrassing that Anton saw my flaws so easily. Duly chastised, I sat back down on the empire chair and read the contract. Thankfully, it was concise with none of that convoluted lawyer crap.

After skimming through the first few clauses, I reached a worrisome one which stated I couldn't be sexually involved with a third party unless Anton ordered it. Did that mean he intended to lend me? Marcus hadn't been the faithful type, always pushing me for an open relationship. But that didn't work for me – I didn't share and didn't want to be shared. However, even if Anton confirmed that's what he meant, I was in no position to argue with him. Since I would sign regardless, leaving that fight to a later date seemed wiser.

Once done reading, I pressed my thumb on the signature box. He didn't hide the look of triumph on his face when I handed the datapad over. This was too easy. I came expecting to beg and plead. It almost felt like a setup. Disturbed by the thoughts racing through my mind, I watched him sit behind his desk and tap the com.

"Anton?" William's voice asked over the com.

"William, please see that Ms. Hopper's creditor issue is settled immediately. And make it clear, any further debt incurred by Marcus Gayle is his alone. Grace is under my protection."

"On it."

Anton ended the call. His pitch-black eyes rested on me with a predatory glint. "At last, Ms. Hopper, you're mine."

CHAPTER 2
ANTON

I couldn't stop feasting my eyes on the beauty before me. Grace became my obsession from the first time I saw her on the dingy stage of Jeruna. I wanted her from the moment I laid eyes on her. Everything was wrong with her show; it was vulgar, amateurish, and she clearly lacked vocal training. And yet, when I heard the first notes sung by her raspy voice, they penetrated my soul and set my blood on fire. I knew then, no matter the cost, she would be mine. I had to have her.

The only reason I was on that backwater planet was to conclude the deal that would cement my rising fortune. To celebrate the signing, the investors and I decided to see a performance I was told would fit nicely in my lineup. Grace happened to be the opening act. She claimed to be eighteen when she had actually been sixteen, too young to legally perform on that stage.

When I tried to talk to her, the young beauty shunned me, repulsed by my brutish face. At twenty-two, being a Braxian-human hybrid, I was used to rejection, though my increasing wealth made that a less frequent occurrence. But hers left a deep scar on my heart. The rejection, I could accept. Why would she want an ugly bastard like me? But it was the mockery and public humiliation she and her friends subjected me to that I couldn't… wouldn't forgive. She didn't remember our first encounter, but Braxians never forgot a slight to their honor or clan.

I didn't retaliate back then; Marcus protected her well. So I bided my time. In the shadows, I created the opportunities that would lead her to me on the Venus Hive pleasure barge when the time was right… when that delectable forbidden fruit was ripe. That her deadbeat ex-boyfriend delivered her onto my lap was an added bonus.

Grace's kiss was a pleasant surprise. I expected her to struggle to accept my touch, but the scent of her arousal clung to my nose. The softness of her lips, her heated response as I plundered her mouth… This opened a plethora of new possibilities. I would have to revise my plans. Over the next six months, I would break her for the Jeruna offense, and then remold her into my obedient little pet. Right now, I intended to fully sample what I fantasized over for more than six years.

I sauntered over to the sitting area on the opposite side of the room, under Grace's watchful gaze. Sitting down in the middle of the brown leather couch, I spread my arms on the backrest.

"Come," I said. Obedient, she strutted towards me. "Stop," I said as soon as she stepped onto the shaggy beige rug in front of the couch. Once again, she complied. "Strip for me. Take your time and make it good."

Grace licked her lips slowly, but this time it wasn't deliberately. She was a performer to her sexy core and right this minute, I loved the exhibitionist in her. By her scent and sparkling eyes, the thought of putting on this little show clearly excited her. The quick glance she cast at my sound system didn't go unnoticed.

"Music on. Derzenia, track five. Play," I said, my eyes glued to Grace.

She gave me a saucy smile and swayed to the sensuous music. Her hands ran over her body while she shimmied up and down. Turning around, she pulled on the knot of her sarong dress tied behind her neck. After releasing it, she looked at me over her shoulder with yellowish brown eyes full of promises. The colorful fabric slipped down before coming to a stop below the small of her back, teasing me with a peek of the seam of her ass. I stared at her naked back and the delicate curve of her spine. Blood rushed to my groin and my cock swelled in my pants.

Grace faced me, one hand holding the loose sarong between her breasts. I could hardly believe this was happening, at last. With the other hand, she removed the barrette that imprisoned her silky reddish-brown hair. She had amazing hair. Even now, I wanted to feel it brushing against my naked chest while she rode my cock.

She shook her head, letting her hair cascade down to her waist. Shimmying up and down again, she used one hand on each breast to keep the sarong from falling. It parted in the middle, giving me a glimpse of her flat stomach and black thong every time she swayed. I licked my lips, wanting to run my tongue over her creamy skin. Soon, I would. I shifted on the couch, forcing myself not to readjust my confined cock.

She twirled, her arms raised, holding the sarong above her head like a flag. I nearly moaned at her naked beauty. Grace stopped, facing me, and dropped the sarong at her feet. Eyes sparkling, the little minx was enjoying teasing me. She caressed her full breasts. Dusty pink nipples stood erect, winking at me, begging to be tasted. She pinched them, rolling the nubs between delicate fingers. Her hands ventured south over her stomach. Grace hooked her thumbs in the straps of her thong and slipped it, revealing a beautiful shaven pussy. She spun the tiny piece of fabric around the tip of her finger before throwing it at me. I caught it in the air and brought it to my nose. The musky scent of her arousal made my cock ache with need.

"Get on your knees and crawl to me," I commanded, my voice raspy.

To my pleasant surprise, she didn't balk at the order. Instead, she dropped to her hands and knees and crawled with feline elegance towards me. I always suspected Grace might be submissive and was elated to have it confirmed. As she closed the distance between us, I spread my legs wider. It took every ounce of control I possessed to hide my hunger for her touch. My cock jerked in anticipation when Grace settled on her knees between my legs.

I drew in quick, shallow breaths as I watched her soft hands free my cock. She gasped upon seeing my girth – I wasn't a small man. Her skin flushed and her eyes darkened with her arousal. Undeterred, her hand stroked my length up and down. The heat building within felt like molten lava in my stomach. My body tensed as her pink tongue showed between perfect straight teeth. Grace bent down to lick the pearl of pre-cum weeping from my slit. Grinding my teeth, I dug my fingers into the couch.

Between strokes, she touched her tongue at the base of my cock, and it slid up my length. Pausing at the top, she teased the head before sliding back down. Her hand moved faster. She swirled her tongue around one of my balls then sucked it into her mouth. So many nights I had dreamt of her mouth on me, tasting me, swallowing me. This exceeded even my wildest fantasies. Although it felt incredible, there was something else I wanted in her mouth. As if she had heard my unspoken plea, her luscious lips wrapped around my cock. The contrast of her blood red lipstick against my olive skin made me even harder.

I couldn't hold back a hiss of pleasure when the wet warmth of her mouth closed around me. Her head bobbed over my crotch, taking more and more of me each time. The lustrous curtain of her reddish-brown hair felt like butterfly wings caressing my thighs with each of her movements. When my cock hit the back of her throat, I couldn't help thrusting up. Grace swallowed and I cried out with bliss. She sucked me with feverish vigor, her teeth gently grazing the shaft and head on each upstroke. I stopped withholding my moans of pleasure as the fire of impending release built. The silky mass of her hair flowed through my fingers.

When did I grab it?

The thought vanished as the head of my cock hit the back of her throat again and she began to hum. My vision darkened and I exploded. The violent, unexpected orgasm tore a shout of ecstasy out of me. Grace swallowed and licked my cum as it shot out.

Destroyed, I lay my head back, looking up blindly at the spinning ceiling. Grace, kneeling between my legs, stared at me with obvious self-satisfaction. It pissed me off that she had made me lose control.

But fuck… that was the best head I'd ever had. Now, it was time to turn the tables. She needed to know who was running this show. My breath still labored, I ran my thumb over her glistening lips.

"Lie on your back, and pleasure yourself."

She sat down from her kneeling position and crawled a couple of feet backward. The hard, dusty nipples of her breasts made my mouth water. Grace lay down on her back, her long, firm legs slightly parted. I watched her dainty fingers fondle her breasts. She plucked at her nipples with blood red nails matching her lipstick. Her luminous, satin skin demanded to be caressed and tasted. She slid one hand down her belly to her opening.

Grace parted the lips of her pussy with two fingers, scissoring alongside her swollen little nub. She was deliciously pink, her slit weeping with her increasing arousal. My nostrils flared at the scent of her musk. The little seductress let go of her pussy long enough to lick her fingers before going back to gently circling her clit. The motion was deliberate. I could feel her stare on me, but my eyes were riveted by the hypnotic movement of the hand between her thighs. Her fingers dipped into her wet opening, gathering moisture, then resumed massaging her clit, the speed steadily rising.

With a half moan, half growl, I tucked myself back into my pants. Her beautiful amber eyes widened, a fleeting hint of apprehension glinting through them. Grace didn't know how hard I was struggling not to ram my cock into that juicy cunt of hers and fuck her within an inch of her life. I got off the couch and kneeled next to her on the soft, shaggy carpet.

"Don't stop," I said when her movements faltered.

After kissing her breasts, I softly rubbed my face against the perfect, silky globes. I inhaled her heady scent. Grace's moan went straight to my groin, making my shaft jerk against my pants. Her body, her scent, the salty taste of her skin and those sexy as hell sounds she made were intoxicating. I grabbed the hand she'd pleasured herself with and licked her juices off it. Crawling back between her thighs, I lifted her legs over my shoulders and buried my face in her core.

"Anton!" Grace cried out.

Her hands sunk into my hair, fisting it almost painfully. She lifted her pelvis to meet my mouth. I grabbed her ass with both hands to still her, while I licked and sucked on her engorged nub. As her whimpers grew, I dipped my tongue in and out of her opening. Fuck, she tasted good. Pleasuring a woman was no challenge for me. But seeing this particular woman fall apart under my touch drove me crazy. I could feel my cock throb in tandem with my tongue, wishing it was the one inside her instead. My thumb massaged her clit. Grace's back arched off the floor. Her legs trembled – she was close to the edge. Sucking her clit into my mouth once again, I slipped my fingers inside her, stretching her in the process.

With her climax imminent, I pulled my fingers out of her and licked them slowly. She whimpered, toppling back to the floor. I didn't want her coming in my mouth. This time, my dick would take her to completion. Sitting back on my haunches, I feasted my eyes on the woman lying on her back before me, her reddish-brown hair splayed around her enraptured face, her hard nipples pointing at the ceiling, and her opening glistening with arousal.

But her face… her stunning heart-shaped face enthralled me. High cheekbones framed a slightly upturned dainty nose. Her big, amber eyes darkened by desire, shone like liquid gold. And her lips… those luscious, pouty lips had made me come harder than I've ever had. I'd never felt such ravenous hunger for another woman.

"Time for me to fuck you, my little pet."

Her wary eyes fell to my hand as it freed my cock from my leather trousers and gave it a couple of strokes. She drew in a shuddering breath and held onto my shoulders when I leaned over her. There was something strangely erotic about getting ready to fuck a naked woman while fully dressed. With a swipe of my knees, I parted her legs wider. I reveled in my power over her, this woman who had dismissed me, humiliated me. Now she would writhe under me, scream for me. When I placed the tip of my cock at her slit, she tensed.

"Relax," I said in a commanding tone.

She jumped at the sharpness of my voice and breathed in through her mouth. I wanted to ram my cock inside her, but damaging her wasn't my goal. She would be punished and humiliated as she had me, until my honor and that of my clan was restored. You didn't maim such beautiful woman. I had plans for her.

Rubbing my cock against her, I coated it with her slick juices. I pushed inside her. She felt exquisitely tight and warm. As expected, my cock was too big. I tried pushing further but met with resistance, her folds squeezing in on all sides. Controlling my breathing, I struggled to squash my impatience. I inched forward, slowly, deliberately. Rocking in and out, I gained a few inches at the time. I snaked my hand between us and rubbed her clitoris. She shuddered, her legs relaxing around me. Her resistance faded and my cock slipped in deeper until my balls rubbed against her.

At last… at long last, she was mine. I could die from the blissful warmth that gripped my length. My obsession with her was absurd, but I had never wanted a woman as much as I wanted her. The whole time I was taking possession of her, my gaze never left hers. There would be no doubt in her mind whose cock was fucking her. She lay still beneath me, the rapid rise and fall of her chest brushing against mine. I gave her a moment to adjust to my girth. Though I'd never admit it, I was also reining myself in. She felt so damn good, it wouldn't take much for me to come again. But I hadn't waited all these years to have her, only to spill after two strokes.

"You're nice and tight, my pet," I said against her lips as I began to rock in and out of her. "Nice and wet for your master's cock… your Braxian master's cock."

She didn't get the hint; that was fine. We had plenty of time for her to remember how she claimed never to let a Braxian cock near her. Each stroke sent coils of fire in my belly. I couldn't let her see the power she held over me. I fisted her hair with more force than needed. She winced. I accelerated the tempo.

"Whose pussy is this?" I demanded.

"Yours," she said breathily.

"Whose cock gets to fuck you, however, whenever, wherever?"

"Yours… Your cock."

"Who do you belong to, pet?"

"You, Anton. I belong to you."

I crushed her lips with mine, my tongue taking over hers. Her heated response and her sexy moans sent me over the edge. Ramming my cock in and out of her, I devoured her mouth. Her hands on my shoulders sneaked around my back, as she pressed herself against me. I nipped at her shoulder and sucked on the delicate flesh of her neck, made salty by a thin coat of perspiration.

For a moment, I regretted not having stripped before I took her, wanting to feel her skin against mine. There was no stopping now though. The fire building inside me was about to erupt. Initially, I hadn't planned on bothering with Grace's pleasure. She was here for mine and for my vengeance. But the thought of her screaming in ecstasy while wrapped around my cock made me so damn hard it hurt. I changed my angle until her blissful shout confirmed I had found her sweet spot. I felt her nails trying to dig into my back through my shirt.

"Anton!" she cried out. "Yes! Yes!"

I wasn't good enough for you, yet how you scream my name now.

Her shouts sent a blistering bolt of lust straight to my balls that were already drawing up. Grinding my teeth, I slipped my hand between us and rubbed her clit while slamming my dick into her sweet spot. At last, her body seized. She stared at me, her mouth stretched in a silent 'O' while her inner walls clamped down on my cock. I exploded with a roar, my seed shooting out in blissful spurts within her. Her head tilted back, and the air rushed out of her in a rapturous moan. I covered her neck and jawline with kisses while the involuntary contractions of her pussy choked the last drops of semen out of me.

I ached to pull her into my embrace and savor the warmth of post-coital intimacy. Instead, I pulled out of her and sat on my haunches while getting my breathing under control. I pretended not to see the hurt and confusion on her face – gentle cuddling wasn't in the nature of our relationship. The sex had been mind-blowing though, even better than the blowjob.

Grace's passionate response was an unexpected treat I wouldn't mind indulging in a while longer. The Braxian delegation wasn't due for another week. Maybe I should revise my plans for the next few days. Revenge, after all, was a patient beast. A few more days to enjoy the clueless beauty would make no difference to the retribution that awaited her.

After tucking myself back in my pants, I got up and walked over to an unassuming little box on my desk.

"Stay as you are," I said when she started to sit up.

Dana delivered the box this morning. I picked it up while casting a fiendish smile at Grace. She eyed me warily as I grabbed a towel from the mini bar on my way back to her. Kneeling between her thighs, I opened the box. When I reached for its content, she instinctively tried to close her legs. My warning gaze stopped her.

"Put your feet flat on the floor and spread wide," I said with a stern voice.

Grace licked her lips, her throat working, but complied. She was a delightful sight fully naked but for the pumps on her feet. Too bad the heels weren't higher. Using the towel, I wiped some of our mixed essences leaking from her. I took the Kegel beads from the box and rubbed them gently on her wet pussy. Once they were fully coated with her juices, I slowly pushed them inside her, grazing her clit with my thumb at the same time. She shuddered prettily then remained still while I cleaned her. I wiped my hands with the towel then helped her up. Her face was flushed and her lips swollen.

I crushed the desire to take her again.

"Brace yourself, sweetheart," I said as sole warning.

The beads vibrated inside her, activated by the remote in my hand. Grace cried out and clung to me, trembling with pleasure. My arm wrapped tightly around her for support. Unable to resist the call of her milky skin, I covered her neck with soft kisses. Meanwhile, I adjusted the setting of the beads until Grace's moans dwindled to a light panting.

Once confident she was steady on her legs again, I released her. "Get dressed and wait for me by the lift in five minutes. I'm taking you out for dinner."

She gaped at me and placed a hand below her navel. "With this thing?"

I smirked. "Yes. Let's see how much control you have."

Grace swallowed but nodded. Cupping her face in my hands, I gave her a hard kiss. "I'm going to enjoy owning you, Grace."

I released her and strolled out of the room. "Don't forget, no thong," I said over my shoulder before closing the door to my office.

CHAPTER 3
GRACE

Anton's hand on the small of my back coaxed me into Risqué, the fanciest restaurant on the Venus Hive space station. For years, I dreamt of entering the VIP section of any of the Hive Network pleasure barges. Who would have imagined that dream would come true in the mother of them all?

Every single eye in the room was on us as we headed to Anton's personal table. Though discreet, I could feel their assessing gazes, weighing and judging. No doubt they found me lacking. My dress was decent enough but nowhere near the quality of the sinfully wealthy clientele around me. Pulling my shoulders back, I walked with false confidence, trying to look like I belonged. For some reason, I wanted to make Anton proud and spare him any kind of embarrassment. The overwhelming need to please, especially whomever I considered my current partner, was one of my many flaws. It often made me do or accept things that, deep down, I knew were wrong.

My last boyfriend, Paul, would often hold my arm so tightly bruises formed. Yet, I kept smiling. I always smiled.

I knew my reaction to Anton was completely irrational. Sure, I was a superficial girl. As long as it looked beautiful or glittered, my interest perked up. However, what really mattered to me was having a place to call home, a warm bed to sleep in, food in my belly, and ideally, someone to look after me. That didn't mean you shouldn't spoil me with fancy stuff, but I wouldn't be miserable without it.

Marcus had been my childhood best friend, before growing up into the gorgeous, sweet-talking man who took good care of me. He loved the way I flaunted my assets, which also helped my career. However conceited that may sound, my body was hot and I craved attention. I loved having men – and women – drooling and fantasizing about me. It turned me on. My usual dress code made sure I never went unnoticed and gave those who saw me plenty to dream about.

But Anton's face didn't fit my attraction requirements, even though he had the body of a god. I kept him as a last resort because I didn't think I could submit to him sexually without being repulsed. And yet, my girly bits seemed to have a will of their own. The minute I touched him for that first kiss, I became instantly aroused. Going down on a man never tasted so good. The salty spiciness of him still lingered on my taste buds. And that tongue of his when he returned the favor? Holy shit! Anton was extremely well endowed – I had never felt so full. The way he took me… I couldn't believe I was getting wet again just thinking about it. No man had ever made me come so hard. And those beads… When did he intend to use them? The anticipation was driving me insane.

However, something was off between us. He wanted me; the way he looked at me, couldn't seem to keep his hands off me said it all. But sometimes, there was a cold, hard, almost cruel glint in his eyes. And the way he pulled away from me as soon as he climaxed had been… strange and hurtful. Anton owned me. I was officially his property, to do with as he pleased for the next six months. If he wished to be cold, I would have to suck it up. Hopefully, it wouldn't be the case. I didn't fare too well without affection and caring.

We reached our table on an elevated dais with a perfect view of the stage and dining room. The beige walls made the room look even bigger and made a sharp contrast with the shiny dark brown wooden floor. Wall lamps, propped at the top of pillars strategically placed not to obstruct the view of the stage, provided a soft ambient light. The restaurant was almost full. The patrons were mainly couples with a few larger groups alongside the walls. Only one other booth on the elevated dais was occupied.

Anton sat next to me on our circular leather seat. He lifted the hem of my skirt and rested his hand on my lap. His fingers drew slow circles along my inner thigh.

I liked that.

A sexy waitress in a skin-tight white leather uniform made a beeline for our table. Matching red shoes, red hair and lipstick made her pop.

"Welcome to Risqué, Mr. Myers. What can we offer you today?" the waitress asked, pushing forward boobs whose size defied gravity.

"Want to have a look at the menu, Grace?" Anton asked.

As if I could recognize half the items on the list. "Would you mind choosing for me? Something surprising, exotic."

"Do you want meat?" he asked.

"I always want meat," I said without thinking.

My face heated at his raised eyebrow. I didn't mean it like that. Well, okay, maybe my subconscious did. It had been too long since I got laid. After that orgasm, I wouldn't object a round two. While Anton sorted out the details of our order, I discreetly observed the patrons in the room. They were all humans or humanoid-looking. The Commons, the popular section of the space station – translate that as the paupers' area – had more diversity and also more risk of interspecies brawls. Quite a few patrons held leashes to half-naked men or women kneeling at their feet. I didn't know Risqué allowed masters to bring their pets inside.

"They are here for the grand opening of Sade next week," Anton said in response to my unspoken question.

"Sade? The fancy new S and M club?"

"The fetish club," he corrected. "Marissa, the owner, spared no expense to make sure every possible non-vanilla fantasy will be satisfied. Needless to say, those in the lifestyle are eager to put this boast to the test."

My eyes flicked back to one of the pets. He was a good-looking, androgynous young man. His master tossed him a bit of food which he licked off the floor. I flinched and glanced at Anton.

"Have you ever owned a pet?" I asked.

"Isn't that what you are?" His hand on my thigh slid up higher and his fingers teased the seam of my pussy. I couldn't help an involuntary twitch as my skin flushed. "You are mine to do with as I please. There is no question I want submissive obedience from you." Anton turned on the beads and I gasped at the sudden wave of pleasure. "How that will translate, time will tell. For now, however, it's your pleasure I want, in all its forms."

"Anton... please."

My hands clenched the edge of the table, white knuckled. I panted, beads of sweat pearling on my forehead. I wanted to throw my head back, moan with pleasure, and spread my legs wider to give his wicked hand better access. But I couldn't. Not here with every eye pretending not to be spying on us. The light ambient music would never cover the sound I would make. I wasn't a screamer but I wasn't quiet either.

"Please what, Grace?" His tone was falsely innocent.

"I can't... They're going to hear..."

"I want you to come for me, Grace. Right here, right now. And I want you to be discreet. Can you do that for me?" Anton whispered, his lips brushing against my ear.

"Anton..."

"Do you have any idea how fucking hard it makes me when you say my name like that?" Anton said through gritted teeth. His thumb started rubbing my clit. "Kiss me, Grace, and come for me."

Anton's commanding tone made my stomach flip-flop. My skin tingled expectantly. Grateful for an excuse to hide my face from the patrons' prying eyes, I crushed my lips against his. Anton's tongue took over my mouth and, at the same time, he increased the intensity of the vibration of the beads. He swallowed my barely repressed scream of ecstasy as my orgasm overwhelmed me. The vibration blessedly slowed, then stopped. Anton broke our kiss. Shaking, I brought my legs together. I leaned against the backrest, trying to collect myself.

"Good girl," Anton whispered with a soft kiss on my temple.

The buxom waitress returned with our drinks. Her knowing smile told me she delayed bringing them to us to give us a bit of privacy. Avoiding eye contact with her, I took a large sip of wine, forcing myself not to down the entire glass in one go.

"You shouldn't have done that," I said after the waitress left.

He swirled his wine in his glass. "Why not?"

I took a quick look at the room. "People could have seen us… probably did see us the way they're all staring."

One of the patrons winked at me while a few others averted their eyes.

"And you loved every bit of it," he deadpanned. At my incredulous stare, he continued, "The thought of getting caught excites the fuck out of you. You like being watched. Even now, you love that every single person in this room has their mind on you, wondering what I'm doing to you. The thought of them watching my hand slip into you makes you wet. Tell me I'm wrong."

Trying to hide the heat creeping up my cheeks, I took another gulp of the fruity wine. I would never admit how right he was. A shiver ran up my spine, realizing how well he seemed to know me.

I gave him an inquisitive look. "Doesn't it bother you what people say?"

Anton shook his head while taking a sip of his wine. "I don't give two shits what these people think about me. I'd have air locked myself into space a long time ago if I did. The only thing that matters to me is the fact that I finally have what I want."

The weight of his eyes on me made clear what… who he was referring to. Our food arriving prevented me from asking him to clarify what he meant. This was the second time Anton hinted at having wanted me for a while.

The meal was on a whole other level. Not only was the plating beautiful and refined, but the flavors and textures were divine. I didn't know what the food was, only that the meat was juicy, tender and seasoned to perfection. The side dishes were fresh and ideally paired with the main course. I especially liked the sautéed vegetables. Crispy, just on this side of spicy hot. They didn't set your throat on fire but gave your tongue a nice little tingle. How could I ever go back to the greasy gruel I once believed the epitome of fine dining?

A stunning woman walked into the restaurant. I recognized her as Sheila Vincent. While I was fairly confident in my own beauty, Sheila took hot to the extreme. The platinum blonde was tall and sexy, with out-of-this-world curves. Thigh length curly golden hair framed a breathtaking face with sharp cheekbones, startling blue eyes, and plush lips made to wrap around a man's cock. Like me, she was a singer. Unlike me, she performed in her own big-ticket show in the Hive's VIP section. A number of patrons greeted her along the way, while others were content to admire her from a distance. As she walked past our table, Sheila cast a smoldering look at Anton and saluted him with a nod. He returned the gesture and watched her strut her way to a table near the stage.

Fuck that bitch.

Taken aback by my bout of jealousy, I looked away. Why should I care who he looks at? I knew better than to fall back into my old patterns, especially this soon. Marcus cheated on me so many times I had grown numb to it. Anton wasn't my boyfriend – I was his exclusive property for the duration of our contract, not the other way around. It scared me that after a single tumble, I was already getting this territorial. But Sheila was no joke.

"Why did you enter into this agreement with me?" I asked, genuinely confused. "What's in it for you?"

Anton's gaze roamed over me meaningfully. "Isn't it obvious?"

"Well, yes but, like you said, twelve million credits is a lot. With your position, you can have pretty much any woman you want, for free. Or at least, for way cheaper than this deal." I glanced at Sheila giving her order to the same buxom waitress that had served us. "Not that I'm ungrateful. You literally saved my life. But I can't help wondering why."

Anton took a bite of meat – he had requested his rare – and chewed slowly, as if pondering how he wanted to answer my question or whether to answer it at all. He swallowed and leveled his dark eyes on me.

"Do you remember the first time we met?" he asked.

"On Lilith Hive?"

"No, Grace. A few years ago."

My eyes widened. I couldn't recall meeting him before. While Braxians, and especially half-breeds, weren't all that frequent in my usual circles, I had met a number of both over the years. But I never paid them much attention; they all looked the same to me. Come to think of it, I had noticed an unusually high number of Braxian half-breeds on the sanctuary planet Haven when I last performed there a year ago.

"I thought you were the most beautiful thing I had ever seen," Anton said, a strange glitter in his eyes. "From that moment, I never stopped fantasizing about you writhing under me as I plowed into that pussy of yours, or how you'd look with your lips wrapped around my cock."

That should have offended me, but instead, I felt moisture pool between my legs. Damn that man.

The lights in the room faded while the spotlights on the small stage lit, saving me from replying. The beautiful Seria Gallant walked onto the stage in a skin-tight red dress with a side slit that ran up her thigh. Her small orchestra on the side began playing a jazzy ballad. I watched in awe as Seria swayed to the first notes. Her deep, throaty voice was the sexiest thing I had ever heard.

"Watch her carefully," Anton whispered in my ear. "Even though she has nothing on you vocally, the type of performance you do would never grant you a spot in elite venues. Look at the way she moves, the way she interacts with her mic. Do you understand the difference?"

Seria was mesmerizing. Her movements were slower, measured, and more delicate than mine.

"She's more elegant," I said.

Anton shook his head, frowning. "The end result is elegance, but it's the intention that makes all the difference. When you sing, you treat your mic as a cock that you're stroking and aching to deep-throat. You're essentially fucking on stage."

He gestured at the mic stand. "Look how she handles the stand and the mic. That's a lover she's slowly, sensuously making love to. See how she caresses the length of the stand with her fingertips? It's the same way you would the thighs of your lover. The way she softly brushes her mouth against the mic is like fluttering kisses on his lips. Each time she rubs her thumb under its length, she's stroking her man or licking his cock. And when she holds the stand and mic tightly like that with both hands, swaying from side to side, that's penetration."

Anton turned to face me and gently brushed my hair aside before softly kissing my lips. "Anyone can fuck, Grace. If you want to move to the next level, learn to make love."

CHAPTER 4
GRACE

Three days had gone by since I had become Anton's indentured servant. He gave new meaning to the word workaholic. People often referred to him as Mr. Ant or The Ant. I always assumed it was just them shortening his given name, but Anton literally worked like those little critters from dusk 'til dawn. No wonder he built such a massive empire by the age of twenty-eight. Still, he managed to have plenty of time for me.

Though he owned me for the next six months, so far, Anton treated me more like a girlfriend than property... and I was falling quickly for it. Dr. Hazan, my former therapist, wouldn't be pleased.

Anton was insatiable, which was pretty common in new relationships. Oddly, he didn't fuck me often. It's not like he suffered from any kind of erectile dysfunction; he could all but get it up on command. I should know. My throat and that glorious prick of his had become quite intimately acquainted over the past few days.

But it wasn't just sex with him. Every time we went out, with surprising patience, Anton taught me something new. First, that impromptu mentoring session while observing Seria. The second day, I learned proper table etiquette dealing with the slew of utensils and glasses in multiple course meals. Last night, we attended a wine tasting event. I never realized there was such a science and community of connoisseurs around it. If nothing else, I now understood the basics of wine pairing.

The only cloud in that perfect sky was that he wouldn't let me share his bed or have one of my own. While he didn't have me on a leash or make me eat from a bowl, I was his pet. My bed was a large, plush cushion on the floor at the side of his bed. When he first indicated where I would sleep, I laughed, assuming he was joking. He didn't smile.

Anton confused the hell out of me. One minute he was tender, passionate, and considerate, and the next, he looked like he wanted to crush my bones.

By the time we returned from Risqué, William not only handled the creditors hounding me, but he also retrieved all my things from the hotel. Anton loved my fuck-me shoes. He often made me parade for him wearing nothing else. My sarongs were a hit, and not only because of their versatility. They offered little obstruction to Anton's wandering hands. However, the fabric didn't meet his quality standards and he intended to remedy that problem. As for the rest of my wardrobe, he asked William to dump it all in the incinerator.

Anton didn't mind that my other clothes did nothing to hide my curves or that there was very little fabric to them. I was an exhibitionist and he didn't mind. It's the clothes themselves and their cut he didn't approve of. Over our first couple of days together, Anton made me examine the way the women in the VIP section dressed. He then compared it to my own aesthetic.

Many didn't show half as much skin as I did while others wore outfits even tighter than mine. They were sex on legs and yet still looked classy. As Anton pointed out, it wasn't necessarily how much skin you showed, but how and which parts. You wanted to flaunt just enough to get a man's cock to perk up with interest, but not so much that his imagination didn't even get a chance to kick in. In short, the way I dressed made me look cheap and slutty, which wasn't okay for his woman.

His woman…

It caused a strange fluttering in my stomach. Braxians had a thing about human women. It was major bragging rights for them to have one as their pet. So Anton parading me around wasn't surprising and had nothing to do with my personal merits. Still, I loved being a trophy.

I had mixed feelings about what Anton was doing. On the one hand, he showed me all the things I had been too blind, lazy or stupid to realize. On the other, he turned my life upside-down, opening me up to things I never thought accessible to a girl like me. Only three days in, and I was already addicted to him, to this life.

This morning, Anton took me to Aphrodite's Vault. The price of a single dress there could feed a family of four for a year — or two. The minute we stepped inside the boutique, Ms. Braddock, the owner, treated us like royalty. She took us to an elegant room at the back of the store. Our own reflection greeted us in the ceiling-high mirrors covering the walls. They were separated by light brown draped curtains hiding the changing rooms. Anton and I sunk into a comfortable khaki couch, surrounded by throw pillows. A glass coffee table, laden with fresh fruits, cheeses, and a platter of amuse-bouche reminded me lunch time was fast approaching. The champagne set to chill in the ice bucket drew my attention. I recognized the brand from last night's wine tasting.

It made me feel worldly.

While waiting for Ms. Braddock to bring in the racks of clothes, I distractedly traced the dark linear patterns on the beige rug covering the marble floor with the tip of my shoe.

Three pretty models gave us a private fashion show. Any piece either of us liked was set aside. In the end, it was my turn to model for Anton. The girls assisted me in and out of the clothes — right in front of Anton — and brought whatever accessory would complement the outfit. Thinking to earn extra points, one of the girls tried to cop a feel while helping me wiggle my way out of a second skin of a dress. I put a quick stop to it with a slap on her wrist and a stern stare; I wasn't looking for some girl-on-girl action and didn't want Anton getting ideas.

We returned to the boutique's entrance where Anton settled the bill with Ms. Braddock. The elegant older woman beamed at us, multiplying the niceties. I couldn't blame her. She was a shrewd businesswoman. Her boutique was renowned for a reason. Anton bought me a full wardrobe, including lingerie – that I had no clue when I would ever wear it since he wanted me commando all the time. It struck me that this shopping spree alone would cost close to, if not more, than my entire debt.

Tucking my hair behind my ear, I realized one of my earrings was missing.

"Anton, I'll be right back. I lost my earring. It probably fell off while I was trying on clothes."

He nodded. "Go ahead. There's no rush."

I smiled and headed for the private room at the back. The door stood ajar. Beyond, the conspiratorial voices of the models stopped me.

"I don't agree that 'clever slut' is the right term to describe Mr. Ant's new squeeze. Well, the slut part sure, but clever, not so much," a voice said.

"Aw, come on, Mary. What would *you* know about being clever?" The high-pitched voice belonged to the brunette model.

"A lot more than you, Jenna." Mary's voice dripped with contempt. "Everyone knows she was Marcus' pet. All he had to do was point and tell her to show her tits. And bam! That show of hers wasn't singing. She all but masturbated on stage."

Ouch.

I knew my show wasn't exactly classy, but I thought it was sexy, not slutty.

"Marcus did use her and I agree that she never struck me as particularly smart. But you're only pissed because she didn't let you eat her pussy," a third voice said.

"Why the hell would I want to go down on that cheap whore?" Mary asked.

"Cut it out, Mary," the voice sounding like Jenna said. "We remember how you attended most of her shows like a lovesick puppy. Grace is a hot piece of ass and we all know which way you swing."

"You don't know what the fuck you're talking about," Mary snapped.

"I was there when Grace told you she only liked dicks," Jenna said. "You're hurt she didn't remember you today. By the way, groping a customer without permission – especially Ant's girlfriend? Not a good idea. Don't be surprised if Ms. Braddock tears into you."

My mind was reeling. I got hit on a lot before and after my performances, by both men and women. It didn't bother me, quite the opposite. But for all that, I didn't fuck around. Sure, I enjoyed sex. However, despite finding a woman's body sexy, they held no attraction for me. I liked men. And I couldn't recall turning Mary down. Sadly, she was one face among thousands of would-be lovers.

"She's not his girlfriend," Mary muttered under her breath.

"He sure treats her like it," the third voice said. "Ant is always generous with his lovers, but this was crazy. If the rumors about her debt are true, he just bought her a second time."

"So you see, Mary," Jenna said, "Grace is the clever one. I'd spread my legs for that ugly bastard any time he wanted for that kind of royal treatment. He could even fuck me in the ass."

A dull pain in my hand made me realize I was clutching the doorframe, my fingertips whitening from the strength of my grip.

The third voice chuckled. "I wonder if he's already rammed hers."

"I overheard Sheila talking with Ms. Braddock yesterday," Jenna said. "Sheila saw them at Risqué a few days ago. Word on the street is Ant had Grace coming all over the leather seats."

"No! Right there, in front of everyone?"

"Sure did. It seems Ant is all over her all the time, and she bends over willingly, taking it like a champ," Mary said.

The clanking sound of hangers falling on the floor was followed by a muttered curse.

"Wouldn't you in her shoes?" Jenna asked. "That's a butt load of credits she owed. That she managed to get him to pay that kind of debt in exchange for riding her is a feat in and of itself. I'd like to know how to get in good with him like that."

"You'd fuck Mr. Ant?" the third voice said, sounding disgusted.

"Hell yeah, as long as he shows me the money," Jenna said. Chuckling, she added, "Plus, his body is hot. I'd just picture Caleb's face instead."

That was enough. I held onto the wall, wavering. Those bitches needed an earful. I wanted to storm into the room and put them in their place, but I couldn't – the thought of confrontations made me anxious. My hand slipped down the wall and fell to my side. Head down, I returned to the front of the boutique.

I hated the way they spoke about Anton. Granted, he didn't have a pretty face, but he wasn't ugly either... Plus, if you ignored the pet bed, he treated me pretty well. A gentle soul lurked behind his brutish face. If I were honest though, what upset me the most was that some of their comments echoed my own thoughts when I planned on begging for his help. Even if Anton had been a complete douche, I would have spread my legs, taken it like a champ, and begged for seconds to keep him happy.

"Did you find it?" Anton asked when I rejoined him.

I shook my head with a strained smile. "No. I guess it must have dropped somewhere else."

Anton's eyes narrowed and he cast a speculative glance at the back of the store. He was a little too perceptive for my liking.

"If it turns up, please have it forwarded to the penthouse, Ms. Braddock," Anton said.

"Of course, Mr. Myers. I'll personally make sure of it."

Without another word, Anton placed his hand on the small of my back and led me out.

CHAPTER 5

ANTON

For the past few days, Grace hadn't acted quite herself. Something happened at the boutique that shook her self-confidence. She kept saying everything was fine but the way she wouldn't make eye contact and chewed on her nails told me otherwise. It had to be the models that somehow upset her. Under different circumstances, I would have lashed out already at anyone who messed with my woman.

My woman…

She wasn't and I needed to stop behaving that way. I still couldn't believe she belonged to me, even if only for a while. By granting myself one week to enjoy her luscious body, I fell into my own trap and got lost in the pleasure of being with her. The truth was, I wanted to experience what could have been. She starred in my wildest fantasies for so long…

I was addicted to Grace's eagerness, willingness to please… to be mine. It also took little to make her happy; a bit of attention, a gentle touch, a kind word and she melted. That too was addictive. She was so keen to learn – humble in her ignorance yet hungry for every tidbit offered to her. Grace never asked for anything but her gratitude for the slightest scrap given to her was heartfelt. The way her face lit up during that shopping spree made me want to buy the whole damn store

– I nearly did too. Her wardrobe needed a change anyways. As she would be considered 'my woman' by everyone for the next six months, I couldn't have her looking trashy on my arm.

You didn't need to spend sixteen million credits on clothes to achieve that, though.

Whatever, credits didn't matter. But I hadn't acquired her to seduce or please her. It was time to silence the softer emotions she stirred within me. She was here to receive her punishment. If nothing else, my kindness towards her this first week worked well as part of my revenge. The shock would shatter her once she realized fun times were over and not coming back anytime soon. The day of retribution had finally come.

A quick glance at the clock confirmed we would meet for breakfast soon. Chastising myself for all the time spent musing – fantasizing – over Grace, I tried to reset my focus onto the reports on my monitor. Her intrusion completely ruined my perfect routine, setting me behind in my work. This was unheard of for me. With a will of their own, my eyes wandered to the shaggy carpet across from my office desk where Grace had stripped and pleasured herself so prettily.

Growling at my inability to stay focused, I closed the report and left my office. While crossing the living area on my way to the kitchen, I nodded at the two men cleaning the room. Startled by my presence, one of them looked at his watch, wondering if they were behind. The staff knew I treasured my privacy and usually worked around my schedule to remain invisible. William was the exception. But then, he was more than just staff. Aside from being my Head of Security, William was my friend and had saved my life fifteen years ago.

I entered the gourmet kitchen where the cook was busy preparing breakfast for Grace and me. On the island behind him, a plate of freshly cut fruits sat by a full pot of coffee. I poured myself a cup before walking over to the dining table. The cook, also surprised by my early arrival, rushed to pull out the dishes from the cupboards to set up the table. It was large enough to seat twelve people, although I'd never entertained more than six in the penthouse. Sitting down, I read the latest news on my datapad. Minutes later, the object of my obsession walked in. Her high heels clicked on the floor tiles as the cook plated the steaks to go along with our scrambled eggs and toast.

"Good morning," Grace said and kissed my forehead. I nodded in greeting and gestured for her to take a seat.

The cook served our food and refilled my cup. He brought a fresh pot of coffee, the plate of sliced fruits, and cream before leaving.

In the last week, Grace relaxed a great deal around me. Sometimes, she seemed to forget she signed herself over as my indentured slave. It was foolish for either of us to indulge in the illusion that we were a regular couple. Her pet cushion was but one reminder of her true position.

We ate breakfast, making light conversation. The laid-back atmosphere didn't last. It was only a matter of time before she brought up the topic of her career. However, Grace probably wouldn't like where that conversation would end.

"Anton, I want to start singing again."

I stopped chewing for a second and looked at her. I swallowed and washed the food down with a sip of coffee.

"Ok."

Grace heaved a sigh of relief. "Awesome! If you don't have plans for me this afternoon, I will go see Peter to ask—"

"No."

She recoiled. "Excuse me?"

"If you want to sing, I have no problem with it. But what you were doing at Peter's didn't qualify as singing." I meticulously cut a piece of steak. "Right now, you are my pet, Grace. As long as you're mine, I will see you do better."

I popped the meat in my mouth, waiting for the storm to hit. Grace clenched her jaw. Some truths needed to be said for her own good. Whatever the outcome of our current agreement, hitting the reset button on her career was a sound investment. With proper training and the right show, she could be a top selling act in one of my VIP lounges.

And she would be.

"Ah... So the real Grace is too trashy for Mr. Anton Myers? You don't want to be embarrassed by my *performance*?"

"The real Grace is exactly who Anton Myers wants. The Grace you project isn't her and yes, she's too trashy. I don't want my pet walking around with her ass and tits spilling out for every bastard to gawk at."

The hurt in her eyes didn't move me.

"We fool around for one week and you know me better than I know myself?"

I wiped my mouth with a napkin then casually discarded it on the table. "It is my business to read people; to see them for who they truly are, their potential and what makes them tick. You, sweetheart, are so starved for attention, you do whatever you think will bring you the most of it, over what you personally want."

Grace snorted, shaking her head. I leaned forward, my gaze seeking hers, but she looked away.

"I was there at the boutique with you. I saw the way your eyes lit up when you tried on the outfits that spoke to the true Grace. Each time I asked you which clothes we should take, you pointed to the ones that excited you the least but showed more skin."

"That's not true!" She glared at me, her knuckles white from holding her utensils too tight.

"Really? You're going to tell me you didn't love that bare-back silver dress or the blood red one?" She didn't answer – didn't need to. The way she averted her eyes spoke volumes. "You passed on them because they weren't skimpy enough to draw the kind of attention you're used to."

Grace pushed away her half-eaten breakfast.

"You're doing the same thing with your singing career; being who Marcus told you to be, rather than who you want to be."

"And who would that be, since you know everything?" Her voice dripped with resentment.

"You want to be courted by places like Risqué. You dream of red carpet treatment, where people scream your name and faint with excitement over your touch. You hunger for the kind of respect and deference women like Seria and Sheila get wherever they go. But Peter won't give you that."

Grace's anger slowly abated as I spoke, her eyes full of longing. She tucked her hair behind her ear and looked at me.

"That doesn't happen to girls like me."

"There is no such thing as *a girl like you*," I said, gesturing for her to continue eating. "You are yourself, period – not whatever label anyone wants to give you. And if you want to prance in the elite circle, take the steps to get there."

"As if it was that simple," she said, nibbling on a triangle of toast.

"Nothing is ever simple, especially things that are worthwhile," I said in a conciliatory tone. "And nothing is ever guaranteed either. But with hard work—"

Grace frowned.

"Yes, Grace, with *hard work*, you have a chance to achieve your goals. And even if they don't reach the height you were aiming for, you will still end up in a much better place than where you started."

Looking dejected, Grace dropped her half-eaten toast on her plate and crossed her arms. "What kind of *hard work*?"

"First, you need a vocal coach to get your voice in shape. You thought Seria was good, yet she has nothing on you, other than training. Then a stage presence coach so you learn how to enthrall your audience like a singer, not a stripper. At the same time, you will start preparing a show that puts your audience's expectations first. That means, researching and analyzing your audience."

"Man, you sure are all work and no play. You're right; I want the glitz and glamor. However, I don't want to become you. Sure, you're all kinds of rich now, but you never relax, and you never have fun."

"Oh, but I do make time to have fun. In fact, we're going to the grand opening of Sade tonight," I said, keeping my expression neutral.

"Oh wow!" she exclaimed, her eyes gleaming. "Everyone here is bending over backward trying to get tickets for it. I bet you've got VIP tickets with a private booth."

"Naturally," I said, spreading a generous layer of cream cheese with chives on a piece of toast. I took a large bite from my toast and leaned back in my chair.

"I can't wait to see it. I hear it's wild in there."

"So the owner claims. I will have very special guests accompanying us tonight," I said, choosing my words carefully. "Braxians. The heirs to the leaders of some of our most prominent clans."

She poured herself some orange juice. "Ok."

"You will be *nice* to them."

She paused pouring juice, her eyes snapping to mine.

"How nice is *nice*?" she asked.

I held her gaze. "Extremely nice."

Her face shut down. She put the bottle of juice down and sagged in her chair. She pinched her lips, her chest heaving. "I'm not fucking some random Braxians."

My voice hardened. "You will do whatever the hell I tell you to do. And if sinking their cock in your cunt is what those Braxians want, you will bend over, spread those creamy thighs and take it. Understood?"

She shook her head. "No, I won't."

I leaned forward. "You read the contract. I fucking own you. You will do what I tell you or face punishment."

"Then I'll take the damn punishment," she said, lifting her chin.

"Are you sure?"

"Yes," she snarled.

"As you wish," I said, draining my cup.

After wiping my mouth and my hands, I rose from my chair and headed out of the kitchen.

"Come," I said over my shoulder without checking if she followed.

Her chair scraped against the floor, then I heard her light footsteps behind me. I called the lift. The door opened seconds after Grace caught up with me. I gestured for her to get in before following after her. She stared at me, bug-eyed, as I pressed my thumb to the scanner before pressing the button to the secured lowest level of the space station.

"Where are we going?" she asked with a thin voice.

"You'll see."

She wrung her hands while the lift made its quick descent to the bowels of Venus Hive. The door opened to a long, narrow corridor with rows of locked doors. I walked to the one at the very end and placed my eye in front of the retinal scanner, then my thumb on the print scanner. The door slid open with a soft swish.

It revealed a large, semi-circular room. The arched wall flowed as one continuous window displaying the endless void of space. Starlight lit the dark room. Grace's wary gaze drew my attention. I met it head on.

"Strip."

She glanced at the room, chewing her lip, then complied. She untied her sarong which she had knotted at the front and the luxurious fabric slid off her body. I extended a hand and she gave it to me with shaky fingers.

"Shoes."

She hesitated. Her mouth opened and closed a couple of times. Grace swallowed audibly then bent to pull off her high heels. I took the shoes from her and walked to a section of the back wall, by the door. A panel slid open, revealing a shelf onto which I placed the scarf and shoes.

"Ring," I said, and a faint circle lit the ground in the center of the room.

I motioned with my chin for Grace to go stand in the middle. She looked at it, then at me, her lips quivering.

She wrapped her arms around her midriff. "What are you going to do, Anton?"

"Go," I said, showing no emotion.

Not knowing what was about to happen, terrified her. It was intended.

She swallowed again before taking hesitant steps towards the ring. Once she reached the center, she faced me. Even now, naked, trembling in the stark empty room with nothing but a curtain of stars behind her, she was the most beautiful creature I'd ever beheld. I fought the urge to drag her back to my room and fuck her senseless.

"Last chance," I said. "You can come with me, and do as you're told, or you can spend the next twenty-four hours here. Your call."

Her eyes welled, and the trembling of her lips spread to her chin, but she shook her head. I couldn't help admire her determination. This display of strength was unexpected… and refreshing.

"As you wish," I said with a nod. "Bars."

No sooner had I spoken, a tight ring of bars rose from the ground, caging her. She yelped, looking around her as they lifted to the ceiling. As they made contact, they stopped with a clank that echoed loudly through the empty room. Grace stared, wide-eyed, as a circular grid descended from the ceiling towards her. She tried pushing against the grid, her arm shaking from the strain. The pressure forced her down until she buckled, her knees slamming onto the metal plated floor.

"Anton!" she cried out, fearing she would be crushed.

The terror in her eyes tore at me. Pushing my shoulders back, I steeled myself in my resolve. The top grid stopped its descent, a little under four feet above the floor. Grace looked at me horrified through the narrow space between the bars. The cage was too low to stand in, too small to lie down in and just enough space between the bars for her to wrap her hands around them.

"You can't leave me here!"

"I'll see you in twenty-four hours." I turned and walked towards the door.

"What if I need to pee?" she shouted in desperation.

Looking at her over my shoulder, I said, "Then do. There's no one else here to mind."

I walked out to the sound of her voice shouting my name until the door closed behind me.

CHAPTER 6
GRACE

When the door swished open and Anton's silhouette appeared in a halo of light, I thought my foggy mind played tricks on me. Everything hurt. My extremities were swollen. The bones of my ass felt as if they were trying to pierce through the skin onto the cold, hard floor. The bars of my cell were all but embedded in my back. I couldn't feel my legs anymore they were so numb. In a way, it was a relief compared to the vicious bouts of cramping that had seized them at various intervals over the past twenty-four hours. I tried to shift, but there wasn't enough room. The sharp pain along my spine convinced me it was a bad idea anyway.

Imaginary Anton approached the cage and crouched in front of me. His black eyes roamed over me.

"I didn't pee," I said with a wispy voice.

"I see that."

Frowning, I blinked at Imaginary Anton. It was the first time the hallucination responded.

"Bars," Anton said.

The sound of the top grid ascending the bars startled me. Looking up, I watched it fly to the ceiling.

I can stand again.

Except I couldn't feel my legs. I hissed at the burning sensation of the bars sliding against my naked back as they lowered into the floor. Losing their support, I collapsed. Anton's hand caught the back of my head, saving me from smacking it against the metal plating.

He's real! I'm free! It's over!

Blood rushed through my outstretched limbs, bringing with it fresh pain and feeling. They awakened in a chaos of pins and needles, stabbing every inch of them. I whimpered and attempted to roll to my side but cried out when my leg cramped. I tried to roll back to my initial position but my other leg cramped too.

I groaned and wept at the pain, unable to find relief. My numb hands couldn't massage the cramps away. An incredibly warm blanket landed on me. The heavenly heat seeped into my tortured muscles all the way down to my bones, loosening the tension. Anton started rubbing and massaging my legs over the thin heating blanket, making swift work of smoothing my excruciating knots. Soon the pain receded, leaving my legs jerking involuntarily to random spasms.

Anton wrapped the blanket around me then carried me in his arms, bride-like, to the lift. By the time we reached the penthouse, I still hadn't regained enough motor control to walk on my own. Anton set me down by the bathroom. I limped inside, leaning on the wall for support. My bladder sang with blessed relief. I didn't know why it had mattered so much, but I refused to pee myself.

I wasn't an animal.

I crawled to the tub and leisured in a hot bath, eyes closed. Interspersed spasms ran through my muscles. When I returned to the bedroom, food was laid out on the small breakfast table. Though it smelled good, I wasn't hungry since William brought me water and an energy bar every six hours of my incarceration. I almost declined the meal but I didn't know what Anton had in store for me. Eating seemed the wiser course of action.

Chewing slowly, I forced myself to clean my plate under his watchful gaze. When I finished, he stood in front of me.

"Sade's launch was a resounding success," Anton said, casually.

My stomach knotted, waiting for the other shoe to drop.

"The celebrations will last for three more days. Night after tomorrow will be the grand finale, which I am expected to attend."

His cold, dark eyes connected with mine. I shuddered.

"My friends were quite disappointed by your absence last night. They're hoping you won't be… indisposed for the finale."

My hands fisted around the hem of my dress, twisting the delicate fabric.

"I don't need your answer now," Anton said as I opened my mouth to speak. "You have two days to decide how you want to spend your evening… and following hours."

He headed towards the door.

"Why are you doing this?" I whispered.

He paused and faced me. "Think, pet. I'm sure it will come back to you."

Anton walked out without another word.

I knew better than to get attached so quickly. Dr. Hazan and I had spoken plenty about it when things got out of hand with Paul. After I broke up with Marcus over his endless cheating, I hooked up with one of my biggest fans. Paul was gorgeous, worldly, and wanted to spend every minute of every day with me. How could I not fall for him? He was so sweet – when he was sweet. It took me a while to admit the number of times he wasn't nice quickly outnumbered the number of times he was. The day I changed my stage outfit to hide bruises, Marcus went ballistic and forbade me from seeing Paul again. He also forced me to meet with Dr. Alicia Hazan. According to her, I had a Dependent Personality Disorder, Accommodating Subtype.

I just called it falling for the wrong guy and trying to make a doomed relationship work.

My first week with Anton had been good, great even. He was growing on me and I thought, maybe, he liked me. The way he spoiled me, taught me things and couldn't seem to get enough of me… I hadn't imagined it. For a brief window of time, I believed my six months with him would be fun. He even seemed willing to help my career. Then, out of nowhere, he turned into this heartless monster.

It didn't even make sense. He went from changing my entire wardrobe because he didn't want my tits and ass exposed to the whole world, to wanting to pass me around his Braxian buddies.

Braxians...

Yes, I was superficial – Marcus had called me out on it enough to be aware. They weren't a pretty bunch. Everything about them was just too damn much. Their forehead was too prominent, their nose too wide and too flat, their jaw too square and broad. But it wasn't just the Braxians unattractive faces that made the thought of them pawing me repulsive. Their bodies were massive with hands bigger than my face. Their freaking thumb alone was almost the size of a human dick, so imagine what lay between their legs. If they tried to fuck me, they'd split me in two. Braxians didn't have cocks, they had tree trunks.

At least Anton, being half-human, was scaled to reasonable proportions. He was big compared to standard humans, but his body was fucking spectacular – big, lean and muscular. To my shame, even now with all this shit going around in my head, thinking of Anton naked made me wet. His face wasn't as brutish as theirs, the Braxian traits being more subdued, refined. And those lips... Anton had amazing lips and he knew what to do with them.

The first time we had sex, I might as well have been a virgin it had been such a tight fit. There's no way I could take on his buddies without tearing apart. Surely he could understand that? And I didn't want to fuck other men. Even when I was with Marcus and he stepped out on me, I never did. Anton and I may not be in a relationship per se, but for me, it was no different. Giving head to some other guys, I could consider, but not my pussy. Somehow, I needed to get through to him.

The cage had been more than I could stand. I couldn't go back there. My muscles twitched just at the prospect. I never did well with pain and couldn't have imagined how excruciating extended periods in a confined space could be. Another session there would drive me insane.

There was only one hour left before it was time to head out to the club. I already told Anton I would come. He became distant over the past two days, giving me no opportunity to plead my case. He only called me when he wanted me to suck him off, then he'd dismiss me. I actually liked giving him head. He smelled good, tasted good, and I loved seeing such a strong man fall apart beneath my touch. But I didn't like what was happening between us right now.

He no longer touched me or tried to get me off. Before, he always made sure I climaxed and only after would he find his own release. Now, he treated me like a fuck hole. This felt like an extension to my punishment, a way for him to get back at me. Yet, I knew it must be more than my refusal to sleep with his friends. When I asked, he simply told me to figure it out.

It was so frustrating.

The bedroom door opened and Anton walked in. I rose to my feet, flattening out the non-existent wrinkles on my dress. It was a long, silver dress with a thigh high split on the side. Anton particularly liked it when I tried it on at Aphrodite's Vault. I took special care of my appearance tonight, hoping to please him. He gave me a once over, and I felt myself warm at the glimmer of approval. His words though felt like a cold shower.

"Nice outfit, but it will not do for tonight. You will wear this," Anton said, extending a small box I hadn't noticed he was holding. "I will leave it to your discretion whether to wear black stilettos or your knee-high leather boots."

My stomach knotted. I placed the box on the breakfast table and opened it. After I parted the purple silk paper, my heart dropped. Within, a black leather bustier and matching leather thong sat next to a fluffy cat tail butt plug with a small bottle of lube. My lips parted in shock. I looked up at Anton, disbelieving. He held my stare, waiting for me to argue. When I said nothing, he gestured for me to get on with it.

I complied.

Under different circumstances, I would be excited by this outfit. It looked ridiculously sexy on me, especially with the stilettos I settled on as they made my legs look infinite. I didn't even mind the butt plug.

Marcus loved anal, so I'd done that rodeo plenty of times before. A bit of roleplaying also had its own appeal. Riding Anton while wagging a fluffy tail might be fun. However, tonight I would attend the biggest event on Venus Hive. All the A-listers would be there. I expected to make a grand entrance on the arm of the big boss, as a peer to the elite. Instead, I would trail behind as a pet. Tears of humiliation pricked my eyes.

Sheila would no doubt be there, looking down on me along with everyone else. They would wonder how I went from sharing lunch with Anton as his companion at Risqué to being his leashed animal. This was not the type of attention I craved.

Anton's eyes roamed over me, assessing. Closing the distance between us, he pulled out the pins in my hair, ruining the elaborate do I had spent hours perfecting. My hair cascaded down my back and he nodded in approval.

He bent me over the silky covers of the bed. Although my pet cushion was comfortable, this bed was ridiculously soft. Anton covered two fingers in lube before probing my ass. I forced myself to relax. This was the most intimate touch I had gotten from him in three days. But even then, it felt mechanical. His fingers pulled out followed seconds later by the pressure of the plug pushing its way in. It was thicker than I realized and slightly burned going in. I whimpered. To my surprise, Anton's rough hand caressed my ass soothingly. After giving me a moment to adjust, he pushed the plug in and out of my tight hole a few times before pushing it all the way in to the stopper.

He helped me back up and stepped into the bathroom to wash his hands. I felt full, but not in an unpleasant way. On instinct, I turned to the mirror to look at my tail. It was humiliating but I couldn't deny I looked insanely hot. I'd fuck myself looking like that.

I could tell Anton thought so too. His shaft strained against his pants. Under different circumstances, I would have playfully helped him with this problem. Right now, however, I just wanted to claw at his face for the cage, this outfit, and his plans for me tonight. He pulled a small object out of his pocket before lifting it before me.

A leather collar.

"You've got to be shitting me?" I whispered.

"Lift your hair," Anton said, his voice frigid.

"Anton—"

"Lift your fucking hair," he snapped.

Pressing my lips together, I did as ordered. He tied the collar around my neck. I heard it click into place. Under different circumstances, I might have been in awe of the collar. Leather repoussé technique had been used on the dark material. Intricate tribal patterns were raised along its length and the embedded amber colored gems matched my eyes. In the middle, a large gem hid the hook for the leash. Anton ran his fingers the length of the collar, a strange look on his face.

His eyes locked with mine then lowered to my lips. Before I knew what happened, he kissed me. My lips parted on their own, welcoming his tongue. I could taste the brandy on his breath as he deepened the kiss. His hand slipped between my legs, pushed the thong aside, and his fingers dipped inside my pussy. I moaned as wetness pooled within my core.

Anton pushed me against the wall while freeing his shaft from its confinement. Putting his hand beneath my ass, he lifted me up against the wall and rammed his cock home in one swift movement. Being unprepared, it hurt going in. His mouth swallowed my shout. With the butt plug in my rear, I felt full to bursting. Anton fucked me hard and fast, his thick cock grazing my sweet spot with every stroke. I thought my spine would split open from the blinding orgasm that ripped through me. Seconds later, he grunted his own release in my ear. Rubbing his face against my neck, he whispered my name so softly I almost missed it.

He kept me pressed against the wall. His face was buried in the crook of my neck while we both came down from our high. My legs wrapped around his narrow waist, my fingers weaved into his long hair, I rested my face against his. This was the most intimate embrace we'd ever shared, savoring each other's closeness in the aftermath. Anton never held me after sex. A beat later, I felt him pulling away and instinctively tightened my arms around him.

Without thinking, I pressed my lips to his ears and words tumbled out of my mouth.

"Don't let your friends fuck me."

I felt him stiffen against me, then he tried to push me away. I tightened my hold with both legs and arms.

"They'll tear me apart, Anton. They're too big. They'll kill me. I'll do whatever you want. I'll suck them off if you ask me. But don't let them fuck me. Just you. Please… Please, Anton. Just you."

I felt the tension bleed out of him as I spoke. Relaxing my hold slightly, I turned my face so our eyes connected. His were unreadable but contained none of the frequent cold glimmers.

"Obey me, without delay, without hesitation, and no harm will come to you. Embarrass me or humiliate me, and whatever you may fear from my friends will be nothing in comparison to what I'll do to you. Is that understood?"

"I won't, Anton. I promise. But please, just you, ok? Just you."

He stared at me for a while. I would have given anything to know what was going through his mind. The way he whispered my name sent shivers up my spine. It gave me hope. Deep down, Anton cared for me. It might be twisted and torn in places, but I could see it. I needed to capitalize on that to survive the next six months. He made as if to kiss me then changed his mind.

Anton pulled out of me and put me down on my feet. I leaned against the wall for support. He went into the bathroom to fix himself. On his way out, he paused in front of me.

"Clean yourself up, then meet me in front. Be quick."

I nodded, watching his retreating back.

"Anton," I said as he opened the door. He looked at me over his shoulder. "Whatever I've done that's made you angry with me, I'm sorry."

Emotions flickered over his face, too quick for me to identify. "No, Grace. You're not sorry yet," he said. "But you're starting to be."

Speechless, I watched him walk out and close the door behind him.

S ade wasn't the over the top, dark and creepy extravaganza I expected. I thought to find the usual red, black or purple walls, chains and shackles dangling from the ceiling, crosses, benches and flogger racks. None of the usual paraphernalia made an appearance. The octagonal entrance gleamed with granite-looking light beige and gold flooring. The tiled walls shimmered with a slightly lighter shade of beige. At the center of each wall, a white-stone entrance led to one of the various fetish themes of the club. They were easily identified by the symbols around the doorways: roleplaying, BDSM, pet playground, voyeurs/exhibitionists, swingers, and orgies. In the center of the hall, dancers and contortionists in skimpy outfits performed an erotic ballet on a circular stage. All along the walls, in the periphery, elevated daises provided cushioned booths and tables for VIP patrons.

Once again, I was out of my depth. My whole life, I'd trudged from one dive to the next, thinking I was climbing the ladder. More glitz, bigger lights, flashier neon always meant better to me. Looking at the understated elegance of this place, and all the others Anton had taken me to, it finally sank in that what I used to call glamour was vulgar. 'Less is more' and 'quality over quantity' started to make sense.

The women's dresses were anything but innocent. Yet, looking at them, no one would even consider grabbing their asses, flicking a lecherous tongue at them or asking them if they'd like a quick romp in a back alley. That was reserved for girls like me.

Half of these women were powerful entrepreneurs, wealthy intellectuals, or famous artists who had achieved success on their own merit. Them, I admired and envied. The other half were bitches who had fucked their way to the top. I wasn't even a tenth the slut they were, and still, because of my own dumb choices, I would never command the respect they received.

Interestingly, barely anyone wore leather. For some reason, I assumed everyone would. Goes to show how clueless I was about the lifestyle. Those who did, or wore role-play costumes, hid them under an over-garment they discarded at the entrance of their chosen section.

I tried to keep my head high and my expression neutral as we weaved through the throngs. Anton mostly ignored me except to make sure the thin golden chain that served as my leash didn't get stuck or tangled anywhere while he led me around after him. Four times we needed to stop for Anton's sycophants to suck up to him. Among them, Ms. Braddock, the owner of Aphrodite's Vault.

I was mortified.

She raised a perfectly shaped eyebrow when she noticed my outfit, her eyes following my tail. She seemed at a loss as to how to address me, if at all. You were not supposed to talk to a pet without its master's consent. Not even ten days ago, she unfurled the red carpet for me. Anton treated me like his girlfriend, spending millions of credits to give me a whole new wardrobe. From the look on her face, she wondered if we were merely roleplaying or if I got demoted. No doubt, Ms. Braddock had expected to see me rocking one of her finest gowns tonight. Instead, here I stood in leather underwear with a fluffy cat tail up my ass. At least, Anton spared me the cat ears. I'm not sure which one of us was more uncomfortable. I put on a brave face as if it was normal but was grateful when she quickly excused herself.

We were stopped many more times before we reached Anton's reserved alcove. While he talked, I let my eyes roam over the crowd. It was during one of those stops that I identified which booth belonged to Anton. The four massive Braxians sitting on the couches within were impossible to miss. My fearful gasp didn't go unnoticed. Anton followed my gaze, recognized his friends and gave me an unreadable look. He opened his mouth to say something to me.

"Anton!" Caleb called out before Anton could say a word. Cutting through the crowd, he made his way to us, Sheila hanging on his arm.

Fuck.

"Caleb," Anton replied, shaking his hand. He nodded at Sheila who blew him a kiss.

Bitch.

Caleb Jennings owned Risqué and a couple of lesser venues in the Commons. He was ridiculously handsome, lithe and well-toned. With his piercing blue eyes, short curly dark brown hair, a noble nose and elegant thin lips, Caleb was the type of man I usually went for. Except,

I didn't like that fucker one bit. There was something slimy about him. While there was no proof, rumor had it that his women didn't have a good time and were in no condition to speak of it when he was done with them. Marcus made it a point to keep me far away from Caleb whenever he dropped by the Commons looking for a 'companion' to entertain him.

"What a lovely pet you have there," Caleb said, his eyes slowly examining me. "I didn't know you were into that."

Anton turned slightly to look at me. I hoped the subdued lighting would hide the heat creeping into my cheeks at Sheila's smirk. A light pull on the golden leash made me step forward, closer to him. Anton wrapped his arm around me, his warm hand resting on my ass. It felt comforting.

"What is anyone ever really into?" Anton asked. "Sade boasts it can fulfill any fetish or fantasy. I can't think of a better place for Grace and me to discover what pleases us."

"Ah, experimenting then," Caleb said, giving me an assessing look.

Sheila narrowed her eyes. I didn't know if it had been intentional or not, but with those words, Anton turned my humiliation into consensual kinky role-play. I wanted to hug him in gratitude. Anton replied with a non-committal smile.

"And what else do you intend to experiment with, Mr. Myers?" Sheila asked, shifting slightly so the slit of her dress parted, exposing the entire length of her stunning leg. "I hear they've been extremely creative in the swingers' section."

I barely managed to swallow the shocked gasp that almost escaped me. Could the tramp be any more obvious?

Caleb chuckled. "Ah yes, they've got much to keep a couple entertained. If you were so inclined, I would gladly take care of your pet while you explore that section with Sheila."

My heart stopped. I didn't want that bitch anywhere near Anton. But worse, I did *not* want Caleb 'taking care' of me. Whether or not the rumors were true, the man gave me the creeps. I tried to school my features but couldn't help a wary glance at Anton.

"A tempting offer," Anton said, his thumb caressing the curve of my ass. "One I must decline, however. I have no doubt, Caleb, that you will have no problem finding a trade partner with such a delightful woman on your arm," Anton said, bowing his head at Sheila, "but I am quite set on discovering the kinks of my own delectable companion tonight. Maybe another time."

Sheila smiled but I could see the venom in her eyes. Though I knew better, I couldn't help casting a triumphant smirk her way as Anton led me to our booth, and the Braxian delegation.

CHAPTER 7
ANTON

The tension oozing out of Grace was palpable as we approached my booth. My 'friends' ogled her with lust-filled expressions. Not for the first time since leaving the penthouse, I berated myself for making her wear that outfit. She looked stunning. The dark leather accentuated the narrow curve of her hips and cupped her perky tits. And that tail… that damn tail fluttering this way and that with every step, drawing every eye to her perfect ass. I wanted to rip it out and bury my cock in her tight hole instead. And I would… soon. But all her beauty was meant for my eyes only. Grace was mine. Yet, here I was, like a fucking idiot, exposing her assets to every bastard on the station. I was doing exactly what I'd told her was wrong about her clothing choices.

Fucking moron…

And Caleb… I would never let that sick fuck anywhere near Grace. He'd maim her, scar the hell out of that perfect creamy skin like he had poor Evelyn. The bastard liked cutting girls with flawless skins, then fucking and whipping them while they bled to create blood splatter art.

Art my ass.

By the time he'd been done with Evelyn, not an inch of her body or

59

face had been spared. She'd gone into shock from blood loss. The cuts performed with a slightly heated scalpel left horrible scars that no amount of surgery could fix. The poor girl was so broken she took her life. I knew Caleb still indulged in his sick games but took the girls off station, outside of my jurisdiction.

Grace's obvious reluctance to go with him both surprised and pleased me. She liked pretty men. I expected her to be dripping wet for him. Maybe she had better survival instincts than I gave her credit for.

We climbed the stairs to the booth, and I once again cursed myself for her outfit. It was meant to humiliate her as she had humiliated me six years ago. And yet, Sheila's mocking smile spurred me to protect Grace rather than twist the knife further. I rubbed my hand over my face. I was fucking pathetic. Maybe the purebloods were right, and I was just a weak mutt.

These six months were meant to punish her and regain my honor. But here I was, panting after her like a lovesick puppy. Even now, I ached to drag her back home and fuck her into next week. The way she felt around my cock when I took her against the wall... I had wanted to stay in her embrace forever. Six years living among humans softened me. Now that I possessed the object of my obsession, I needed to cure myself of my weakness.

I saluted my guests as they rose to greet me. The leader of the Veelan Clan, Pattel, was a respectable, older Braxian. Unlike most Braxians, he promoted peace over violence. Sitting next to him was Gerwin, the firstborn son of the Caldes Clan leader. I hated that bastard. He was a bully and wielded his clan's status and power like a whip over those he considered inferior. As a mixed-breed, I was his favorite target. Toran and Jarvis were Gerwin's bitches. Both also firstborn sons of their respective clan leader, they followed Gerwin's lead in all things.

As the firstborn son of my own clan leader, I should have become my father's heir. But a mutt, a half-breed, couldn't become more than a servant or a slave. Women, who were viewed as property and broodmares on Braxia, received more respect than one of tainted blood. Gerwin made sure to remind me of it on a regular basis. However, despite my lack of status, my achievements and failures all reflected on my clan. Entertaining the Braxian elite elevated the prestige of my clan, and so I suffered their presence even though I fucking hated it.

Today, though, was special. They weren't simply my guests as part of my clan duty, but as witnesses and participants to Grace's punishment as I reclaimed my trampled honor. I sat across from my guests on the burgundy leather love seat. Grace settled at my feet on a padded cushion.

"We thank you once again, Anton, for your generous invitation," Pattel said, his eyes gliding over Grace before resting on me.

"My pleasure, Elder Pattel," I said, my smile gracious. "They've promised quite the spectacle tonight."

A taunting grin flickered across Gerwin's face. "Indeed, very considerate of you, Myers."

I gritted my teeth at the slight. Myers was my mother's name. As a half-breed, I wasn't allowed to bear my father's name. You only called someone by their last name to indicate they were strangers, of lesser rank or as a mark of contempt. He was baiting me, hoping I'd challenge him to fight so he could prove his physical superiority. I wouldn't give him the satisfaction.

"I'm always happy to extend my good fortune to the clans," I said, with a mocking grin of my own.

His smile faded.

To elitists like Gerwin, my growing wealth and power were insulting. Mutts should be grunts. My success further highlighted Gerwin's ineptitude and failures. He had no accomplishments of his own; he lived off the success and wealth of his father's clan.

"Glad to hear it," Gerwin said, his eyes falling to Grace. He licked his thick lips. "You've brought additional entertainment. How generous of you. I wouldn't mind a better look." He turned to the other Braxians. "How about you?"

"She looks like a nice piece," Toran said.

"Yeah," Jarvis said, "I wouldn't mind seeing how fluffy that tail is."

Pattel pursed his lips but said nothing. Grace's eyes weighed heavy on me. I ran my hand through the silky strands of her hair. She was trembling. Her fear should have pleased me, not put a nauseous cramp in the pit of my stomach. Keeping my face neutral, I ran my thumb over her lips. My eyes warned that I wouldn't tolerate disobedience.

"My friends want a better look at you, Grace. Why don't you show them what a lovely pet you are? Go on, they won't hurt you." I unhooked the gold chain leash from her collar.

Grace swallowed and her hand clenched around my ankle before she rose to her feet. She was statuesque, with legs for days, perfectly round ass, flat stomach, impertinent perky breasts, flawless luminescent skin, and the face of a goddess.

My woman…

I couldn't help puffing my chest at the Braxians mesmerized expressions. Braxians considered human women willful, independent creatures, but beautiful nonetheless. Human women wanted nothing to do with Braxians, both because they considered us too ugly and demanded equality. I couldn't blame them, but they'd never get that on Braxia. To own a human female, obedient, submissive, and as gorgeous as Grace, was considered a great feat and a great source of pride.

Grace approached Pattel and stood facing him for a few seconds before slowly turning so he could admire every side. Once she completed her rotation she looked at him for his permission to move on. He lifted a massive hand and caressed the length of her upper arm with his knuckles. He dropped his hand and reclined in his plush chair. A slight nod indicated she could go. His touch had been gentle but watching her before him made me understand her plea earlier.

My whole life, I despised women as selfish bitches. You could say I had mommy issues. Like Grace, my mother indentured herself to my father to get out of a bind. Three months into the one-year contract, she became pregnant despite her contraceptive implant. Once my father found out, he forbade the termination. As she was under contract, she had to obey. I was born premature, three weeks before the end of her contract. In exchange for bringing me to term, my father released her early. I never saw or heard from her.

Now, looking at Grace moving towards Gerwin, I couldn't even fathom how my mother had managed to take my father, to begin with. Braxians *were* too big. How did he not split her in two? Like with Pattel, Grace stopped before Gerwin and rotated. As soon as she had her back to him, Gerwin placed his hand on her ass. His hand was so big, it almost covered it fully. I clenched my teeth so as not to tell him to unhand her.

"Hmmm, very nice," Gerwin said, rubbing his hands over her body.

Grace bit her lip but otherwise withstood his attentions stoically. He grabbed one of her breasts and gave it a rough squeeze. She winced. I watched her face for further signs of distress but there were none. Gerwin's hand was on the move again. It slid over her stomach before forcing its way between her legs. She needed to part them to accommodate its size. Her eyes flew to my face, but I only spared her a quick look before focusing on how the bastard was handling her.

"How tight are you, little slave?" Gerwin asked, rubbing a thick finger against her pussy.

My hand gripped the edge of my seat's cushion, fighting the urge to rip his arms off. He roughly pushed a finger inside her and she yelped in pain.

"Careful!" I snarled. "I allowed you to look, not damage her."

"My apologies," he said, smirking. "I assumed you had stretched her already. But then, it is true you don't share a true Braxian's girth."

I ignored the chuckling from Toran and Jarvis.

Gerwin pulled his finger out of her slowly, then licked it. He didn't break eye contact with me. I gestured with my head for Grace to move. She didn't hesitate. Leaning back in my seat, I crossed my legs and dusted non-existent lint off my pants. I cast a swift glance at Toran who clumsily caressed her legs as she turned around for him, before setting my eyes back on Gerwin.

"I realize that until this moment, you've never touched a human female, let alone fucked one," I said. "Having bedded more than my fair share, I can tell you unless you intend to tear them, you have to start gently until they adjust to your girth."

"To hell with gentle!" Gerwin spat. "After her offense on Jeruna, she should be begging for any sliver of kindness she gets. Any true Braxian would have fucked her cunt to a pulp for the disrespect she showed your clan, then stuffed her throat full of his cock so she never speaks another insult again."

Grace's eyes widened, pausing mid-rotation in front of Jarvis. She blinked, her forehead wrinkling in concentration as she tried to piece the clues together. She still hadn't figured out what she had done. How could anyone be so clueless of the harm they caused others?

"It would have been too bad to wreck such a pretty pussy," Jarvis said, rubbing his thumb over her slit. "She must be nice and snug. Her throat though, why didn't you silence her like Darla? You could still enjoy fucking her mouth."

Grace slapped a hand over her mouth, her eyes bugging in horror. At last, she remembered. Now, the real game of retribution would begin.

"The answer to your comment," I said looking at Gerwin, "and question," I continued, looking at Jarvis, "is the reason why *I* am the one who built the Hive empire, and not either of you." I gestured to Grace. "Come here, pet." While she approached, I turned back to Gerwin. "I could take your approach and break her in one night like a rabid beast. Or, I could take mine and get to fuck the sexiest pussy you've ever seen, every day, anytime I want, any way I want, and wherever the hell I want."

Once Grace stood before me, I rested my arms on the backrest of the couch and spread my legs just enough for her to fit between them, never breaking eye contact with Gerwin. She got down on her knees and reached for the magnetic clasp of my pants. I couldn't repress the mocking smile stretching across my lips when Gerwin clenched his jaw, spite burning his muddy brown eyes.

"You see that, Jarvis?" I asked, waving at Grace sucking me off.

"You don't mess with a mouth like that. Not only does she give the best head this side of the galaxy, but she's also got decent pipes on her. Once I've had my fill, and she's completed her vocal training, she'll be the hottest ticket on this bucket."

I fisted my hand in her hair while she bobbed up and down on my shaft with the energy of despair.

"Watch and learn, Gerwin. This is how you teach them respect. She said she'd never let a stinking hybrid cock anywhere near her. Look at her now. Every fucking day, she sucks my cock, swallows my cum, and rides my dick. And when I'm done stretching that tight little ass of hers, I'll be fucking the hell out of that too. Isn't that right, pet?"

Eyes brimming with tears, she paused her ministrations long enough to whimper, "Yes, Master."

"Good girl," I said, swallowing the bitter bile of shame and self-disgust wrenching my gut.

Pattel chuckled, his broad shoulders shaking with the deep, rumbling sound. "Now that is impressive, young Anton. I have seen many well-trained human females, but none so stunning, let alone this skillful. You have done well for yourself. Your honor has been masterfully regained. I will apprise the clans of your accomplishment."

I smiled, triumphant at the praise. Pattel was a respected elder on Braxia. With his testimony, my dishonor would be cleared. It took three years after that fateful day when Grace publicly humiliated me for the shunning of my clan to be lifted. Three years because three stupid girls thought to amuse themselves at my expense.

Despite my warring emotions about Grace, Gerwin, and this whole messed up situation, her lips on me were divine. I wanted to surrender myself to their blissful caress, but not without tending to my guests first. I waved a waitress over.

"Yes, Mr. Myers," she said with deference, pretending not to see Grace deep-throating me.

"Please bring us three bottles of your finest wine, and I would have each of my guests well taken care of." I gave the waitress a meaningful glance towards Grace.

"Of course, Mr. Myers," the waitress said with a bright smile. "Drinks and entertainment coming right up."

Seconds later, four reasonably pretty girls lined up in front of the Braxians and went to work on their cocks, too massive to fit their mouths. Despite that, Gerwin gave me a begrudging nod of appreciation. Satisfied that my host duties were fulfilled, I gave myself over to the pleasure of Grace's expert lips.

CHAPTER 8
GRACE

Last night had been a fucking nightmare.

Stupid, stupid, stupid girl.

Anton didn't give two shits about me. He hated me. He didn't want me maimed the same way one takes care of a favorite sex toy. And that whole spiel about training me to advance my career? It had never been about me. He always intended to continue taking advantage of me once our contract was up.

I'm such a fucking idiot.

I wanted him to care. If I could start caring about his brutish face, why the hell couldn't he like me? Why couldn't anyone love me? Granted, I wasn't the most educated chick in the world but I wasn't a bad person. I was loyal, dependable, and did what I was told. Why couldn't that be enough? Alright, I fucked up back in Jeruna. But dammit, we were kids! It was just a stupid joke. I had gotten in trouble so many times in those days and done far dumber things than that. Who would have imagined it would be the one to come back and haunt me?

Back then, Darla and Steffie were wannabes like me. Both had their own shows while I mostly did opening acts. Darla even did a few guest appearances in elite clubs. The three of us were hanging out when a delegation of Braxians showed up, apparently there to conclude some big business deal. Although I had seen Braxians before, they always scared the shit out of me. They were colossal, hulking guys with massive everything. And their faces... holy fuck! They looked like those neant... neon... nerthal... whatever the hell those cavemen were called, with big, brutish faces.

I thought they looked fugly but as long as they didn't bother me, it was all good. Darla and Steffie couldn't seem to leave the subject alone. They were your typical vanilla pretty, popular girls, top of the in-crowd, and I wanted in. So I laughed with them, bitched with them, strutted like them. And boy did they strut. They made it a point to flaunt their stuff in front of the Braxians and glared when they looked.

Marcus didn't like me hanging out with the girls. He said they were trouble, but their connections could boost my career. There was one funny looking Braxian – a half-breed – that kept staring at me whenever I went to the bar or bathroom. While bigger than a human, he looked scrawny compared to the other Braxians. His face wasn't as messed up as the purebloods, with his Braxian traits being less pronounced, but that still didn't make him pretty. Marcus believed he had the hots for me which I thought sounded pretty gross.

Like an idiot, I told the girls what Marcus said. They figured it'd be funny to lead the hybrid on a bit and see if he would work up the courage to talk to me. It was a shitty thing to do. However, being my stupid, eager-to-please self, I went along with it. I thought once he made a move, I'd tell him to fuck off, we'd laugh at his embarrassment and call it a day.

How fucking naïve.

Darla made me rehearse the lines I'd say when he approached me. They were pretty hurtful. If only I'd listened to Marcus and stayed away from the girls, none of this would have happened. I remembered only wanting to get it done and over with. It turned out Darla planted her wireless microphone on me without me noticing. When the half-breed came to talk to me after I'd teased him one too many times, she aired my whole rejection speech on the com. Everyone heard. I was mortified. He was livid. For a minute, I thought he might beat me. I ran.

The girls, however, didn't think we'd done enough. They went on talking shit about Braxians for a while longer, making ape sounds until someone eventually cut the feed. Marcus dragged me out of there, screaming. He didn't let me leave my room for three days. I thought he was way overreacting. Yeah, it had been kind of cruel, but no one died. By the time he let me out, the Braxians were long gone and so were the girls. I never heard from them again, their careers having apparently burnt out overnight. It wasn't rare in our industry, but I wondered back then if they'd gotten blacklisted over that little stunt.

That was six years ago. Now, however, I feared they had fallen victim to Anton's trampled honor. Honestly, I had forgotten about that incident. Despite being a shitty prank, Jeruna had been such a minor thing – at least to me – compared to some of the other idiotic stunts I allowed myself to get lured into back then. Not once did I consider the possible consequences. To think Anton nurtured his rage and resentment for all these years…

Anton and I hadn't spoken since the party last night. He was already up and off to work by the time I woke. Somehow, I needed to fix this. But above all, I needed to know how far he intended to take his revenge. From what I'd heard in recent years, Braxians were really anal about honor and respect. The violence suggested last night by his friends freaked me out.

My worry escalated when I noticed the little present Anton left by my sleeping cushion: an anal plug bigger than the cat tail and a bottle of lube. His promise to fuck my ass haunted me. Anton was big. Really big. This was one tumble I wasn't looking forward to. Seeing how he was hell-bent on revenge, he wouldn't be gentle. Not after last night.

Our contract would hold up in any court in this galaxy. I couldn't flee. The consequences in the Eastern Quadrant for breaching an indentured servant contract were far too dire. I could only hope that if I took whatever punishment he had in store for me without a fuss, it would be a one off. Then we could go back to the way things were last week, when he was nice.

Yeah, keep dreaming.

My alarm went off, reminding me that my first vocal training session would start in thirty minutes. How was I going to do that with all this mess in my head? Anton insisted I find my own trainer and start doing things for myself. Dana, the receptionist, saved me. I liked her a lot. She was friendly, smart, resourceful and always willing to help. She didn't do the work for me but helped me narrow down a list of viable mentors and got me their contacts.

Most turned out to be pretty stuffy. They'd ask me to perform for them to evaluate my level. It didn't take a genius to see they weren't impressed. Yet, they were all eager to become my trainer, no doubt to garner Anton's good favor. However, I wasn't interested in a teacher trying to score points with my lover. Scratch that, with my master. I wanted someone genuinely interested in helping me out.

That someone was Romero.

He was the sixth trainer out of the seven I lined up. I liked him instantly. Tall and skinny, his body looked like it got confused as to what gender he was supposed to be halfway through puberty and settled for the status quo instead. Romero was a pretty man, with a baby face and an easy smile. That he also didn't look down on me after my performance sealed the deal.

Now wasn't the time to reminisce though. I needed to get ready.

It took me nearly five minutes of cringing, cussing and half the bottle of lube to get the damn plug in my rear. Another ten minutes to walk without showing – too much – that I had something huge up my ass. Then I went to meet Romero. The auditorium sat on the ground floor of the penthouse complex. Dana reserved it for me, two hours every day.

Like Anton, Romero thought my voice sounded good. Actually, he loved my voice and said it would be amazing once I learned some vocal techniques. That gave me a much-needed mental boost after my crappy week. My repertoire and performance, however... He made me swear to dump every bit of it and never speak of either again. I should have thrown a tantrum. Instead, I laughed.

I missed laughing.

We devoted the first hour and a half to singing techniques: posture, breathing, vocalizations, and diction. In the upcoming weeks, we would work on sound coloration and vocal effects once I mastered the basics. I couldn't wait to rock the same kind of vibrato Seria used during her performance. We dedicated the last thirty minutes to – yawn – theory.

"Focus, young lady," Romero said with a friendly scowl. "It may not be as fun as working your vocal techniques, but it's just as important. Now, why do you think your 'performances' never landed you a contract in the elite clubs?"

"Well that's a no-brainer," I said. "My show is a slut fest. The elite is too stuck up for that level of sexy."

Romero shook his head. "That's not true, and you know better. Everyone wants sex, but there's a difference between fucking and making love."

My stomach knotted at his words. They echoed almost perfectly what Anton said on our first date… Well, our first time out at the restaurant that felt like a date. I wanted that Anton back.

"The elite doesn't want to be caught watching porn. It's unseemly," Romero continued, not having noticed my dampened mood. "That's why you need to give them the same level of excitement by wrapping it into a more palatable presentation. They need to be able to brag about watching your performance in fancy circles, for its elegance, its eloquence, its pizzazz," he said with a flourish.

"So, I put on a sexy but fancy dress, pick a song from the 'acceptable' repertoire, and make minimal movements on a stage and boom, I'm respectable?" I mumbled, sitting down on the stage, legs crossed.

"That's the first step," Romero said with a chuckle. "But sweetheart, that will only increase your chances of getting the right doors to open. You need talent and charisma – which you do possess, you little diamond in the rough. But above all, you need honesty."

I blinked. What the hell did honesty have to do with anything? Romero smiled at my confusion. He brought a chair close to where I sat on the stage. Flipping it around, he sat on it backward, his arms resting on top of the backrest.

"You cannot fool your audience, darling. They will know if you're faking it. It's the difference between a B-movie actor and an Academy Award winner. The difference between the singer living off the bar gigs and a superstar. It's just like a relationship. If you're not honest with your partner, there is no hope. You can rarely get away with faking an orgasm or faking your affection. Sooner than later, your partner will know, he'll feel it. The same honesty must flow between you and your audience. Treat them like a lover and they'll worship you."

"Well then, I might as well give up now because I fucking suck at relationships."

"Sugar plum, the key to success in business, on stage and in a relationship, is figuring out what your customer, your audience, or your partner truly wants and give it to them."

"My partner wants revenge. He wants to hurt me." My voice broke down. I looked away. "He hates me."

Romero stared at me quietly as I sniffed, kicking myself for my loose tongue. I shouldn't be talking badly about Anton, let alone airing out our problems like this. Worse, Anton was paying Romero's bill. Instead of the tongue lashing I expected, Romero rose from his chair and sat down on the stage, next to me, our shoulders touching.

"No, pumpkin. Nobody spends twelve million credits to get revenge on someone they hate."

My eyes bugged. "How—?"

"Everyone knows. I'm afraid the creditors weren't very discreet," Romero said with a sympathetic smile. "Mr. Myers doesn't hate you. If his reaction towards you is unfriendly, then it's the symptoms of you not giving him what he wants, what he needs from you. The same way a disgruntled audience will boo an artist off-stage if they fail to meet expectations."

Folding my legs, I wrapped my arms around them. I started rocking back and forth but quickly put a stop to that; the butt plug having reminded me of its presence.

"But I do everything he says, everything he asks."

Romero put a comforting hand on my shoulder and gave it a gentle squeeze.

"People only tell you what they want you to hear. *You* need to learn to read between the lines. The signs aren't ten feet tall and all blinking neon, but they are plain to see if you pay attention. Remember when you sang for me before hiring me?"

I nodded, staring at him, hopeful.

"After you noticed me smiling when you held that high note then modulated it, you made sure to repeat it twice more during your performance. You noted what I liked and catered to my tastes. This is what you must do on both the professional and personal stage."

He tapped a finger on the tip of my nose. Rising, he dusted the seat of his pants then helped me to my feet.

"Now, sugar pie, for your homework…" Romero shook his head at my pout. "Yes, darling, homework… you will analyze your target audience and make a list of the things that make them tick and tingle, both negative and positive. That includes the triggers and quality of their response. We will use your observations as the foundation for your new show; one that will mesmerize your audience and get them eating out of your hand."

After training, I returned to the penthouse and headed for the kitchen. It was only a few minutes after noon and the cook would have lunch ready. I opened the door and saw my usual place all set with my plate sitting on a warmer. Until that moment, I hadn't realized how anxious I felt coming to the kitchen. Deep down, I feared Anton might have ordered the cook to put down a set of dog bowls on the floor for my food and water. Since he forbade me to remove my collar, I could only assume he wanted me in the role of a pet for the long haul.

This whole situation was so messed up, I didn't know which way was up anymore. Although I was pretty submissive, roleplaying a pet never appealed to me. The memory of the men and women eating directly off the floor as their masters tossed food at them at Risqué made my stomach squirm. If this was Anton's plan for me, I didn't know how I would make it through.

The food was good but I don't think I tasted any of it. Problem-solving had never been my forte and figuring out how to solve this particular situation used every single one of my brain cells. I washed down the braised pork with a glass of wine, put away the dirty dishes, and wandered back to Anton's bedroom.

It was a large room with a massive Blackwood bed propped against the back wall. A small breakfast table, large enough to comfortably seat two, sat in the corner across from a floor to ceiling vidscreen. When turned off, the screen blended with the sleek, light gray walls. Anton often set it to display nature sceneries, as if it was a window onto a breathtaking outdoors view of some exotic planet. Otherwise, he would set it to news feeds. You could watch movies, but that would mean rest and relaxation, two words that didn't fit in Anton's vocabulary. My pet cushion lay on the other side of the bed, between the nightstand and a large Blackwood dresser. Across from the bed, a set of sliding doors gave way to a mammoth walk-in closet and a fabulous in-ground tub – more like pool – a separate shower with massaging showerheads, and a sauna.

This was another reason Anton's behavior towards me confused me so badly. The first week, he had taken me out every night, buying me a completely new wardrobe – which occupied half of his walk-in – and ensured I got off every time we had sex.

But he stuck me on that stupid pet cushion at night.

The staff waited on me, he paid for my trainer, and I got to use his awesome bathroom and personal gym. Even now, I was sitting at the breakfast table with a state-of-the-art holographic keyboard to do research on the kick ass vidscreen. These weren't the living conditions of someone you hated.

Maybe Romero was right. Maybe Anton just wanted me to apologize for that stupid stunt. And then, we could go back to nicer Anton. I would like that. He didn't look down on me or talk down to me even when he gave me speeches about being lazy, my outfits or my shows. He took the time to teach and explain things to me like I was worth the effort. Hanging out with him was fun and he seemed to enjoy my company too.

Anton wasn't pretty but he wasn't ugly either – his face was actually growing on me. I liked pleasing him and he seemed to like caring for me too, at least that first week. It felt nice not to be treated like trash or like I was too stupid for someone like him.

I just needed Anton to like me again. I wanted him to whisper my name like he did last night when he fucked me against the wall, and hold me the way he had, as if he cared. I wanted him to flaunt me around like he did at Risqué that first time, as if I was a precious jewel – as if he was proud to be with me, to own me.

A lot of girls hated that idea of being owned, but for me, it meant I belonged. Someone cared enough to want to keep me, take care of me. Not just use me then discard me. I mean, everyone uses everyone, so what's the problem? Marcus used me all the time to draw in crowds and keep his 'special' customers happy. And I used him too, in my own way. As long as I sang, showed my stuff, and did what I was told, he kept me safe, made sure I ate well and had a good place to sleep. Except for his cheating, we had a pretty good life.

But now, my life was with Anton, at least for the next five and a half months.

With a heavy sigh, I turned on the vidscreen. I navigated the menu to the entertainment library Romero recommended for my homework. The large folder contained a few hundred recordings of some of the Hive's elite clubs' top performances. They were sorted by Artist. Feeling petty, I skipped the entire section with Sheila's name. I resented that her name appeared on this list. Sure she had talent, but dammit, you shouldn't hit on a man who accompanied another woman. Anton was mine, so the bitch needed to fuck off.

Mine? Really?

Whatever… I didn't have the energy to set the mental record straight.

I loaded the footage from one of Eliza's shows. The controls allowed me to focus on the performance or switch between the various cameras displaying the audience, and even zoom in on them. I settled as comfortably on my chair as the butt plug allowed and started 'analyzing' the performance. Eliza was pretty amazing. Too amazing I suppose because I lost myself in her song and forgot to analyze the audience. When I wasn't gaping in awe, my mind was wandering back to Anton.

Screw it.

Unable to focus, I put Eliza on full screen and curled up on my pet cushion, rocking softly to her hypnotic singing. The butt plug annoyed me, but I didn't dare remove it. It made lying down and sitting in certain positions rather uncomfortable. In spite of that, I must have dozed off because the com startled me awake.

"Yes?" I said, answering the call groggily.

"Hi Grace, it's Dana," the receptionist's voice said over the com. "You asked me to tell you when Mr. Myers returned. He's on his way up to the penthouse as we speak."

"Oh right," I said, rubbing the sleep from my eyes. "Thank you."

"You got it," Dana said before hanging up.

I raced to the bathroom to splash cold water on my face. Knowing Anton, he'd probably head straight to his office. I debated whether to ambush him there or give him a few minutes before we had 'the talk.' After fiddling and fussing over my appearance worse than when getting ready for a night out, I paced the room, trying to work up the courage to see him. I fingered my collar. I'd been doing that a lot since Anton put it on me last night.

Whatever my feelings about being collared, it was a fine piece of jewelry. Incredibly soft, and airy. At first, I feared the leather around my neck would make me sweaty and irritate my skin, but it felt like silk. Hoping to pacify Anton further, I chose a black and amber sarong that complemented the collar, echoing the gems embedded within.

Stop procrastinating and get it done already!

Taking a deep breath, I steeled myself and marched out of the room to Anton's office. I knocked, entering when he bid me to come in. His eyes narrowed when he saw me. My stomach dropped at the dead look in his eyes. Biting my lip, I considered making a hasty retreat and trying another time. Anton gestured with his chin towards the red leather empire chair across from his desk – the same chair I sat in when I signed the contract.

I closed the door behind me and quietly sat in the chair while Anton concluded his call. His dark eyes never wavered from me the whole time he talked over the com. Unnerved, I couldn't help fidgeting and once again considered retreating. By the time I decided to make a run for it, Anton ended the call. He leaned back in his chair, and raised an eyebrow at me.

This was such a bad idea…

I swallowed.

"Anton, I… I wanted to apologize for what happened back in Jeruna."

Wow, really? That's the best opening I could come up with?

"I mean, I was just a stupid kid but it doesn't make what I did okay," I said twisting my hands in my lap. "It was wrong, and… it was cruel. But I swear to you, I didn't know they were going to push it that far. It was stupid… I already said that," I mumbled to myself. "Truly, if I could go back and change any of it, I would in a heartbeat. What… What can I do to make it up to you? You name it… I'm so sorry."

He tilted his head, his jaw setting in a hard line. "That's your apology? You think you can stroll in here, say you're sorry, and make it all go away? How stupid are you?"

I flinched.

"We were just kids!" I said, my voice rising. "Yeah, it was shitty, but come on, Anton! It was just a prank. That was six fucking years ago. It's not like we killed anyone."

Wrong answer, dumbass.

As if in slow motion, I watched his eyes fill with rage, his lips distort into a furious snarl and his knuckles whiten as he gripped the armrests of his chair.

"Just a prank?" he said in a low, menacing tone.

"Anton, I—"

"Just a fucking prank?" he shouted.

He exploded out of his chair

I withered in mine, heart pounding, and watched him circle around his desk towards me. My lips parted in fear, I shrunk into my chair, pushing myself away from him.

"Do you know what your 'little prank' cost me? Cost my clan?" Anton asked through his teeth. "For three fucking years, my clan was outcast and shunned from the Empire for being dishonored. THREE FUCKING YEARS!" He slammed his hand against his desk. It resounded through the room like a thunderclap.

"I'm s—sorry," I sobbed, curling into myself.

I had never seen him, or anyone, so enraged. For the first time, I truly feared for my life. The thugs at the hotel would have violated me and maybe even sold me, but I doubted they would have injured me permanently. This Anton standing before me had murder in his eyes.

"Sorry?" He fisted my hair and brutally pulled me to my feet. I whimpered in pain, pressing my palms against his chest for support. "Now you're sorry? You three cunts almost cost me EVERYTHING! Had you pulled your little prank one hour earlier, the elder clans would have canceled the investment contract I'd spent ten years putting together."

He shoved me away from him and I stumbled to the floor. It was a bad fall, with my knee and elbow taking the brunt of the impact. Although it hurt, I watched him while rubbing the sting from my scalp where he had gripped my hair. He circled around me like a shark, his face twisted with fury.

"This… All this," he said, waving at the room, "everything I built would have never existed had the deal not already been signed by the time you bitches decided to fuck with me. Do you know what Braxians do to those who trample their honor and shame their clan?"

I shook my head, my vision blurry from the tears drenching my face.

Anton leaned forward, his face inches from mine. "Ever wondered what happened to your friends? Why their careers ended so abruptly?"

I slapped a hand over my mouth to hold in my choked sobs, leaning away for fear he would strike me. But Anton straightened and resumed his predatory pacing around me.

"Your fate would have been just as unpleasant had Marcus not locked you away. So no, *pet*, your apology is not accepted. I have waited a long time to regain the honor you so casually spat on, and you will pay every credit with interest."

My mind was reeling. I couldn't think straight. The venom, the hatred in his eyes... How had I not seen the depth of his contempt for me in the past two weeks? Darla... Steffie... What happened to them? And what would happen to me? Whatever punishment Anton planned for me would be painful.

"I'm sorry.... I'm so sorry."

Distantly, I knew it wasn't the right thing to say.

"No Grace, you're just starting to be. Remember your words that day? 'You seriously think a girl like me would let a half-breed Braxian cock anywhere near me?' Remember that?"

Did I ever... That had been part of the little speech Darla designed for the occasion. Braxians were rabid in their need for revenge, and it always directly tied to the nature of the offense. That explained why last night his friends said he should have fucked me to death and wrecked my throat. However, Anton saw me as an investment and didn't want to damage my vocal cords. Some other parts, though, weren't as essential for stage performance...

"Well guess what? You're about to be full of that half-breed cock. Get on your fucking knees."

Anton stood before me, undoing his pants. I wanted to run for the door but scrambled to my knees instead. Where would I go? Who would protect me? He contractually owned me and had the right to do anything he wanted short of killing me. By rights, he could beat me, starve me, degrade me, but he hadn't.

My only consolation was that as his indentured slave, he was obligated to release me in the same physical state he found me when we entered into this deal so he couldn't maim me. However, these days, doctors could fully heal plenty of grievous wounds. If Anton wanted, he could put me through hell before fixing me.

Guilt for what I had done to him and the painful consequences his clan endured, burned in my guts. I didn't want to be punished, and although I didn't fully understand the Braxian honor system, there was no question Anton and his clan greatly suffered because of our actions. I didn't begrudge him the right to his vindication but hoped he wouldn't take it too far. Maybe if I didn't fight, he wouldn't hurt me too much.

As if to contradict my hope, Anton painfully fisted my hair again. My cry of pain turned into a heaving choking sound as he shoved his cock in my mouth. It hurt. The blunt head hitting the back of my throat felt as if a hammer punched my tonsils. My gag reflex kicked in and I dry-heaved. I slammed my palms on his thighs to slow the brutality of his movements, but it didn't help. Anton kept up the punishing pace, barely giving me enough time to breathe.

Each impact of his cock radiated pain down my throat. My skull throbbed.

He rammed his dick in further, holding my head with both hands so I couldn't pull away.

"Take it," he ordered.

My lungs burned within me, begging for air. Panicked, I clawed at his thighs, trying in vain to pull away. My vision blurred and black dots appeared before my eyes. Just when I thought I would lose consciousness, he shoved me back and I collapsed to the floor, gasping for air. I dry heaved, my stomach cramping horribly. My face felt sticky with tears, snot and drool. Yet, I was stupidly grateful my meal had been long ago enough that I didn't vomit on his fancy carpet. That might have angered him more.

Please, let that be enough.

But brutally fucking my mouth wouldn't be deemed sufficient retribution for three years of shunning. I tried to swallow the saliva pooling in my mouth, but it felt like a million shards of glass ground their way down my throat.

"Are you amused now, Grace? Do you still think it was funny?"

I shook my head, blubbering, and curled into a ball. For some reason, I wished he was yelling instead of grinding out his words. This felt even more ominous.

"No? That's too bad because we're just getting started. Get up!"

Please, Anton. I'm so sorry. Please...

I didn't want to get up and fought the urge to curl up tighter on the ground. But I couldn't anger him further. I struggled to my feet, steeling myself for round two. Before I could get my bearings, Anton shoved me against the wall. I threw my hands up just in time to keep me from smashing face first into it. My wrists wrung from the impact. Before I could fully straighten, Anton bent me forward again and kicked my feet apart. His hands roughly lifted the hem of my sarong.

The sound of him spitting was swiftly followed by his massive cock pushing its way inside my pussy. Despite his saliva, being so dry and tense, it burned like hell. The added pressure of the butt plug only made it more agonizing. A metallic taste filled my mouth from biting inside my cheeks. Fighting to silence my whimpers, I searched for a quiet place in my mind to take refuge. So I wouldn't feel...

Anton wrapped his hand around my neck and pulled my head back. I gritted my teeth against the pain, while he continued pounding his length in and out of me. Each stroke burned going in and pulled at my insides going out. The worst part was his pelvis slamming against my ass, pushing the butt plug in. I was never good with pain. Coming from him, it hurt even more.

At least, he's not hitting me.

Anton's hot breath brushed against my ear. "That cock fucking your pussy belongs to a half-breed. That cum you've been swallowing the past two weeks and that's been filling that tight cunt of yours, belongs to a half-breed. That half-breed Braxian cock is going to continue fucking you senseless for the next six months."

This 'punishment' needed to end so that I could forget it ever happened. As if hearing my silent plea, Anton pulled out of me. The horrible burning sensation made me cry out but was followed by intense relief. I didn't know which hurt more between my vagina and my battered throat – both throbbed in counterpoint to each other. My legs wobbled beneath me. I wanted him to be done so I could crawl back to my cushion.

But he wasn't.

Anton dragged me by the nape to his desk and pressed my face against the top, his hand holding me down. Even though I didn't deny him the right to his revenge, this was too much. My throat and my pussy, I could manage, but not my ass. I wasn't prepared enough for someone so big. Imagining the damage he was about to do to me, I began trembling all over, my breath catching in my throat with terror.

Anton pulled the butt plug out of my ass in one swift motion. I screamed, feeling like my insides were being torn out. Searing pain radiated along my spine and down my legs. I felt a trickle of cold liquid over the seam of my ass and the citrusy scent of Denax filled the room.

As if in a dream, I heard my broken voice plead to him.

"Please... Please n-not... this. Not this."

I hadn't meant to beg for mercy, fearing to incense him further. Time seemed frozen. His hand still held me down but nothing else was happening. Despite my blood roaring in my ears, I could hear myself sobbing in the otherwise silent room.

Please, please, please don't do this.

Anton suddenly let go of me. Boneless, I let myself slide off the desk and crumbled to the floor. Everything hurt. Too battered to move, I just lay there, weeping.

His polished black shoes entered my line of sight. I didn't have the strength to look up at him but felt his gaze on me.

"Now, Grace... Now, I finally believe you truly are sorry," Anton said, his voice void of emotion.

His feet moved away from me, and I heard his office door close.

Anton was gone.

CHAPTER 9
ANTON

It wasn't supposed to be like this… feel like this… Yesterday should have been a moment of triumph; of vindication. The cleansing of my disgrace and reclaiming of my honor. Not this miasma of shame and self-disgust. Not the churning bitter bile of remorse and self-contempt that ate at me. Six years I waited to confront her, punish her for the offense against my clan and me, to humiliate her the way she humiliated me.

Six long years…

My eyes wandered back to William. Stiff-backed, he sat in a chair next to the couch I occupied. I sat at the same spot as that first time Grace's lips made me touch heaven. Over the years, William's role with me alternated from the hero who saved my life, to a father figure and big brother, to a business partner and right-hand man. But through all that, he always remained my one and only friend. Arms crossed over his chest, his hard stare made me feel small, alien in my own office.

The condemnation in his eyes cut deep.

The silence hung heavy between us, like a living, breathing entity. I shifted, finding it difficult to hold his gaze. I felt like a child facing a disappointed parent.

A long, drawn-out sigh pushed through William's nose.

"When you set out to punish Grace, I thought you intended some mild humiliation like you did at Sade and to spend the next few months fucking her. I could accept that. But what you did last night—"

"Will never happen again," I interrupted, my eyes cast down.

I didn't care much what humans thought of me. But William was different. His opinion meant a lot to me.

"It better not."

My eyes snapped to his at the sharpness of his tone. The coldness of his stare, his lips set in a grim line, gave me chills. I tried to swallow past the lump in my throat, but my mouth was too dry.

"I realize Braxians have their own set of rules and that your contract gives you certain *rights*," William said, "but I'm human. I cannot accept a woman being treated this way, least of all by someone I call a friend."

"I already told you, it won't happen again." His words irritated me, mostly because they echoed my own thoughts. I wanted him to stop. Without thinking, I blurted out, "I merely followed Braxian rules."

My argument rang hollow to my own ears. Shoulders sagging, I shut my eyes, unwilling to see the disapproval on his face.

"By Braxian rules, you should be dead."

My blood ran cold.

William continued without mercy. "Your father followed his conscience rather than the rules. Learn from him. Some things you do cannot be undone. They will haunt you for the rest of your life. Think long and hard what kind of man you want looking back at you in the mirror."

Rising from the couch, he leveled me with a hard stare. "Braxian honor isn't everything, Anton."

He headed for the door with heavy steps and closed the door behind him.

Honor...

Humans had no real understanding of honor, at least not the way Braxians did. A man without honor was nothing, no one, not fit to live. As a half-breed, upholding my honor was a matter of survival. Unless they were females, most half-breeds were killed at birth or terminated during pregnancy so they wouldn't taint the bloodline.

On Braxia, women were always welcomed, whatever their species. As they were considered inferior beings, the purity of their blood was irrelevant. They lived to entertain the men. Being pureblood only meant they received the honor of birthing the next generation of Braxians.

My father's decision to spare my life stained our clan's honor and lowered our status. Every day, growing up, I dreaded the moment he would give in to the clan's pressure and smother me to cleanse our bloodline of my tainted presence. I needed to work harder, be smarter and make myself indispensable to justify the mercy my father had shown me. But I was small and weak compared to the purebloods. When I wasn't working, I would hide or dodge bullies like Gerwin determined to kill me for bragging rights. However, what I lacked in strength, I more than made up for in business savvy.

I hustled and bustled, scraping every credit possible until I could open a strip club on Braxia, exclusively featuring human females. For all their bluster, Braxians craved the delicate elegance and beauty of human women. Most Braxians never had the opportunity or means to travel off-world to seek them out, so I brought them home instead. I saw a need and catered to it. In no time, I opened a second club, then a third before expanding with new locations off-world. My clubs provided work, income, and status for my clan. While they still despised me for being a half-breed, they no longer wanted to see me harmed – I benefited them too much.

It took nearly ten years of relentless wheeling and dealing before I garnered enough credibility to grovel before the elders' council. I needed them to invest in my Hive Network venture. Even at the time of the signing on Jeruna, some of the elder clans hesitated to enter into business with a mutt. That day should have been my consecration, my redemption. With that deal, I was going to build the greatest entertainment empire anyone had ever seen. We would no longer be a lesser clan. The wealth generated by the Hive would increase our clan's status. I could still see the pride in my father's eyes when the contract was signed.

I was no longer the shameful bastard of the clan leader. I was the hero that would turn the tide for our struggling clan and lift us to the top of the Braxian elite. A decade of hard work followed by a mere hour of celebration before my descent into hell because of three stupid girls. The contract already being signed, and therefore binding, was the only reason I still lived. The elders couldn't retract themselves, and my clan needed to meet the revenue commitments of the contract. They didn't have my business knowledge and connections to see it through.

The trouble was, the girls didn't just humiliate me and my clan by extension. Darla and Steffie ridiculed Braxians as a whole. Their punishment didn't come from my clan but from the elder clans. Had Grace mocked us through the intercom, they would have gotten her as well. But Grace only offended the half-breed. The elders didn't give a shit about my disgrace beyond the fact that they were now engaged in a business deal with a dishonored man.

As a consequence, they shunned my entire clan. Three long years during which no one would buy from us, trade or do business with us. We weren't welcomed at any social event or gathering. No one would even speak to us. For most clans, a shunning was a death sentence. Sometimes, banishing the clansman that caused the shunning was enough for it to be lifted. In my case, it wasn't an option, or I would have been banished... or killed immediately.

It was a difficult time for my father with senior members of the clan demanding he step down as leader because of me. However, my father was strong and held onto his power, sometimes by breaking a few jaws and limbs. Thankfully, the Hive Network became a resounding success. By the second year, I already owned four hives and began construction of a fifth. I generated enough revenue to keep the clan living comfortably and provided work for all those who needed it. By the end of the third year, I returned the elder clan's investment, four years ahead of schedule. In response, they lifted the shunning.

At the time, Braxia had entered the worst of its financial crisis, and many clans turned their eyes to us – to me – for work, business collaborations or financial assistance. Today, half the main clans on Braxia were beholden to me in one way or another, be it through loans, supply chain, or employment.

For all this, I should have reveled in Grace's pain. Instead, watching her choke on my cock, tremble before me, and crying with heart-wrenching sobs had torn me apart. However, my duty to my clan wouldn't allow me to back down. I guess Gerwin was right about me after all – I was weak, a poor excuse of a clansman. A true Braxian would have gotten his rocks off handling Grace the way I did, fucking her in every hole while she begged for mercy.

But no, not me. Not the pathetic mutt of a half-breed.

I couldn't even do it. Her asking me to stop once was all it took to break my already fragile resolve. Right now, I felt nothing but shame, fighting the urge to throw myself at her feet and beg for her forgiveness. Maybe my father should have smothered me as a child. I would never be a true Braxian – I didn't have the spine for it.

I rubbed my face with both hands, fighting the depression settling in. We were only two weeks into the contract. Despite my threats to her, I wouldn't be able to treat Grace like this again, let alone for another five and half months. Like a coward, I avoided her since our confrontation. I couldn't bear the look of despair in her eyes. What the fuck was I going to do?

And to make matters worse, that asshole Gerwin and his goons would come by the penthouse in a couple of days to discuss business. Technically, I already displayed my mastery over Grace. Publicly. Yet the clans would expect her to wait on me during their visit. I didn't need this shit right now.

My com rang, pulling me out of my dark musing.

"Yes?"

"Mr. Myers," Dana said, "there is a Mr. Marcus Gayle at the reception requesting an audience with you."

Are you fucking kidding me?

This day was just getting better. What the hell did Marcus want? Why would he show his face after abandoning Grace? When the hell did he get back on Venus Hive? I considered telling her to send him away, but I needed to know what he was up to.

"Send him up," I said, terminating the com.

I checked the time on my monitor. Grace would be in her vocal training session for another forty-five minutes. Marcus would need to be gone before her return. I didn't want him anywhere near her. Especially not now while I was trying to sort out how to handle her. Grace was mine and no one, least of all him, would take her from me.

William escorted Marcus into my office, then left without another word. I didn't miss the curiosity on his face. By now, all of Venus Hive would buzz with the news that my woman's ex-boyfriend was back.

"Hello, Mr. Myers," Marcus said, taking two hesitant steps towards me. He outstretched his hand but then withdrew it when I remained seated.

I leaned back in my chair and gave him a once over. His tussled dirty blond hair looked as if he just fell out of bed. With his striking green eyes, a perky nose and cleft chin, his face was everything mine wasn't. Despite his bargain suit, worn shoes, and cheap fragrance, Marcus was a good-looking man. He could make hand-me-downs look like couture. Marcus was tall and lithe with average muscle mass. I could probably toss him across the room with one hand without breaking a sweat.

"Mr. Gayle," I replied, "did you get lost?"

Marcus chuckled. Fiddling with his collar, he took another two steps forward.

"No, not lost, Mr. Myers, though I can see why you would think that."

I gestured with my chin at the red empire chair in front of my desk. Grace's chair.

Had it truly only been two weeks?

Marcus took a seat, thanking me. "So, you must wonder why I'm visiting?"

I stared at him in silence. He shifted in his chair and cleared his throat.

"Right. So, I wanted to thank you for rescuing Grace. I never would have left her behind had I known they would come after her. They've never acted like this before."

Indeed, threatening relatives and loved ones over bad debt was unheard of in 'civilized' circles. Low-level thugs and criminals still did on some backwater planets and mercenary space stations. Then again, creditors rarely received strong incentives to make sure the damsel in distress would have no other choice than to beg for my assistance.

I smirked.

Marcus clenched his jaw, putting two and two together. He knew he could never prove it. Good looking, and smart. Under different circumstances, I could have used someone like him.

"I didn't rescue her," I deadpanned. "We signed an agreement."

"Yes, about that…"

My eyes narrowed. Pretty boy better tread carefully. I had no intention of ever releasing her, not even after the six months were up.

"…I was able to rectify the situation that put me in this predicament, to begin with," Marcus said, his eyes flittering between mine. "Which means I'm able to buy back Grace's contract from you if we can agree on terms."

What the fuck?

When Dana announced Marcus' arrival, a lot of scenarios played through my mind. But this? Who the hell would pay over twelve million credits to buy back the contract of some chick he wasn't even mated to? How deep was the bond between them?

"Why the fuck would you do that?" I asked. "This is more money than you've ever had. You're a free man, cleared of any debt. Why not walk away? And don't tell me some shit about being in love with her; we both know you're not."

He tilted his head to the side, his gaze assessing. The silence stretched for a few seconds and my irritation bubbled to the surface. I was about to snap at him when he snorted as if in derision of whatever thought crossed his mind.

"I can see why you would expect me to cut and run. After all, I'm a hustler and peddler of 'exotic' goods. But I'm not a con man. You don't last long in this line of work if you screw over your business partners. I'm not an overly proud man, but I do have my honor."

Marcus reclined in his chair and crossed his leg. I didn't like this sudden change of attitude. I wanted back the nervous man who walked into my office a few minutes ago.

"You've also got another thing wrong, Mr. Myers."

I raised an eyebrow at him.

Marcus smiled. "I do love Grace."

His words struck me like a slap in the face. The smug, confident tone of his voice made me wonder if they truly shared deep feelings. Had Grace given her heart away?

"You're going to come into my office and lie to my face?"

"I'm not lying to you, Mr. Myers," Marcus said calmly. "I'm not *in love* with her, but I do love her. Grace and I have been together since we were nine. We grew up together in the same orphanage."

"Ah, so now it's childhood love?"

He curled his lips but continued as if I hadn't interrupted.

"Grace was always pretty, but she became gorgeous at twelve. Mr. Carston, the son of a bitch who ran the orphanage, was quick to notice. It took me a while to realize what he was doing to her. I killed him and took Grace away. I've been taking care of her ever since."

"Touching story, really. However, child abuse on fringe colonies is commonplace. Those who survive move on. We all have our own growing pains."

My own childhood had been no cakewalk. I'd have taken someone trying to get into my pants any day over everyone looking for an opportunity to maim or murder me. At least, I think I would have preferred that. However, the thought of that Mr. Carston abusing Grace, especially as a helpless child, made my hands twitch with the need to shatter his bones. It was a good thing Marcus already disposed of him. Otherwise, he'd be getting a visit from me.

Marcus nodded. "I have no doubt you've faced plenty of hardship, being half-human. Surely you can understand that I would want to do this for the person who helped me through my difficult times?"

No, I didn't. No one ever helped me survive any of my own nightmares aside from my father's distant protection.

That's a lie. William saved you.

That was true. I owed William. If he ever found himself in a bind, no price would be too high to help him.

"Unfortunately, her contract isn't for sale. You'll have to find yourself a new cock bait."

His expression hardened. Marcus pressed his lips together, clearly holding back. I doubted it was fear making him pause. He wasn't in a position of force in these 'negotiations' and knew better than to antagonize me more.

Marcus sucked in air through pinched nostrils, his eyes piercing me. "Alright, Mr. Myers. Let us speak plainly."

I leaned back in my chair, a bored expression on my face, and gestured for him to proceed.

"I know you're still angry about Jeruna… with good reason."

My lips twisted into an angry snarl, fury boiling in my veins. It took all my willpower to rein in my rising temper and school my features. He had balls bringing up Jeruna. Pretty, smart, and with a backbone. I couldn't help feeling a begrudging respect for him. This was unexpected. He held my still furious gaze, his unwavering.

"Grace didn't want to do it and felt horrible about the whole deal. She's a pushover. She needs to please. You can get her to do almost anything if she thinks it will make you like her in the end."

"And that should absolve her?" My hands fisted over the armrests of my chair. Thinking of Jeruna made my blood boil. Self-control normally wasn't much of an issue, but right now, mine was beyond thin.

"No, Mr. Myers. It shouldn't and doesn't. I'm merely explaining how it happened," Marcus replied. "You have every right to demand retribution for the offense and to restore your honor."

"How kind of you to grant me your permission."

What's my problem?

I was acting like a snotty brat. This was not how I wanted to portray myself to Grace's former lover – the man who owned her affection from childhood. Showing more class than I was, Marcus pretended not to hear my childish outburst.

"Grace has been with you for the past two weeks. You must know by now that she's nothing like Darla and Steffie. They were cruel and spiteful. What punishment they received was a long time coming."

Marcus uncrossed his legs and leaned forward. While his posture could be perceived as begging, the expression on his face belied its submissiveness. Though he was pleading with me, he was also doing a lot of convincing.

"Grace is a good girl, loyal to the bone. She doesn't have an ounce of malice in her. Granted, she's no rocket scientist, and she can be a little superficial, but she'll do anything for those she cares about. All she wants is to be loved."

"Didn't you just say you loved her?" I asked.

"I'm a man whore. As long as it's tight, warm and willing, my dick is happy to dive in. Grace isn't down with that. The whole time I was stepping out on her, she didn't cheat once, even when I gave her permission. Hell, I even tried to convince her to participate in my orgies, but it's not in her. It makes her feel dirty. Grace wants to belong to a single man who will only want to belong to her. That will never be me."

Images of Grace begging me not to let the other Braxians fuck her flooded my mind, her words echoing in my head.

"Just you. Please… Please, Anton. Just you."

And how she shied away from Caleb when he suggested we swap partners at Sade. That had been so unexpected, not that I would have ever let that twisted fuck anywhere near her. I would never admit it, but I was pleased by the thought that she wanted no other cock but mine.

"Fascinating, but what does that have to do with anything?" I said, tapping my fingers on my armrest. The clock was ticking. I wanted him gone before Grace returned.

Marcus straightened in his chair and gave me a speculative look. "I understand Grace has been punished for her trespass, and your elders considered your honor restored at Sade."

How the fuck did he know that?

"Therefore, I would reiterate my offer to buy back the remainder of Grace's contract. This would be the full amount of the original debt with all interest regardless of the two weeks she has served so far. I have found a man whom I believe can be everything Grace wants. He will be faithful, give her a home, a family, the stability, and love she's always craved."

I jumped out of my chair and heard it scrape against the floor. My fists resting on my desk, I leaned forward, glaring at him.

"Fuck you, fuck your offer, and fuck that man. Grace is mine. So take your offer and get out. You're not getting her back."

The bastard didn't flinch. Instead, he barely repressed a smug smile. He'd baited me and I'd jumped in headfirst. I wanted to break his neck.

Marcus slowly rose from his chair, smoothing his suit.

"I don't need her back," he said. "I need her happy. If I were smarter, I'd marry her. You've had your revenge, Mr. Myers. Grace is a wonderful, beautiful girl. A smarter man than me would play for keeps and realize what a treasure he holds."

"I do not need advice on how to manage my property," I said, straightening.

Marcus glanced around the room with an amused smile. "That, you definitely don't. I've taken enough of your time. Thank you for hearing me out."

He sauntered towards the door. After opening it, he paused in the doorway and turned to face me.

"By the way, if Grace starts kissing you on the forehead, it means she considers you're a couple and she feels affection for you." With a final nod, he walked out.

I touched my eyebrow, then stroked across my forehead. Grace had kissed my forehead – just once, as a good morning greeting. Ten minutes later, I had stuffed her in a cage for twenty-four hours because she didn't want other men fucking her.

I dropped back into my chair with a heavy sigh. Resting my elbows on my desk, I held my head between my hands.

CHAPTER 10
GRACE

I watched another recording, trying to analyze the patrons better than last time. Like yesterday, I couldn't focus. This time, it wasn't because I itched to go stir the hornet's nest, but because I ached. Everywhere. Despite my comfortable chair, I stacked a pillow on top. My throat hurt like a bitch. When I checked in the mirror this morning, I could see purplish red bruising in the back of my mouth around the tonsils. Swallowing, eating, even talking was painful. It felt like my throat was riddled with tiny cuts. My pussy was sore too but that was more bearable.

Romero was fairly upset when he realized I was in pain. I didn't tell him anything, but he guessed the soreness was courtesy of Anton. Thankfully, he didn't pry. He merely reminded me that it was vital I figured out what my target wanted. Well, I knew what he wanted; revenge. And I gave it to him with my tears and pain. I just needed to survive the next five months.

He called it a day after fifteen minutes. With the state of my throat, singing or even discussing anything wasn't an option, but I had wanted out of the penthouse. The stiff way I moved made performance training impossible. We would reconvene in a couple of days. While sorry I didn't spend more time with Romero – he was a really cool guy

– I was quite happy to go curl up on my pet cushion and wallow in self-pity.

After tossing and turning for an hour, I gave up and crawled to the breakfast table to fire up the vidscreen. My training day wouldn't be a total waste. Half an hour into my homework, the bedroom door opened.

Surprised by my presence, Anton froze in the doorway. "Shouldn't you be training?"

A coil of dread seeped down my spine. Clasping my hands to hide their trembling, I faced him. Fear weighed so heavily on my chest, I could barely breathe.

"R-Romero c-cancelled today's l-lesson."

My voice sounded raspier than normal.

Anton frowned, his eyes dropping to my throat. He marched towards me, and I instinctively shrank away, raising shaky hands before me.

He stopped in front of me. Head bowed, I silenced a whimper.

Don't cry. Don't move. Don't make him angry.

"I'm not going to hurt you," he snapped. "Get up."

Shuddering, I lowered my hands hesitantly and obeyed, looking at him with pleading eyes. I thought of running, hiding, throwing myself at his feet, but knew better than to antagonize him. When he raised both hands towards my face, I flinched.

"Stay."

His voice was as hard as the look he gave me. Cold sweat trickled down my back. I blinked away the tears welling in my eyes – I didn't want to survive another punishment. I swallowed, wincing halfway through. My throat felt like some vicious beast had raked its claws through it. Anton's frown deepened, and he placed his fingertips on the sides of my neck. I felt him apply a slight pressure while studying the reaction on my face.

"Does that hurt?"

His voice was muffled by the frantic pounding of my heart.

"A l-little… B-but mostly when I s-swallow or t-talk."

Lips pursed, his hands remained gentle on my neck. My chest

heaved from my semi-panicked breathing. Although Anton didn't appear to be angry, he wasn't happy. What did that mean for me?

"Open your mouth."

I complied. That hurt as it stretched the muscles in the back of my throat. But I didn't want to give him any reason to hit me. By the hard set of his jaw, I knew what he saw displeased him. While I could deep throat with the best of them, yesterday was different. No one could handle that.

Anton took a few steps back, then gestured for me to approach. Confused, I closed my mouth and did as ordered, trying to hide my stiffness and the limp from my bruised knee.

"That's enough," he said, glancing at the pillow on my chair.

At first, my face heated with shame, then I felt myself pale with worry. What if he begrudged me seeking that bit of comfort? Without a word, Anton circled around me and stepped into the bathroom. Not knowing what to do, I stood still, waiting to see what he was up to. He came back carrying a spray bottle, some ointment, and a hand towel.

My heart seized in my chest.

All tension bled out of me as I watched him approach. I felt like a puppy eagerly awaiting to be petted by my master. Dr. Hazan would be disappointed with me. It was wrong to respond to kindness this way, but I couldn't help it. I loved having someone take care of me. Even now, knowing I needed care because of the trauma he'd inflicted on me, a warm fuzzy feeling spread through me. Anton placed the ointment on the table.

"Open," he said, raising the spray bottle in front of my mouth. "Don't swallow until I tell you."

I nodded and he pushed three times, coating the back of my throat. Cold at first, it started tingling, the feeling growing in intensity before quickly fading.

"Close your mouth and swallow."

I did as he commanded. It hurt but not as much as earlier. Anton massaged my throat and I leaned into the touch. Romero asked me earlier if I was familiar with the spray. Of course I was, like any decent singer. It worked wonders on sore throats and laryngitis; two things you couldn't afford before a show. When he asked why I hadn't used any, I gave him the runaround and he let the matter drop. Truth was, I didn't know how Anton would feel about it. It wasn't uncommon for masters to refuse painkillers to a pet they had personally punished.

"Open again."

Anton repeated the process twice more. On the third time, when I swallowed, my discomfort became faint and distant.

"Sit on the bed," Anton said while putting down the spray and picking up the ointment. After I complied, he approached and looked at my groin. "Are you sore?"

What do you think? I thought bitterly.

But I simply nodded. He gently pushed my shoulder backward, indicating for me to lie down. He lifted my skirt, exposing me to him. Noticing the bruise on my knee from when he had shoved me to the floor, he rubbed some ointment over it first. The effects were almost immediate, numbing the dull throbbing there. I always bruised easily. For a while, Marcus and I thought it might be some medical condition, but the doctors found nothing. My pale skin didn't help either, making the slightest scratch look worse than it was.

Once done with my knee, Anton parted my legs and crouched in front of me. Lifting my head up to see what he was doing, I watched him spread some ointment on top of two fingers then carefully insert them into my swollen opening. The coldness of the cream, my raw insides, and the thickness of his fingers made me flinch.

Anton put his other hand on my thigh and caressed it with his thumb in a soothing motion. My eyes pricked, and I blinked away the tears. I wanted to hate him. I should hate him. It wasn't right that I was this hungry for the slightest sign of caring. Just like it wasn't right that I had been so brutally punished for something stupid I did years ago. I watched Anton gently slip his fingers in and out of me, coating my inner walls with the healing cream. This was the man I liked and wanted to see. The gentle, caring, careful Anton.

Why couldn't he always be like this? Why did the men I like always end up hurting me?

He pulled his fingers out. "Better?"

I nodded, fearing my voice would betray the turmoil raging inside me.

"How is your rear?" he asked after lowering the front of my skirt.

I froze. The terror from last night creeping back in. Nothing ever scared me more than when he almost fucked my ass. I believed he would damage me beyond repair. Kill me even. Pictures of me lying in a pool of my own blood flashed in my head. I shuddered, goosebumps erupting all over my skin.

It didn't happen. He stopped. You asked him, and he stopped.

He did stop.

That didn't make anything that happened last night okay. But for me, it changed everything. Paul never stopped. Begging him only brought me greater punishment.

"Grace?"

Anton's voice snapped me out of my daze. Yes, my ass did hurt. Nowhere near as bad as my vagina had, but it was sore, nonetheless. I could still feel the burn from when he ripped out the plug.

I considered saying no, not wanting Anton anywhere near my ass in case he decided to finish the job. However, nothing indicated he wanted revenge right now and I really didn't like pain. It felt silly to punish myself further.

"Yes, a bit," I whispered.

"Move up the bed and get on your hands and knees," he said.

I did as ordered, my pulse rising. He applied a small pressure on my shoulders so my face rested on the mattress with my ass up. That position made my butt hurt. Then again, since last night, any position hurt. While eager for the relief the ointment would provide, I dreaded the moment Anton would insert his fingers into my tight hole.

As if sensing my growing panic, Anton's calloused hand gently caressed my butt cheek in a circular motion to make me relax. His wet fingers touched my rosette, and I tensed up. He didn't try to push his way in though. While still caressing my cheek, his fingers softly applied the cream around my inflamed opening, soothing it. With a slow, painstaking process, Anton eventually managed to slide a single finger inside me to coat my rear with the ointment.

When he finished, he wiped his hand on the hand towel and helped me back to my feet. He made me walk around the room to assess my level of discomfort. It wasn't as magical as the throat spray, but I no longer walked as if a stick was stuck in my behind.

"In half an hour, have something to eat," Anton said. "And before you go to sleep, we'll put on a bit more ointment."

"Yes, A... Thank you."

I almost said his name but thankfully caught myself in time. After last night, I wasn't sure where I stood. Should I call him Master? He only ever asked me to call him Anton, though.

He gave me a strange look then nodded. I watched his retreating back as he headed for the bathroom, wondering what thoughts were going through his mind. Did guilt drive him to take such thorough care of me? Did he fix me only to break me again later? Was yesterday enough punishment or was it only the first of many?

After washing his hands and putting away the spray and ointment, he quietly walked out of the room.

The next two weeks were like sitting in the eye of a storm. Things remained peaceful, quiet, yet you knew some serious shit would go down soon. Anton reverted to the distant, but mostly kind man of our first week. After soothing the bruising he had inflicted, he didn't touch me for three days.

I felt in limbo, not quite knowing my purpose or what he wanted from me. Worse, wondering if more punishment awaited twisted my stomach with fear. I really wasn't good with pain. At least, Anton didn't want to do severe damage to me, which was a major relief. Despite his rage, Anton used Denax on me – a fast-acting muscle relaxant – right before I asked him not to take my ass. Even without giving it enough time to take effect fully, a few seconds would have spared me from tearing but not spared me from pain.

But he stopped.

And that gave me hope.

On the fourth day, we returned to our previous routine. He called me into his office to suck him off. Quickly, my initial fears that he would savagely fuck my face alleviated. Anton showed no aggression. He was almost tender in the way he caressed my hair and my face while I deep throated him. I was ok with this Anton. But would it last?

On the sixth day, he didn't let me finish. Half-way through, he pulled me off him, laid me down on his desk and went down on me. I had forgotten what Anton could do with his tongue. I hadn't had an orgasm since the day he took me against the wall with that cat tail in my ass. That wicked mouth of his got me off like a rocket. He didn't stop. I climaxed once more before he took me.

Until that moment, I hadn't realized how hollow I felt. How I had missed having him inside me. Not only the fullness but especially the gentle, careful way in which he took me until I adjusted to his girth. Only then did he surrender to passion. Despite still being torn by what he had done to me, I couldn't help melting. He kissed me while riding me, which felt good. Anton's mouth was heavenly, whichever set of lips he used it on. We didn't kiss often. Kissing created intimacy and he wanted none of that between us. At least he didn't seem to want to punish me anymore. I was content with this Anton.

Initially, I rejoiced finding out the Braxian delegation's scheduled visit was delayed by another week. Yet, as the days trickled by and the date approached, I wished they hadn't postponed. At least the nightmare would be over by now. However, wishful thinking wouldn't change a thing. I pushed the unpleasantness of tomorrow away from my mind.

I didn't know if Anton realized tonight marked our first month together. Well, okay, not together, but of the signing of our contract. Could that be the reason we were going to Risqué tonight? Wondering for hours what outfit he expected me to wear almost drove me insane. I wanted to flaunt one of the countless gorgeous outfits Anton bought for me. A little over two weeks passed since 'the incident' and I was all but under house arrest. Aside from vocal training, there were no opportunities to show off those outfits. And now I feared Anton would bring me another pet costume.

I remembered those human pets eating food off the floor as their masters tossed bits of meat to them. I shuddered, my hand unconsciously reaching for the collar. Is that what Anton had in mind for me tonight?

We'd be leaving soon, and I was running out of time to prepare. Bracing myself, I made my way to his office, hoping my inquiry wouldn't trigger his anger. I hesitated in front of his door, itching to turn around and hightail it back to the bedroom. I shouldn't be scared. Unlike the previous time, I wasn't bringing up a sensitive topic. But Anton was too mercurial; a sweetheart one minute and a vicious monster the next. Inhaling, I knocked on his office door.

"Come in," his muffled voice called out.

I opened the door and took a few hesitant steps inside. The absence of tension in Anton's shoulders and the relaxed setting of his jaw made me breathe easier. He gave me an inquisitive look. A quick glance around the room didn't reveal the presence of a box like the one that had contained the cat outfit.

I cleared my throat. "I was wondering if you have specific clothes for me to wear tonight." I tucked my hair behind my ear.

He frowned. "Why would I..." The expression on his face changed as understanding dawned on him. "Right. No, Grace. I do not foresee the need for special outfits in the near future. You have a full wardrobe you can use."

I couldn't hold back the broad grin splitting my face. Relief and excitement made me giddy. Role-play could be a lot of fun, but not the way we did it last time. I nodded with enthusiasm, my mind already reviewing my wardrobe.

"Ok. I'll go pick something then. Sorry for bothering you."

As I turned to leave, he said, "That silver dress looked good on you."

That was the dress I planned on wearing before he made me change into the cat costume.

"Sure, Anton. I'd be happy to wear that," I said, facing him.

He rose from his chair and sauntered towards me. The light smile on his face reassured me that he held no ill intentions. Stopping before me, Anton let his eyes roam over every inch of my body. He slowly raised his hand and combed his fingers through my hair. I shivered at his touch.

"Leave your hair down," he said with a soft voice, his eyes staring at the strands as they flowed through his fingers. "You have the most amazing hair. I want it unobstructed."

"Okay," I whispered, my breath catching in my throat.

Of course, he would want it down. He liked easy access to everything. His hand slid off my hair to cup my cheek. Eyes locked on my mouth, Anton slowly ran his thumb over my lips. My heart thumped in my chest. Kisses and cuddles were a big thing to me. I couldn't get enough of them, but Anton hardly ever gave any. My lips parted, willing him to proceed.

When he leaned his head down to kiss me, I melted against him. My hands gripped his hair as if to make sure he wouldn't pull away from me. The kiss was slow, deep and tender. He pulled me against him, his arms encircling me in a tight embrace. My nipples hardened and a slow fire ignited in the pit of my stomach. I could stay like this forever. Teasing, tasting, commanding, his tongue explored my mouth like a conqueror. When he broke the kiss, he chuckled at my disappointed whimper.

Our eyes met and something undefinable, yet powerful, passed between us. His thumb caressed my lips again before he let go. It took all my willpower not to pull him into my arms again. I felt cold and flimsy without his body against mine.

I'm so fucking pathetic.

Only minutes ago, I dreaded knocking on his door for fear he would go wild on my ass. Now, a caress and a kiss had me weak in the knees and begging for more. Knowing it and doing something about it though, were two completely different things.

"Go on," he whispered. "There are a few things requiring my attention before I can get ready. I'll join you shortly."

I nodded and left him to his work.

❧

With a spring in my steps, I strutted by Anton's side, clinging to his arm as we entered Risqué. I wore a collar but no leash. Tonight, Anton hadn't brought a pet, but a companion, and he was flaunting me, left, right and center. His hand never left me, whether resting on my waist, my hip or the small of my back. I loved its possessiveness, the way it said to the whole world 'she's with me, she's mine.' Although I knew it was huge bragging rights for Braxians to show off that they owned an obedient human woman, I didn't care. Whatever Anton's motives, he liked showing me off and I loved to be.

We stopped at many tables on the way to our own, the patrons standing to pay Anton respect. And every time, he introduced me as his companion, Grace. It made me warm all over. The crowning moment was when Caleb showed up with Sheila trailing behind while one of the patrons' wife oohed and aahed at my dress. I loved being the center of attention with all eyes on me; the woman's admiration, Anton's pride and Sheila's burning jealousy. All my happy places tingled with pleasure.

I pressed myself closer to Anton's side, returning Sheila's venomous glare. His hold tightened on my waist, as if in approval. A quick look at his face and the small smirk at the edge of his lips told me he knew exactly what silent war waged between Sheila and me. I suddenly wondered how he felt about my possessiveness towards him. I belonged to him, not the other way around. Yet, for the duration of our contract, I couldn't help but consider him mine. After the usual greetings, Anton informed Caleb they would speak later, then with a nod to Sheila, he escorted me to our table.

We sat at the same elevated booth as before. It exposed the entire restaurant to us while providing a perfect view of the stage. The best part was watching Sheila settle at a standard table at ground level below us. Her relationship with Caleb confused me. It wasn't uncommon for venue owners to sleep with their performers. Yet, Caleb wasn't known for doing so. If the rumors were true, it made sense. The performers at Risqué were too high profile to deface in edge-play. But since Sheila started performing here, I often saw Caleb and her together as a couple, though also with other people. Maybe they enjoyed an open relationship.

Once again, Anton ordered for the both of us then patiently described his selection to me afterwards. I recognized some of the dishes. Soon, I'd feel confident enough to order on my own. That's one thing I liked about Anton. He didn't mind explaining things to me. It made me itch to learn more. I had missed that.

We enjoyed the wonderful meal while making small talk. I had never seen him so relaxed. The evening was shaping up to be the most amazing time we'd had.

"So why did you stop at seven space stations? Did you always intend to have seven Hives?" I asked, before taking a sip of wine to wash down the spiciness of the stewed vegetables in a curry sauce.

Anton pushed back his plate and leaned against the cushioned leather seat.

"Seven was always the plan. I just built them sooner than expected," he said, unable to hide the pride in his voice.

"Why not build more then? I mean, clearly, they're all a huge success," I said waving at the room.

"Because that would hurt my business more down the road." At my confused look, he continued, "Each Hive is strategically located to serve a specific sector. Because there are so few, the business owners bid high to win any space that becomes available. That, in turn, ensures they provide quality services to attract the type of clientele that can keep their businesses flourishing."

"So… you're creating rarity to keep the prices up?" I asked, still a little confused.

"In a way, but that's just part of the reason. With rarity, I get quality, but above all, I avoid flooding the market so the Hives don't start cannibalizing each other."

"How?"

Anton lifted his hand and absentmindedly fiddled with the small hair at the nape of my neck. "Ever been to Callan Fall?"

I nodded, leaning into his touch. "That's where I had my second feature show."

It was a miracle that poor excuse for a pleasure barge hadn't caved in on itself. The space station was riddled with rust, leaks and every type of pest imaginable. Mercenaries, mine workers, and small-time traders constituted the bulk of the clientele. It was a third of the size of Venus Hive.

"Have you noticed how many brothels and bars they have?"

I snorted. "More than half the station is brothels and bars."

"Remember how often they shut down before a new owner opened another one?"

Yeah, I remembered. There was a closure every other week, followed by a big reopening. Most establishments lasted a couple of months, six at best. Only a handful managed to last longer, but they offered highly exotic – meaning sick and deranged – services.

"All the time," I said, nodding.

"That's what happens when you have too many similar businesses competing for the same pool of customers. Everyone makes a small share, but not enough to keep them afloat. That's why I regulate the number of businesses of a similar type on each Hive."

"Why do you care though? As long as you have people paying rent, whether they succeed or fail shouldn't matter to you, right?"

He smiled, his hand sliding from my nape to my shoulder, where his thumb followed the line of my clavicle back and forth. The caress distracted me, but I wanted to remain focused.

"It matters because their success increases mine. The more money they make, the better services they can provide, the more refined the clientele they attract. I only rent half the space on each Hive. All other establishments belong to me, including some entertainment venues, every single hotel, food market and power, among others."

"You're crazy smart," I said, impressed.

"And you're smarter than you give yourself credit for."

My jaw dropped at the unexpected compliment. Was he mocking me?

"Right. I can't even order my own meal," I said, trying to hide my discomfort with self-derision.

Smiling, Anton gently caressed my cheek. "Lack of education or worldly knowledge doesn't mean stupid. Aren't you learning now?"

My eyes pricked. I nodded, not trusting my voice.

He gestured at the room. "These people have nothing on you. You're young, beautiful, and smart enough to learn all this shit. You just need to start believing in yourself."

The onslaught of emotions sweeping through me made me dizzy. Aside from Marcus, and more recently Romero, no one ever seemed to think much of me or my potential. Coming from Anton, it touched me deeply.

Feeling awkward, I tried to lighten the mood with a joke.

"You're only trying to make me work even more."

Anton burst out laughing. I loved its booming quality and the way it softened his features.

"Yes. It does involve a bit of hard work."

He got to his feet and extended a hand towards me. Surprised, I rose and placed my hand in his.

"Let's dance," he said, leading me to the dance floor.

An orchestra played slow ballads, mainly as ambient music, but the patrons were welcome to dance. The low hum of conversations considerably lessened as we stopped in the middle of the otherwise empty dance floor. Anton pulled me into his arms, and I wrapped myself around him. Every single eye was on us. I felt happy tingles again. Anton's nostrils flared and he shook his head, incredulous.

"You're such an exhibitionist! This? This makes you wet?" he said with a chuckle.

My face burned with embarrassment. Ok, I was a freak. So what? Anton began to move, and I tensed at first.

"Afraid I'm going to squish your toes?" he asked with a wink.

I bit my lip and lowered my eyes.

"Don't worry, Grace. I know how to lead."

And did he ever. For such a brawny man, his movements were fluid and effortless. While we mostly swayed from side to side, cheek to cheek, occasionally, he would make us – or me – spin.

Did I mention this was the best evening ever?

I inhaled his fresh scent, raw, male, and mixed with his spicy cologne. Wrapped in his arms, against his chiseled body and surrounded by his scent, I felt at home. Unable to resist, I softly kissed his neck. His arms around my back tightened though he pulled back his head to look at me. We stared at each other for a moment in silence. His gaze fell to my lips, and I slightly lifted my head, on instinct. A strange glimmer flicked through Anton's eyes. His face took on an incredibly soft, almost tender expression. He leaned down and kissed me.

That was twice, tonight alone. I surrendered to him, his hand gently fisting my hair as he deepened the kiss. My girly bits throbbed in response, and I pressed myself even closer to him. I wanted him to carry me to the closest table, toss the food and dishes to the floor and take me right there, on top of the table – watching patrons be damned. Well, okay, not damned. The thought of them watching while Anton fucked me into next week had me dripping.

He broke the kiss and I almost whimpered. His hand still gripping my hair, he pulled my face into the crook of his neck and pressed his lips to my ear.

"You're mine, Grace," he whispered. "You belong to me, and I'm never letting you go. Do you understand?"

Lost in the moment, I nodded against his neck, my arms tightening possessively around him. A warm, fuzzy feeling spread through me at his words.

"Say it."

"I'm yours, Anton. All yours. No one else but yours," I whispered.

He kissed my ear, then pulled back to look at me, his eyes burning with desire. "Let's go home."

I didn't need to ask why. The steely length of him strained against my stomach. The thought of his beautiful cock made my mouth water. But as much as I loved sucking him off, right now, I wanted him deep inside me.

When he released me, I was surprised to notice half a dozen couples had joined us on the dance floor. I had been too drowned in a lusty haze to realize it. Unfortunately, fucking Caleb Jennings thwarted our hasty retreat.

"Anton," he said, blocking our path, "I hope you weren't leaving already. There are some urgent matters we need to discuss."

The look on Anton's face said it all. He was in no mood for any kind of discussion with Caleb right now, urgent or otherwise.

"I promise, it won't be long. But we're unable to proceed with the construction work without your approval," Caleb said, his face taking on a sad expression.

"Let's get this over with," Anton said with an aggravated sigh. "Let's go back to our booth."

"Wait." I pulled on his hand as he started towards our table. "I'll go to the ladies' room while you two discuss business."

He nodded and released my hand. I watched him walk back to the table, his gait unusually stiff. I couldn't help but wonder about the cause; annoyance or too hard a shaft? The latter pleased me more. It was only fair considering my trip to the bathroom was to wipe off some of the mess between my thighs. Soaking wet and no undies to dam my arousal, I didn't trust myself to sit down without leaving a trace behind.

Weaving my way through the tables, I entered the bathroom.

CHAPTER 11
GRACE

The gleaming dark marble floor of Risqué's bathroom and the creamy walls made the room enormous. It was divided into two sections; the powder room in front and the stalls in the back. One long sink with motion-sensor faucets occupied the length of the powder room's left wall. Above each faucet, wooden frame mirrors hung on the wall. On the opposite wall, fancy stools with a dark brown and gold brocade cushion rested in front of a long counter. Various high-end beauty products were neatly organized on top, reflected by the ceiling-high mirror that covered the entire wall.

The stalls lined the wall of a circular room with a circular pouf, large enough to seat ten people, in the center. It was covered in the same brocade as the stools. There didn't seem to be anyone else in the bathroom, so I entered the first spacious stall on the left. Seconds later, I heard clip-clopping heels walk into the room. I made quick use of the facilities, chuckling at how soaked my inner thighs were. Walking out of the stall, the most unpleasant surprise awaited me in the form of Sheila.

She sat cross-legged on the pouf, pretending to clean non-existent dirt beneath her red painted nails. The holographic marker above my stall no doubt informed her of my location when it switched to 'occupied.' I nodded politely and walked past her to wash my hands. If Sheila wanted a cat fight, she would initiate it. I wasn't playing her game.

Sure enough, her footsteps echoed behind me. She sat on one of the fancy stools. I glanced at her reflection in the mirror. Her eyes dressed me down, the expression on her face calculating.

"That was quite the show you two put on just now," Sheila said, crossing her shapely legs.

"A show?" I asked, placing my hand beneath the motion-sensor soap dispenser.

"Clinging to each other like you were drowning and sucking each other's faces off."

I snorted. "It's called dancing and kissing, Sheila. Surely you've seen that before."

"No need to get cute with me," she said, her tone hardening.

"Then don't ask for it." I rinsed my hands. "You didn't stalk me here to make small talk. What do you want?"

"I underestimated you." Sheila rose from her seat. "People say you're sweet but a ditz. Yet, I saw you playing the game."

She approached me, hips swaying to her feline stride. The woodsy scent of her perfume tickled my nostrils. I expected her to wear a spicy perfume but the fragrance was refined and suited her. She leaned her hip against the sink, invading my space. I kept a careful eye on her while waving my hands in front of the air dryer. While effective, it was mostly silent and didn't impede our ability to talk... unfortunately.

"Don't get too comfortable. You're a beautiful girl," Sheila said, grabbing a strand of my long hair and gently letting it flow through her fingers. I recoiled but didn't pull away from her touch. "You've done a great job keeping his baser instincts sated this long. However, you don't have the class or mental acumen to satisfy anything else."

I flinched. Of course, the bitch would hit where it hurt. Anton was smart, there was no question about that. He was right about my lack of education. I didn't pursue studies after running from the orphanage a few weeks shy of my thirteenth birthday. He also made it clear he didn't like my trashy clothes or behavior.

Sheila smirked, knowing she had scored a hit. "Since I, too, can be a nice girl, consider this your advance warning that Anton is going to be mine. I am far more suitable for him than you and my performances won't embarrass him, unlike yours."

Taking a deep breath in an attempt to control my anger, I faced her. "Any well-trained monkey can perform with distinction for its audience," I said, quoting something Romero taught me. "But real class starts by not throwing yourself at the feet of the man who already declined your shameless offer at Sade."

Sheila gasped.

"It's also not stalking the woman of the man you covet all the way to the bathroom in a desperate attempt to undermine her confidence."

"Now you listen to me," she hissed, straightening.

"No, *you* listen to me," I snarled getting up in her face. "I'm not playing your stupid games. You can't intimidate or scare me. Your skinny ass was around here long before I arrived. Anton never came sniffing after it. That should tell you something."

"It tells me I'm not some cheap whore he could buy!"

Although I did sell myself to Anton, I wasn't a whore – not that I cared what Sheila thought. But I couldn't resist knocking her down a notch.

I laughed. "Cheap whore, really? Has anyone ever happily paid over twelve million credits just to have you? I doubt you'd even get twelve hundred."

Sheila's fists clenched, her pretty face distorted by anger.

"I may be ditzy and trashy, but I'm honest. Anton knows that everything he gets from me is genuine. I truly like him."

Sheila huffed in disbelief.

"What you saw between him and me on that dance floor was real. That's why he still wants me. You can't fool your audience, Sheila," I said, spitting her name with contempt. "He knows you only want his money and status. Pleasure barges crawl with girls like you. But hey, it's a free world. Keep peddling your wares. With luck, he might toss a few pity credits your way. Just spare me your fucking 'friendly' warnings."

I stormed past her, feeling her incredulous stare burning a hole in my back. In spite of my many flaws, bitch bullying was one thing I no longer tolerated. The music industry was riddled with them. Before, I would shrink into myself and take it. Not anymore. While I still avoided confrontations, when someone brought it to me, I fought back. For the time being, Anton was my man, and I was his woman. If Sheila thought I was going to roll over and let her snag him, she had another thing coming.

Closing the door behind me, I flattened the nonexistent wrinkles of my dress. I lifted my chin and strutted back into the dining room. Crossing the dance floor amidst the dancing couples was the shortest route back to Anton's booth. From where I stood, he seemed to be having an intense discussion with Caleb. As I weaved my way through the dancers, a hand grabbed my wrist.

"Marcus…" I whispered in shock.

"Hey, Gracie," he said, pulling me into his arms.

On instinct, my hand slid to his shoulder, and I followed his lead while we began dancing. What was he doing here? When did he get here? Did he know what trouble I inherited from his debt and disappearance?

"How..? What..?"

"I'm so sorry, Gracie," Marcus said, his face filled with remorse. "I never imagined they would come after you. They'd never done that before. You know I would never leave you in harm's way, right?"

"You abandoned me." My initial shock waning, my eyes prickled.

"I didn't abandon you. The deal went to shit, and I had to sort things out before it got out of hand. I thought you'd be safe here. Your hotel was paid for the month, including meals, and Peter was supposed to let you perform for some credits. Honestly, I thought you'd be fine."

"They broke into the hotel."

Marcus' face twisted in anger. "Yeah… those fucking bastards. As soon as I heard, I came back here but it was a long flight. By then, you had already signed with Anton." His eyes searched mine. "Are you alright, Gracie? Is he good to you?"

I sniffled but nodded. "Yeah, he's alright."

"Grace…" Marcus said with that stern tone he took when he thought I was lying.

"Well, he mostly is," I said, shrugging. "I mean, it's only been a month. The first week and the last two weeks were nice."

"And the second week?"

I scrunched my face. "Why didn't you tell me back on Jeruna? I thought you were only punishing me."

"I *was* punishing you, Grace. That shit was stupid," Marcus said, his voice taking an angry edge. "But I was also protecting you. That's my job."

"You should have told me how serious this was, Mar. I didn't understand back then. I'm sure even the girls didn't realize the repercussions for Anton and his clan."

"What would that have accomplished?" Marcus asked. "The damage was done."

"*That* damage was done, but it would have made me think twice about all the other stupid shit I did afterwards. And I wouldn't have been blindsided getting into this deal with Anton."

"You're right. I should have."

"What happened to the girls?"

The look on his face told me I wouldn't like it one bit.

"You don't need to hear that, Gracie."

"I need to know. Tell me." I nudged his shoulder, urging him to answer.

He heaved a deep sigh. "They mixed some kind of acid in Darla's drink. It destroyed her vocal cords and half of her digestive system. She can barely speak anymore, let alone sing. Her stomach can no longer handle solid food. She's been on suicide watch ever since."

I bit my fist in horror but gestured for him to continue. I would know the truth. The song ended and most couples returned to their tables. Marcus held me and we resumed dancing when the orchestra launched into the next piece.

"They had Kranax Beetles lay eggs inside both of Steffie's ears, presumably while she slept. When the larvae hatched two days later, they didn't take the shortest way out. She was left disfigured and deaf. She managed to take her life a year later."

I rested my forehead on his shoulder, fighting back tears. They had been mean in their immaturity but didn't deserve that extreme a punishment for a childish prank.

"Is that what Anton would have done to me?"

Marcus caressed my hair then lifted my chin to make me look at him.

"No, Gracie. Anton didn't punish the girls. The elder clans did. Your punishment was Anton's to decide on. Did he hurt you?"

"Yeah." Marcus stiffened, his hold on my back tightening. "But he felt sorry afterwards and made it all better. He took really good care of me."

Marcus stopped dancing. "Did he hit you?"

"No, Mar. He never hit me."

"And since then?"

I shook my head. "No, he's been nice since then."

We resumed dancing.

"Do you like him?"

My face heated. I nibbled on my bottom lip before giving him a shy look.

He laughed. "You do like him. And you don't mind him being Braxian? You don't mind his face? I know how you are."

I shrugged, feeling slightly embarrassed to be called out on how superficial I could be. "He's only half Braxian and isn't crazy big like the others. Plus, his body is ridiculous. No one should be that perfect – not that I mind." I giggled. "As for his face, well he's half Braxian so it's normal he has that big forehead and flat nose."

"Are you sure you like him? That it's not just—"

"He's not Paul," I said, interrupting him. "Yes, I get attached too quickly and forgive too easily. Dr. Hazan would probably disapprove. Except for that one bad week, he's been good to me. He makes me want to be better."

"Better?" Marcus asked, looking confused.

"He sees me, the real Grace I didn't even know existed. People only see ignorant, trashy Grace. But Anton spends time with me and talks to me, not like I'm an idiot. When I don't know stuff, he doesn't talk down to me or judge me. I've learned and discovered so many new things thanks to him. He's such an important, busy man and yet he makes me feel like I'm worthy of his time."

"You are *not* an idiot, and you *are* worthy of his time."

"But people don't usually treat me that way. He believes in my potential. With hard work, he's convinced I will be better than Seria. And he's making me do it myself because he thinks I'm smart enough to manage. It's hard and it sucks, but I am doing it, Mar. I see my progress and it feels good – it makes me want to be more."

Marcus smiled and kissed my forehead.

"Gracie, you know I love you, right?"

I nodded, my throat tightening.

"I want you to be happy, to have the kind of life and stability you always dreamt of. But I'm not the kind of man who can give you that. You know that, right?" he said, his eyes searching.

The lump in my throat made it hard to swallow, but I nodded again.

"I think Myers really likes you."

I snorted. "Whatever makes you think that?"

"I met him a week ago."

"What?" I stopped dancing in shock. Marcus forced me back into motion. "You've been here a week?"

He gave me a rundown of their meeting, describing Anton's jealousy when Marcus pretended to have found the perfect man for me to test Anton's feelings towards me. My lips quivered and I couldn't resist kissing his cheek. Marcus had been my childhood best friend, my only lover for many years, my protector and big brother for the last year. He always looked after me, which is why it hurt so much when I thought he had abandoned me.

"Careful, Gracie, I might take that as an invitation."

I playfully slapped his shoulder. "As if, you man whore."

"You've got that right." We both chuckled.

The music ended. Couples shuffled about around us but we stayed put until the next piece started.

"I watched the two of you dance tonight," Marcus said. "You seemed happy together. Would you consider staying with him for the long haul?"

"Is that what you want?" I said, my chest aching.

Had Marcus tired of looking after me? We'd never been apart more than a day since we ran from the orphanage nine years ago. Had a month separation been enough for him to want to be rid of me permanently?

"It's not about what I want Gracie, beyond your happiness. I've taken you as far as I can. My lifestyle isn't for you. This…" he said, releasing my waist long enough to wave at the room. "This is where you belong, with a man who looks at you the way Myers does, and you dressed like the lady you are. You should be performing in venues like this, not Peter's."

"Anton doesn't want me performing at Peter's," I said, my heart swelling with affection for my best friend.

Marcus looked pleased. "I hear you're training with Romero?"

My enthusiastic nod didn't hide any of my affection for the friendly trainer. "He's amazing! I'm learning a lot from him. But he makes me work too much."

Marcus threw his head back, laughing. He knew what a lazy bum I was. If we weren't in public, I'd make a face at him. At that moment, I realized how much his absence had weighed on me. Marcus was the one person who always had my back even if he couldn't be faithful. Since we ended our romantic involvement, I hoped he would grow out of the need to fuck everything that moved. Now, it was clear to me that my love for Marcus wasn't that of a woman for her mate. I wasn't in love with Anton, but looking at Marcus' beautiful face, I felt no lust or sexual attraction, just bone-deep affection.

"I think you are where you need to be, Gracie. Myers is doing a lot of good things for you right now, opening new doors and new possibilities for a better future," Marcus said, his tone serious again.

"Yes. I like him a lot, Mar. Today has been so perfect. I love when he's affectionate like that. It makes me want to stay with him forever.

But sometimes he gets angry, and I don't know how to handle that. He punishes me, and that's not ok."

"Tell him that."

"He owns me, Mar," I said shaking my head. "Anton can do whatever he wants to me for five more months and I have to accept it, even the punishments, even when they're not fair. He could torture me every day just for the fun of it if he wanted. I'm just grateful that he's not."

"Aww, Gracie."

"I didn't have a choice, Marcus! I didn't know where you were or what to do."

"Yes, I know and I'm sorry. Look, there are only five months left. Stay out of trouble and keep your head down. Learn everything you can to build the career you've always wanted. When the contract is up, I'm sure he'll want to keep you. Then you can set your terms of what is and isn't acceptable for you to stay of your own free will. For now, start planting the seed that you're not okay with this kind of treatment but don't provoke him either. And keep in mind all that Dr. Hazan has taught you."

"Okay," I said smiling.

"One last thing, Braxians have weird rules about women. If you plan on a long-term relationship with Anton, learn about his people and their expectations. Then you can negotiate. Alright?"

"Alright. I should go back to Anton now," I said, as the music ended.

While I wanted to continue talking with Marcus, I had been gone too long. Dancing a fourth time in a row with him would be pushing it.

"Good point," Marcus said, kissing my cheek before releasing me. "I'll see you soon, Gracie."

"Bye Mar, and thanks," I said with an affectionate smile.

Turning towards our table, I sought out Anton who was still talking with Caleb. Our eyes met and my stomach dropped.

I remembered all too well that cold, hard expression.

CHAPTER 12
ANTON

What the fuck was pretty boy doing here? How dare he touch my woman? Worse, how could she let him hold her like that for all to see? Granted, the surprise on her face when he grabbed her looked genuine. Refusing him that first dance would have been rude. Though it displeased me, I could accept that. But a second and then a third? Whispering, giggling and making fucking googly eyes at each other? As if that wasn't enough, she kissed him. She fucking kissed him right in my face. How dare she humiliate me?

And me, like a damned idiot, let myself be conned into thinking her sweet and affectionate disposition was genuine. The way she held on to me when I said she was mine, the fervor of her response when she said she belonged to me, it sounded so sincere. Stupid fool… I wanted to march down to that dance floor and break pretty boy's neck.

"They sure make a beautiful couple," Caleb said. "Of course, it's all innocent, but I expected her to at least slap him for abandoning her to his creditors."

That freaky bastard. I wanted to smash his handsome face on the table, see how smug he would look then. It was all his fault too. Had he not intercepted me for this so-called urgent conversation, I would be home right now, balls deep inside Grace. I wouldn't have fucked her, as per our usual. I had planned on making love to her, in a proper bed, with actual foreplay. The perfect ending to a perfect evening. Instead, I was sitting here, watching pretty boy grope my woman and pondering what punishment would most suit her latest offense.

"You have no idea how much I envy you, Anton," Caleb said, the taunting glimmer in his eye plain to see. "Such a beautiful girl with such a sweet disposition. Should you tire of her at any point, I'll be more than happy to buy off the rest of her contract."

Like hell you will, you sick son of a bitch.

"You're the last man I would sell her contract to," I said, my voice dangerously calm. I downed my brandy and gestured for the waitress for another. "I know what you do to your girls. You will never set a finger on Grace – not now, not after our contract is over, not ever. Is that understood?"

His eyes narrowed. "Once your contract is up, she's a free woman. If I make her a sweet enough offer, it is her prerogative to accept."

It was my turn to have a smug smile on my face. "Correct me if I'm wrong, but isn't Risqué's rental contract up for renewal? I'm getting obscene offers to put this location up for bid again."

"My restaurant is highly successful," Caleb said through his teeth. "You don't have grounds not to renew."

"That's irrelevant. I have no contractual obligations to renew. If it's you or another tenant, it makes no difference to me. I'll still be making a killing."

"Why the hell do you care so much about this girl?" Caleb asked, his hands fisting on the table. "Look at her." He pointed with his chin towards Grace and Marcus. "She sure doesn't seem to care about you right now."

"What feelings I may or may not have for Grace are none of your fucking business, Caleb. Just stay the hell away from her."

We were both looking at her when the third song ended. To my relief, they parted. Then the bastard leaned in and kissed her. My blood froze. Caleb chuckled and I cracked my knuckles.

"Well, maybe I'm not the one you should be worried about after all."

Half the room watched Grace. She who thrived on attention didn't notice, too lost in pretty boy's eyes and words. They made a spectacle of themselves. Half the patrons glanced between them and me. A pureblood would have already beaten Marcus to a pulp then dragged Grace by the hair out of here. On Braxia, her punishment would be a bloody whipping.

She turned towards us, a dreamy smile on her face. When our eyes met, her smile slipped. Worry lines etched on her forehead, her steps faltering as she walked towards us. A quick look around the room seemed to increase her anxiety. She sat next to me, back stiff and eyes glued to my face.

"You look lovely as always, Grace," Caleb said with a taunting smile. "That was quite the sweet reunion with your lover."

Grace's head jerked towards Caleb, a look of panic on her face. "He's not my lover," she said, her eyes flicking towards me.

Caleb waved dismissively. "Ex-lover, friend with benefits, it's all the same. We're adults. Venus Hive is after all about indulging fantasies."

"Do not project your loose behavior on me, Mr. Jennings," she hissed.

"I'm not—"

"That's enough," I interrupted Caleb. Time to put an end to this farce. Rising from my seat, I added, "Our business is concluded. We're leaving."

"Of course," Caleb said with a slight bow. "I'm sure the rest of your evening will be most... entertaining."

We left Risqué. This time, it wasn't arousal I could smell on Grace, but fear.

It took us only ten minutes to walk from the restaurant to the penthouse. As always, the walkway bustled with activity as patrons went from one venue to another. At this time, most customers finished eating dinner and headed to one of the various entertainments available. Unlike the Commons where flashy signs and glaring advertisement were the norm, in the VIP section, everything was understated, with a quiet elegance. While on the walkways, patrons were expected to cover their more outrageous outfits, but pets could be leashed.

A few customers paused to greet us as we passed them. My expression made it clear I was in no mood to chat so they moved along.

As we neared the gleaming white entrance of the Venus Hive headquarters, Grace's tension became palpable. She opened her mouth once or twice, as though to speak, then closed it.

I spent the entire walk debating which punishment was most fitting. On Braxia, a pureblood would flog her, twenty-five lashes with at least half of them breaking skin. The clan would place the offending female in a cage for three hours before tending her wounds. Depending on the severity of the offense, treatment didn't guarantee painkillers. I dismissed that option.

In spite of the anger raging within me, I could never take a whip to her – or any woman for that matter – and least of all beat her bloody. Growing up, people stronger than me had taken pleasure beating me at every opportunity. I would never be them. There would also be no repeat of the punishment in my office when I… was brutal with her.

That left one option.

We entered the building and headed for the lift at the end of the hallway. The night guard nodded at our approach. My pace accelerated the closer we got to the lift, and Grace skip-ran to keep up. I waited until she stood inside to select our destination. I pressed my thumb on the scanner.

"Anton, what are you doing?" Grace asked with a shaky voice.

I gave her a cold look and pressed the button to the secured basement. Her lips quivered. I faced the door, refusing to let myself be moved. Not after tonight.

"Why, Anton? Why?" she asked, a lone tear rolling down. "I didn't do anything."

She approached me and wrapped her hands around my arm, pleading.

"Please, Anton… Please, don't do this."

I tore my arm out of her grip just as the lift doors opened and marched down the corridor.

"I don't want to go there! Anton, please... please," she said, still standing inside the lift.

I stopped. "Move your ass or I'll drag you," I said.

She took a couple of hesitant steps, tears now flowing freely down her cheeks. Losing patience, I grabbed her upper arm and dragged her after me. After unlocking the cage room, I jerked my head indicating for her to get in. Grace complied. She wrapped her arms around herself.

"Strip," I ordered, standing right in front of her.

"We only danced, Anton. We did nothing wrong. Everyone could see that," she pleaded.

"Only danced?" I shouted. She cringed and shrunk back. "Only danced three fucking times back-to-back, clinging to each other like you were fucking drowning. Yes, everyone... EVERYONE could see. You made a damn spectacle. And then you had to go and fucking kiss him!"

"It wasn't—"

"SILENCE!" She recoiled and stood trembling, still holding herself. "I told you to strip. Don't make me tear it off."

She undressed, her soft sob echoing in the empty room. Her dress slid to the floor, and she stepped out of her stilettos. Goosebumps rose on her skin. Grace lifted her head and looked at me with such gut-wrenching sorrow, my resolve faltered.

"Please don't do this, Anton. Today was so perfect. Please..."

I tore my eyes away from her. "Ring."

Another big sob ripped out of her. Head down, shoulders drooping, she walked into the ring of light.

"Bars," I said, once she reached her destination.

The cage formed around her.

She crouched without a word as the gridded lid descended. Grace's arms circled her folded legs, and she rested her forehead on her knees. I walked out, leaving her dress and shoes on the floor where she dropped them.

⌀

My fingers tapped on my desk as I struggled to focus on my work. This was completely absurd. Why the hell was I so tormented? She deserved it! By Braxian law, she deserved worse.

We're not on Braxia.

And that was the crux of the matter. We weren't on Braxia. Which was a good thing. But I was Braxian. Any disrespect to me reflected on the clan. I fought too hard for what little respect they granted me to let her ruin it.

But they're not here. They don't know. So what does it matter?

Everyone saw what she did. I could see their thoughts in their eyes. When would Anton lose it? What punishment would she get? Even Caleb needled me to fuel my anger. By now, they probably thought I was weak for a Braxian.

Didn't you tell her you didn't give a shit what people here thought of you?

That gave me pause. After pondering the question, I could say I honestly didn't give a shit what my patrons thought. If any of them pissed me off enough, I could airlock their asses into space and grease a few palms to make the consequences go away. There also hadn't been any Braxians there to witness. There rarely were any Braxians in the VIP section unless they were guests. So why had I felt so angry, hurt, and humiliated?

You were jealous.

Yeah but…

You were jealous.

Fine. Yes, I felt jealous. That little pissant shouldn't prowl around my woman. She knew better. Tonight had been so fucking perfect… Even she thought so.

'Please don't do this, Anton. Today was so perfect.'

I wanted to go free her but changing my mind now would make me look weak. She needed to learn she couldn't do things like this. She was mine.

CHAPTER 13
GRACE

My perfect evening kept replaying in my head over and over again. How did it go so wrong? I didn't deserve this. To think, like an idiot, I had been picturing Anton and me living happily ever after. It didn't matter that my actions angered him. Nothing justified him hurting me every time he became upset.

Why did he ruin everything?

The door opened. By the size of the silhouette walking in, I knew William was bringing me food and water. So, the first six hours had gone by. Only the first six hours. I wouldn't survive the remaining eighteen hours. My extremities were numb, and I already agonized through at least a dozen bouts of cramping. One of them had been so bad I passed out. If Anton kept doing this to me, could it cause permanent damage? Whether he realized it or not, he couldn't have devised a crueler punishment for me.

William crouched in front of my cage, a sympathetic look on his face. He wasn't a bad sort though I didn't quite understand his friendship with Anton. We didn't talk much, but he was always polite and helpful. He also never looked down on me. The energy bar and bottle of water in his hands didn't appeal to me. All I could think about was slipping into oblivion and forgetting I ever allowed myself to care for the monster that owned me. Plus, I wasn't feeling too well.

"You should eat, Grace," William whispered.

He held the energy bar through the narrow bars of my cell. I gave him a sad smile and shook my head. I wasn't hungry.

"Can you feel your hands?" he asked, guessing part of the problem.

I shook my head again, feeling my throat tighten. Kindness was the last thing I needed right now. He frowned but said nothing. Scooting closer, he placed a long straw in the water bottle and slipped the tip through the bars. For a minute, I almost declined, but then thought better of it. It would be another six hours before William returned. Leaning forward, I took the straw between my lips and drank.

"You need to be more careful, Grace. Don't you know by now how proud Braxians are?"

Dropping the straw, I rested my head against the cage and gave free rein to my anger.

"I did nothing wrong, William. Nothing! My best friend and I danced and talked. That's it. Anton and I had the perfect evening. And then he goes and does this. For what?"

"He felt humiliated."

I turned my face away with an irritated groan.

"Grace," William said, "it may have been innocent on your part but for Braxians, perception is everything."

"No, revenge is everything," I bit back.

"Look at me, Grace."

Though somewhat reluctant, I complied. William sat crossed legged in front of me. He had a rugged kind of charm. Square jaw covered with a five o'clock shadow, light brown hair sprinkled with silver, and blue eyes leveled on me with a serious look.

"Honor and respect are everything to Anton."

"I didn't disrespect him, though."

"You may not have intended to but that's how it came across to him, and in the end, that's what matters."

I shook my head, refusing to accept this. "That's crazy. At this rate, anything I do will potentially offend him. It can't be like this. If my dancing with Marcus was so upsetting, why didn't he say something? Why not cut in before it became a problem? Am I to be punished every time he feels I sneezed the wrong way? I don't want to live in constant fear of him."

"What do you know of Braxians?"

I shrugged. "The standard stuff. They're giants, warriors, clan focused, treat women like shit and are obsessed with honor."

He chuckled. "That's one way to put it. Do you know what they think of hybrids like Anton?"

The way he said that caught my attention. The memory of that asshole Gerwin came back to mind. He'd tried to needle Anton all evening at Sade.

"Gerwin didn't seem to think much of him," I said.

"Gerwin is an asshole and a waste of oxygen," William snapped. "But Gerwin is only one of millions who think that way about Anton."

How could they feel contempt towards Anton with his phenomenal financial success? As far as I knew, he was the richest Braxian of any clan, period.

"Braxians consider half-breeds a taint on their bloodline. While female half-breeds are allowed to live, the males are systematically put to death."

What?

"But how is he here then?"

"For whatever reason, his father decided to spare him, in spite of his clan. But his clan wasn't the only threat. It is considered sport to hunt down and kill half-breeds. That Anton managed to reach puberty is a miracle. Do you know how he and I met?"

I shook my head, blown away by these revelations.

"A little over sixteen years ago, I ran a smugglers outfit with some regular customers on Braxia. I had just concluded my business when I heard a commotion in a back alley. Two Braxian teens were beating a kid to death."

I already knew where this was going.

"They were too intent hammering him to see me coming. That's the only reason I was able to take them down. Already at twelve or thirteen, those pureblood kids were bigger and stronger than me. Aside from the element of surprise, they also didn't have proper combat training. After running them off, I looked at the kid and realized he was a half-breed, not a human slave as I first thought."

"Didn't you get in trouble for attacking Braxian kids?"

William chuckled again. "No. They kept their mouths shut. Their clans would have shunned them for losing a fight to a human."

Poetic justice.

"Didn't Anton tell on them?"

William shook his head. "No, because they wouldn't have been punished. Killing Anton would have given them and their clan bragging rights. His father was shamed already for keeping him alive."

Those Braxians were crazy. If they hated him so much, why the hell did he want to please them?

"Anton had so many fractures and internal bleeding, it was a miracle he survived. However, I couldn't bring him back to his house. His clan would have finished him off while he was defenseless. He stayed with me for a month while recovering. During that time, he thought of opening a club. I had the connections, he had the funds. A thirteen-year-old fucking kid..."

"So you went into business with him?"

"Yeah, kind of," William said with a reminiscing smile. "At first, I just found him human women willing to come to that hellhole. He paid me a finder's fee. The money he brought in saved his life."

"No, you saved his life."

William snorted. "Only that one time. He saved his own ass every other time. But his success is the one reason his clan shows him any respect, if you can even call it that. It's more tolerance. What you girls did back on Jeruna could have gotten him killed."

A silent tear ran down my face. Such pointless, extreme violence. And the living hell a child went through because his blood wasn't pure. How was that even his fault?

"Anton devoted his whole life earning acceptance from his people. Woe onto anyone who jeopardizes that... even you."

"But why does he even care? Anton doesn't need them. He doesn't even live with them. *They* should be sucking up to him!"

"I couldn't agree more, but you can't expect him to change everything he's built his life around overnight. Learn about Braxia, Grace. Learn their customs and traditions to protect yourself. Five months is a long time. You're a good kid. While you may not agree with me right now, Anton is a good man."

William offered me a bit more water. I drank a few more sips but refused to drink it all. Eighteen hours would be a long time to go with a full bladder. With one last smile, he got up and left.

～

I must have dozed off because the sudden burning sensation of the bars sliding against my skin startled me awake. My teeth chattered slightly, and the insidious cold had me frozen to the bone. Feeling groggy, it took me a moment to realize this shouldn't be happening yet. William only came by once and I didn't think it was all that long ago either. I blinked to make out the silhouette by the door.

Anton.

Before I could think further, the bars disappeared into the floor, leaving me without support. My arms were too numb to hold me up so I collapsed, barely managing to hold my head up. Disbelieving, I watched Anton's retreating back as he left me there, sprawled naked on the cold floor. My eyes prickled and a vise-like grip crushed my chest. Even though he released me sooner than last time, him abandoning me like this killed something inside me.

I rolled onto my back, opening and closing my hands to bring some feeling back to them. They felt like they were stuck in a leather glove too small for them. The dreaded pins and needles began to spread. Seconds later, my muscles contracted, a sharp cutting pain shooting through both my legs. I cried out, contorting this way and that to loosen the cramps. When they finally receded, I tried to get up on my feet, but the cramps came back with a vengeance. My brain felt foggy, my head heavy and that cold bit at me.

Gritting my teeth, I decided to crawl towards my dress still lying on the floor. Tears of pain and anger soaked my face.

Never again… He won't fool me ever again.

Horrible childhood or not, he couldn't excuse this. Marcus and I also had a difficult childhood. That didn't make me want to hurt people every time they upset me. William said Anton was a good guy. For a while, I thought so too. Not anymore. The floor's metal plating squeaked against my skin as I crawled forward. The slick surface provided little grip and the muscles of my arms burned by the time I reached my dress. Putting it on became a challenge. Any attempt to sit up or fold my legs triggered precursor muscle spasms. To make matters worse, I felt dizzy and feverish.

I eventually managed to get into my dress but not the shoes. Walking in those stilettos guaranteed to pull on all the wrong muscles. I crawled to the door, dragging the shoes behind me. Using the door frame for support, I pulled myself onto my feet. Right on cue, a vicious cramp seized the back of my calf. I ground my teeth through it, flexing my leg and foot until it faded. Holding on to the wall, I limped my way to the lift. The corridor swirled around me, and my stomach churned.

What's wrong with me?

The ride up was quick, but crossing the large living area at the entrance of the penthouse would be a challenge. My legs were shaky. There were no walls to lean on between here and the other side of the room where a wide corridor led to the sleeping quarters. Furniture would have to do.

I began the slow journey down the three steps into the living area when I heard the lift chime behind me. Looking over my shoulder, I was surprised to see William who seemed just as stunned to see me. In no time, he realized my predicament. Closing the distance between us, he lifted me into his arms. I almost wept with gratitude. We entered the bedroom as Anton walked out of the bathroom, drying his chin as if he had just shaved.

My blood curdled. Would he consider William carrying me another offense? His expression went from shocked to seething. But it was William he glared at, not me.

"What the fuck are you doing?" he snarled.

"What you should have done," William answered, leveling Anton with a cold stare.

I gawked at William. He carefully put me down on my pet cushion. I curled up in a ball while he pulled my blanket over me. My eyes remained on Anton who never looked my way. Once done, William turned to face Anton.

"My office," Anton hissed, then walked out.

"Indeed," William said, following in his wake.

I wanted to tell Anton not to be mad at William, but my eyes wouldn't stay open.

CHAPTER 14
ANTON

A million thoughts raced through my mind as I stormed into my office. How dare he carry her and care for her? William knew I was the only person with the clearance to disable the cage. If she was out and making her way back on her own, then he knew it was by my will. I went straight to the bar and poured myself a glass of brandy. The sound of the door closing echoed behind me. I tossed back my drink in one shot, welcoming the burn as it slid down my throat.

"How dare you challenge me?" I asked, turning to face William.

The fury in his eyes rivaled mine.

What the hell has gotten into him?

"No, *boy*. The question is rather how dare you treat that sweet girl like that?"

What the hell?

I gaped at him, unable to believe what I was hearing. William hadn't called me 'boy' in more than a decade.

"How I treat my property is none of your business."

William snorted. "Property," he muttered, shaking his head. "So an elder tells you your honor has been redeemed, and you go into full Braxian mode?"

"I *am* Braxian."

"No. You. Are. Not," William said, his tone clipped. "You're a half-breed. Remember who dragged your half-dead body away from the Braxians?"

I took a menacing step towards him. "Tread carefully, human."

"Or what, boy?" he said, taking a step as well. "You're going to use your superior strength to beat me within an inch of my life like the good Braxian you think you are?"

I flinched. Yes, that's what a Braxian would do.

"Why the hell are you trying to provoke me?" I said, running my hand through my hair in frustration.

"I'm trying to stop you from being a fool. You have a sweet, gorgeous young woman who cares for you, and you keep treating her like shit."

"She humiliated me!" I shouted.

"She did not. You felt insecure and jealous, so you punished her for it. Grace danced innocently with her best friend. She didn't deserve this, and you know it. That's why you freed her early."

I turned away, unable to withstand his accusing stare. Everything he said rung true.

I poured myself another drink. The amber liquid reminded me of Grace's eyes. "You didn't see it. The way they were whispering…"

"Marcus told her she should stay with you."

I froze, my glass paused halfway to my mouth.

"She agreed and hoped you'd want to keep her permanently."

My hand shook and alcohol sloshed onto my shoes. I put down my glass. How could that be true? Girls like her didn't like guys like me, only my wallet.

"You don't know that," I whispered. "You weren't even there."

"Seriously, Anton?" William asked. "I talked with Grace this morning when I brought her water."

"Ah," I snorted, understanding at last. I tried to hide my disappointment. "So she sweet-talked you into thinking she liked me, and you bought it."

"No, you stupid boy," William said. "I'm your Head of Security, remember? Who the fuck do you think set up the surveillance system throughout the Hive?"

Oh right... I picked up my glass and swallowed its contents.

"After talking with her, I spent the past hour getting the footage from Risqué and cleaning up all the noise. There are two videos in your inbox you'll find mighty interesting."

I frowned. "Two?"

"Yes," William said, crossing his arms over his broad chest. "Why don't you go have a look? It's quite revealing."

I walked around my desk and sat down. After locating the files, I launched the first video to display on the vidscreen on the wall. A recording of Grace and I dancing at Risqué appeared on screen. My stomach clenched.

"Do you see how she holds you? How she looks at you like you are the most wonderful thing she's ever beheld?" William asked. "The best is yet to come. Wait for it."

I knew what the best was. And a few seconds later, I watched the beautiful, tender yet passionate kiss she gave me.

"That's genuine," William said, pointing at the screen. "You've found yourself a girl who sincerely cares for you. And what do you do? Torture her and drive her away over some stupid culture that never even accepted you, to begin with."

He had made his point. "Enough."

"Yes, Anton. It's enough." William strolled over and placed his hands on my desk, his eyes boring into me. "We've been friends a long time. I've never told you what to do or meddled in your affairs. But this time, you need to wake up. You deserve a bit of happiness. Even now, light years away, Braxia is still fucking with your life. Let it go. Stop giving them power over you. Stop allowing them to twist you. You're a better man than this. They need *you*. It's time you start setting the rules rather than following theirs."

Pushing himself up and away from the desk, William marched out of my office, closing the door quietly behind him. I rubbed my hands over my face. How did it get so complicated? This wasn't the first time

William hinted I should sever my ties with Braxia, but he had never been this blunt before.

I couldn't do it. I would need to renounce my clan, relinquishing the only thread still linking me to my roots. A man without a clan was a man without honor – a nothing, a nobody, a disgrace. Granted, they would never embrace me, but at least now they accepted me. They needed me. And through me, the man by whose mercy I got to live no longer led a second-rate clan but one of the most powerful on Braxia.

My eyes strayed towards my computer. The second file beckoned me. I knew what it contained. William wouldn't lie. Yet, I needed to hear it from her own lips. As the recording played through Grace's and Marcus' conversation, the knot of guilt and shame twisted and roiled with renewed intensity.

"He makes me want to be better."

What she didn't realize was that she was doing the same for me. Grace made me question things I always accepted as normal because that was what Braxians did. However, hurting teenage girls so savagely over wounded pride wasn't right. Brutalizing her the way I had over that same barbaric code of honor was madness. That thought had tormented me for the past two weeks.

"I love when he's affectionate like that. It makes me want to stay with him forever."

Those words played in a loop in my head. I wanted her to stay with me forever, but she no doubt expected it to be as my mate. The clan wouldn't accept it. You didn't mate with human females, you only owned them. And they wouldn't allow me to have male offspring. I would be expected to kill my sons, and if I didn't, they would hunt them down. A picture of Grace's belly swollen with my child sprung to mind. I almost choked with emotion.

Braxians could only mate and reproduce with Braxian females. As a half-breed, I couldn't sully our females with my weaker seed or further taint my clan's gene pool by having offspring of my own. In other words, I couldn't have a future – no mate, no children. If I had daughters, they would become entertainment for any male within the clan. That was complete shit.

So why do I subject myself to this?

Because I was Braxian, and that was our way. And above all, because I owed my father too much and swore never to shame the clan ever again.

Blocking those thoughts, I replayed the recording of Grace and me dancing in a loop.

The delegation would arrive within the hour. Catering to that piece of shit Gerwin and his minions was the last thing I needed. They would expect to see Grace attending me. That was going to be fun news to break to her. I hadn't seen her since this morning's fiasco. The one time I worked up the courage to go check on her, she had been asleep. It surprised me considering how active she normally was. My steps were heavy and reluctant on the way to our bedroom. I expected to find her watching those recordings Romero made her study. Instead, she was still sleeping, curled up on her cushion, her back to me. Worry coiled and writhed all over my skin – something was wrong.

"Grace?" I called out, rushing over.

She stirred but didn't turn. Crouching, I pulled down the warm blanket obscuring her face. Her cheeks looked flushed and sweat beaded her brow.

I touched her skin. "Fuck."

Using my personal com, I called William. "Get Dr. Farland here ASAP. Grace is burning with fever. She's lethargic and struggling to breathe."

"On it," William said.

I carried her to the bathroom and started filling the tub with cold water while undressing her. She put up a bit of a struggle after I submerged her. Her movements were sluggish, and she mumbled incoherent words. My mind raced, trying to figure out what could have happened to make her this ill so quickly. Was it because of something I did? Had the punishment caused her illness? I crushed the fear blossoming in the pit of my stomach that this was something serious. Whatever the future might have in store for us, I needed Grace in mine.

Someone knocked on the bedroom door.

"Come in," I shouted.

I heard Dr. Farland's light footsteps approaching. William shadowed him, carrying a heavy medical bag.

"Hello, Mr. Myers," Dr. Farland said, walking in.

"She slept all day, which was strange," I said. Now wasn't time for niceties. The doctor crouched in front of the tub to have a look at her. "When I came to check up on her a few minutes ago, I found her in this state."

Farland checked her temperature then took some blood samples. He ran them through a portable analyzer.

"Please take her out of the water and to the bed so I can perform a proper exam," he said.

I lifted her out of the bath. Cold water dripped down my arms and soaked my chest. William handed me a thick towel and I wrapped her as best I could. He stepped out of the room to give her privacy but not before giving me a look that fueled my festering guilt.

Farland fluttered about Grace while performing his exam.

"Please turn her on her side and fold her legs," he said, pulling out a vicious looking needle. "I need to perform a spinal tap."

"Why? What do you think is wrong with her?" I said, worry gnawing at me.

"Based on her current symptoms, the speed at which they manifested and the preliminary blood tests I've just performed, I believe she has a case of bacterial meningitis. I will know for sure once I've analyzed her spinal fluids."

I cringed while he inserted the needle at the base of her spine to draw out some fluids.

"Isn't meningitis kind of serious? And I thought that disease was cured," I said, holding Grace's hand. They were cold and clammy.

"Meningitis is indeed serious and can be fatal if diagnosed too late," Farland said while analyzing the sample. "You are correct that meningitis has been cured on most planets, mainly due to vaccination protocols. However, I understand this young lady grew up in an orphanage where medical care is minimal at best. It is doubtful she received even half the standard vaccines. Also, alien species have different mutations of the bacteria."

Reading between the lines, I glowered at him. "What are you saying?"

The analyzer beeped. Dr. Farland nodded and rummaged in his medical bag, pulling out a hypospray and a box containing small vials of blue liquid.

"That she does indeed have bacterial meningitis, and that you more than likely gave it to her," Farland said, matter of fact.

The expression on my face must have communicated that I was close to bashing his head against the wall.

"Please understand that almost everyone in the main civilized species carries the bacteria in the back of their throat or nose — including humans and Braxians," Farland said, shifting on his feet. "Considering the nature of your relationship, you probably transferred it to her through a kiss in the past twenty-four hours. Sneezing or deep kissing are the most common methods of transfer. Had she been properly vaccinated, it wouldn't have happened."

I still wanted to punch him, but I felt too relieved to know her punishment wasn't the direct cause of it.

But I would have noticed sooner without that damn punishment.

Plagued with remorse, I watched Farland inject her in the neck with a hypospray.

"I'm giving her antibiotics that will get rid of the infection. She should be coherent again in the next couple of hours. Here are five more doses," Farland said, handing me the vials. "You must give her a dose every six hours."

"Will she be okay?" I asked, trying to hide my concern.

"Yes, Mr. Myers. We got it early enough. There should be no lasting effects. But have her come see me the day after tomorrow for a check-up after she has taken the last dose. The good news is people rarely catch meningitis again once they've had it. But to be on the safe side, after she's fully recovered, it would be advisable to get her up to date on all her vaccines."

You better believe she will.

"Thank you, doctor," I said, ready for him to leave me alone with Grace.

Getting my meaning, he nodded, grabbed his bag and walked out of the room. I ran my hand over Grace's hair and softly kissed her damp forehead. Walking to the closet, I rummaged through her clothes. I grabbed a red silk nightgown to dress her in. Her breathing improved and the fever slowly dropped.

The Braxian delegation would be here in the next twenty minutes. Reluctant to leave Grace, I tried to come up with a valid excuse to postpone – in vain. I crawled on top of the bed and gathered Grace into my arms. Her eyes fluttered but she merely sighed. I rested her head in the crook of my neck. Pulling the covers over us, I held her close for what little time remained.

We sat the living area to keep the meeting informal and, hopefully, short. Historically, Braxia's wealth and economy mainly relied on hiring out our army. With our size, strength, and speed, Braxians were formidable on a battlefield. However, over the last century, the number of interplanetary armed conflicts significantly dwindled thanks to peace treaties negotiated by the Galactic Council.

The shift destabilized our nation's fragile economy. Only a small fraction of our population had trade skills to adapt to changing times. Gerwin, Jarvis and Toran's clans were among them. From their humbler status, their clans rose to the top of the economic ladder during the transition. Under my grandfather's leadership, my own clan saw its status plummet from elite warrior clan to lesser farming clan, struggling to make ends meet on inadequate lands.

Under the new Magnar's rule, fundamental changes were taking place in Braxia. He wanted to fix our broken economy by educating the population in non-traditional fields for our people – especially science and commerce – and increase the volume of outbound trades with neighboring planets. The success of my Hive Network had piqued the Magnar's interest and he 'strongly encouraged' the elder clans to explore off-world ventures. As an 'expert' in that field, he expected me to provide whatever support I could. Needless to say, being mentored by a mutt didn't sit well with Gerwin.

"I revised some of the proposals you put together," I told Elder Pattel, under the watchful eyes of the three younger Braxians. "I've forwarded you a report for each with pros and cons to consider. There are a couple of them I might want to invest in, assuming certain adjustments are made. Once the stakeholders review them, we can arrange additional meetings."

Elder Pattel sighed with relief, his shoulders relaxing; he didn't want to return to the Magnar empty-handed. It was ironic that a 'lesser being' such as myself could make the call on which project to invest in.

"This is excellent news, Anton," Pattel said, with his usual friendly demeanor. "The Magnar wants us to move quickly on this. But I understand there were a few proposals you wished to discuss tonight?"

"Correct," I said. "The gladiator arena your own clan submitted is of great interest to me. You've been very thorough. It's solid and well thought out."

Pattel puffed his chest at the praise and cast a smug smile at his companions. Gerwin nodded but pursed his lips.

"Well done, Elder Pattel," Toran said, grinning.

"Indeed," Jarvis said with an enthusiastic nod.

Those two took brownnosing to another level. That they would lead their clan after their fathers was a joke in and of itself. They weren't particularly smart and confused leadership with bullying. This was largely due to their enduring childhood friendship with Gerwin, their little group's leader, and role model. Removed from his toxic influence, Toran could possibly be redeemed. Jarvis, however, was a lost cause.

"Your arena concept falls perfectly in line with my entertainment network," I told Pattel. "As such, I would like to propose an exclusive partnership with your clan. Instead of one gladiator arena, it would be seven; one for each of my Hives. The biggest one will be here on Venus Hive and hold an annual championship."

As expected, my four guests gasped. This offer was beyond generous and would completely turn around the future of the Veelan Clan. As their leader, Pattel had done well for them and managed to maintain their elder clan status. However, like my father's own clan, Veelan was mainly a warrior clan. Fertile agricultural lands saved them when Pattel's father swiftly leveraged them. The Veelan Clan wasn't struggling per se, but this contract would propel them to the top.

Pattel raised his massive hand to rub the nervous twitching of his broad, flat nose. "This is an unexpected offer and a most generous one. Obviously, I must discuss it with my clan's council, but I'm sure we will work out a positive outcome."

I liked the old man. He was a behemoth, like most men of his clan. His bloodline produced some of Braxia's greatest warriors. It was smart of him to devise an economic plan that would help leverage the strengths of his clan. I couldn't wait to see his clansmen in action in the arenas.

"Naturally," I said. "Take all the time you need to review my partnership proposal. Please note that as the arenas will be part of the Hives, I will absorb the construction costs; you merely need to state what your requirements are."

And with that, I sealed the deal. The construction cost of the single arena represented fifty percent of their investment. Now, there would be seven at no cost to them. They also knew I didn't do half-measures so their arenas would be state of the art, above and beyond anything they could have built themselves. What he didn't realize is that with this contract, his clan, like so many others throughout the empire, would now be beholden to me for their status and prosperity.

"My clan will be most pleased with this information. We will get back to you promptly on the matter," Pattel said bowing his graying brown head.

"As for Clan Caldes," I said, looking at Gerwin, "I'm afraid yours will not work... at all."

Gerwin's nostrils flared, the muscles of his arms bunching with anger. "Like hell it won't! Our material is lighter and cheaper than titanium. Customers will want it."

"Except no one will build their ships with duralium because it cannot handle the tremendous thermal and pressure requirements of frequent light speed travel," I said. "Selling duralium sheets to shipyards isn't an option. Your clan needs to come up with an alternative market, or transform it into *internal* spaceship parts."

Transformation would translate into a huge financial nightmare. First, they would need to figure out which parts to make, come up with a design that wouldn't infringe copyrights and build the manufacturing facilities. And that still didn't guarantee customers.

A muscle twitched on Gerwin's temple. "That's crap and you know it, half-breed!"

Pattel narrowed his eyes at Gerwin, while Jarvis and Toran gave him a nervous look. Gerwin was walking a fine line. Disrespecting your host in his own home constituted a huge offense. If he did, the other guests would side with the host or become offenders as well. That is, if the host called out the offense. Until then, they would sit back and watch.

I wanted Gerwin to cross the line. He had no idea what I had in store for him. Although bigger and stronger than me, he didn't have my agility and quick wit. It didn't hurt that William and a security detail stood at the ready in case things got ugly. While I expected Pattel to intervene, Jarvis and Toran could go either way.

"Careful, Gerwin," I said. "You're in my house and I'm doing you the courtesy of advising you on—"

"I don't need your shitty advice," he shouted, rising from his seat.

The rest of us all stood in response.

"You may have the Magnar fooled, but we all know better," Gerwin said, taking a step forward. "I know what you're doing, mutt. You're trying to get back at me because I have the balls to tell you what an abomination you are. You do not get to claim host privileges, Myers. Had he any honor, your sire would have killed you like the dog you are. Time for me to rectify his mistake."

Gerwin lunged at me. I dodged his lumbering attack. After

slamming my elbow into the back of his head, I dashed back out of his reach. Pattel barrelled into Gerwin to restrain him. I hailed William on the com. I didn't need to say anything; he would know to come immediately. Jarvis and Toran stared at the scene wide-eyed, uncertain what to do.

"Get off me, old man!" Gerwin shouted at Pattel, trying to shake him off.

"You will not dishonor my clan, you stupid fool," Pattel roared, twisting Gerwin's arm up his back.

"Mutts don't count!"

In an unexpected move, Gerwin twisted free of Pattel's hold. He swung a meaty fist at my face. I barely managed to dodge the blow. It would have crushed my skull, killing me on the spot. Instead, his momentum carried him forward. I whipped around and kicked the back of his head, sending him crashing into the wall. At that same time, the lift's chime announced William's blessed arrival.

Gerwin turned around with a roar, but Pattel and Toran jumped on him before he could come after me again. A good thing too. I probably couldn't do enough damage to knock him out, while a single blow from him could kill me.

"Stand down," William said, storming into the room with four security guards. His blaster, set to stun, aimed at Gerwin.

"You've done enough, Gerwin," Pattel said.

I stood in front of Gerwin, with Pattel and Toran still holding him down. William and the guards closed in on our position, ready to intervene. Gerwin bared his teeth at me, breathing heavily, his hard face twisted with fury.

"Gerwin Caldes," I said, "I have welcomed you into my home, provided you with food, refreshments, and comfort as was my duty as a host."

"You are no host! You're a mutt!"

I ignored him. "And you have thanked me by insulting me, and attempting to harm me bodily, with the intent to kill."

"Your father should have killed you in your whore of a mother's womb!"

"For this offense to my honor and that of my clan, I banish you and every member of Clan Caldes from all seven of my Hive space stations, be it for leisure or work."

All four Braxians froze. Gerwin's eyes widened, the repercussions of his actions dawning on him.

"All trade agreements and business contracts with Clan Caldes are, as of this minute, null and void," I continued. "William, see that they are all expelled within the hour."

"It will never hold. You hear me mutt?" Gerwin shouted. "It will never hold!"

"Get this trash out of here," I said to William.

"Apologies for this unfortunate turn of events," Pattel said while dragging Gerwin to the lift with Toran's assistance.

I nodded. Jarvis, clearly shaken by the fall of his leader, followed in silence. This had been a long time coming. My clan needed to be informed of the situation. I was done getting bullied. It couldn't be delayed, but it would wait for me to check on my woman.

CHAPTER 15
ANTON

Grace rested peacefully when I entered our bedroom. Her skin still looked too pale, but her breathing sounded significantly improved. Her fever had broken. She no longer shivered, and her hands and feet had returned to a normal temperature. I wanted to see her eyes, talk to her, and make sure she felt fine. However, I reined in my selfish desire and let her sleep.

Despite my reluctance to leave her, I needed to reach out to my father before Gerwin's clan did. I doubted Gerwin fully understood the impact of his banishment. After one last kiss on her cool lips, I went to my office to com my father. Although I was the offended party and well within my rights, I couldn't help the worry bubbling in the pit of my stomach.

My father's image appeared on the vidscreen. Like Elder Pattel and most men from warrior clans, my father was a massive man. He stood over seven feet tall with four hundred pounds of pure muscles. Once again, I felt small. Weak. I inherited his pitch-black eyes and raven hair, though gray streaked through his. Humans often compared the Braxians' broad and flat noses to that of baboons, hence the monkey sounds the girls made back on Jeruna. I never understood it. If you tried hard, you might compare our noses to a grizzly bear's snout, maybe. However, I always thought it looked more like that of a feline – a lion's in my father's case.

"Anton." My father's voice boomed like rolling thunder.

"Clan Leader." I bowed in respect. "I'm sorry for disturbing you, but there is an urgent matter I must bring to your attention."

"I'm listening."

His face remained impassive as I recounted what happened. That was the thing with him. You never knew what he thought, whether he would pat you on the back or punch your lights out for fucking up. He should play poker. I folded my hands on top of my desk to hide their twitching while awaiting his verdict.

My father nodded. "You have taken the appropriate actions under the circumstances."

I could have whooped in relief. "He will challenge my status as a host."

"And he will lose. A host has nothing to do with genetics. He was in your home after you welcomed him before witnesses. Whether you are a pureblood, Halfling, human or any other species, the rule applies. And besides, you are clanned."

"That was my understanding as well, but I wanted to confirm."

"Any other response to his actions would have shamed you and our clan. You did right."

"Thank you, Clan Leader."

"The Council and I will need to prepare for Clan Caldes' retaliation against us," my father said. "Be on the lookout. They might come after you as well."

"No, Clan Leader, they won't." I smiled at his raised eyebrow. This was the most emotion my father ever showed. "When Raylor Caldes comes demanding you lift the banishment, you can tell him that the next time his son wishes to disrespect someone, he shouldn't bite the hand that feeds him and his clan."

My father narrowed his eyes. "How so?"

I reclined into my chair, feeling smug. "Over the past three years, I have acquired every duralium shipment contract issued by Clan Caldes.

"Why?"

"Control. Few people want duralium due to its inability to sustain frequent warp speed jumps. Caldes can only find a handful of customers on this side of the galaxy. I can use duralium for my Hives since they're stationary. As I own every single one of Clan Caldes' contracts, they are now beholden to me. I can easily find another duralium provider. They won't find customers unless they try to sell below cost. They *will* come begging for forgiveness, or they'll starve."

My father lips stretched into a ghost of a smile. "Well done, son."

Son...

My heart thumped in my chest. He seldom acknowledged our blood bond. It was deemed inappropriate. How I longed to call him father.

"Just so you know, Clan Leader, almost every elder clan is beholden to us in one form or another."

He nodded, and a glimmer of pride shone in his eyes. I reveled in this too rare display of approval.

"You have done very well for yourself and for our clan, Anton." Despite his casual tone, my father was paying me a great compliment. "Elder Pattel spoke highly of your performance taming that human female. I recall she was a great beauty on Jeruna."

Cold dread spread down my spine. While the offense had been against me, it affected my entire clan. It fell to me to cleanse our honor, which I had done. But technically, the clan could wish to exercise its own revenge.

"I have already punished her for her offense against the clan and me."

"Yes, I am aware. That matter is closed." I swallowed my sigh of relief. "What are your intentions?"

I shifted in my seat. There was no good answer to this. "I own her for the next five months.

My father waved a dismissive hand. "That wasn't my question."

My face heated at being called out on my attempt to dodge. "I will release her, as per our contract."

Like hell I will.

"Why? Why not use this time to bind her to you?" my father asked. "She's beautiful and obedient. Why not keep her as your mate?"

My heart stopped for a moment, and I blinked. Why would he ask me that? He knows I can't.

"She's human. Braxians are forbidden to mate outside our species."

"You're not Braxian." His face was void of emotion. "And you're not on Braxia."

I flinched. I'd heard this many times before, but coming from him…

"Right," I said, proud that the hurt didn't show in my voice. "But the clan would never accept it."

My father stared at me, his expression unreadable. I shifted once again under his scrutiny. For some reason, it felt as if I had failed him.

"You are correct. The clan will never approve," my father said at last. "Goodnight, Anton."

"Goodnight, Clan Leader."

My father extended a hand to end the com but paused at the last minute.

"*I* kept *you*," he said, then terminated the com.

I stared numbly at the dark screen. Yes, to my eternal gratitude, he kept me, despite the clan's outrage. However, in spite of our clan's lesser status at the time, my father was well-respected and a formidable warrior. Hence his detractors couldn't remove him from power when he refused to kill me. Did he just give me his blessing to do what my heart desired? The clan though… I didn't have his strength. They would hunt her down and any offspring we had.

Frustrated and confused, I got up with a sigh and made my way to our bedroom… to Grace.

Why couldn't I have been born human?

Things could have been so much simpler. After checking that my alarm was set for Grace's next injection, I discarded my clothes and crawled into bed next to her. She shifted and mumbled my name when I pulled her into my arms.

"I'm here, Grace," I whispered in her ear. "Everything is fine. You are safe. Sleep."

She snuggled against me without waking. It felt right. She belonged in my arms, in my bed. I wasted one month on my wretched revenge. That stupid pet cushion would be gone in the morning. Whatever lay ahead for us, I was done squandering the time I had left with Grace.

～

For the second time, the alarm's soft buzzing woke me, this time to give Grace her third shot. Reluctant, I untangled myself from her embrace and loaded the hypospray with a fresh dose. I brushed her hair aside and leaned over to inject her neck. Her eyes snapped open and locked with mine before drifting to the hypospray in my hand. While still a little sluggish, she no longer acted dazed and confused. She frowned and gave me a suspicious look.

I paused. "You've been very sick. The doctor came by last night to treat you. This is an antibiotic to help you fight the infection. You have to take it every six hours, which is now."

Her eyes took on a faraway look, probably trying to remember feeling ill. She touched her cheek as if to check her temperature.

"Yes," I said, kneeling on the bed beside her. "You were burning up with fever. I had to put you in cold water to help break it. Okay?" I asked, gesturing at the hypospray.

She nodded. "Thanks."

I performed the injection then went to fetch her some water. "Here, drink this. You need to stay hydrated."

Her grateful smile brightened the room. She drank it all down without pause. I almost told her to slow down. Eyelids drooping, Grace handed me the empty glass. I got back in bed and cradled her body against mine. She stiffened and opened her mouth as if to say something but was too lethargic. The injection probably contained a sedative.

"Sleep, Grace. We'll talk later."

She mumbled something before falling asleep again.

It was a little before six a.m. I didn't need to be up for another couple of hours. When I woke next, I would cancel or postpone everything on my schedule. Too much happened in the past few weeks, and especially the past couple of days. I needed to reassess my situation.

Things that used to mean everything to me – honor, clan, acceptance – didn't matter all that much anymore. William's voice echoed in my mind.

"Even now, light years away, Braxia is still fucking with your life."

And it was. For a smart man, it seemed stupid that I always accepted this as normal. Something had changed. I had changed.

No. I am changing.

More importantly, I couldn't go back. Even though the uncertainty of what lay ahead scared me, I didn't want to go back. Thankfully, I had five months to figure it all out. I looked down at Grace's beautiful face as her head lay on my shoulder.

"I love when he's affectionate like that. It makes me want to stay with him forever."

"I will be," I whispered. "From now on, I will always be."

Sleep eluded me, but that was fine; I was used to functioning on minimal rest. Images of us dancing together replayed in my head and kept me company. By eight, I was up and about. First order of business; getting rid of that pet cushion. When I first acquired it, I convinced myself it was to put Grace in her place, humiliate her. But the truth was I feared her. The emotions she stirred within my soul terrified me. I avoided kissing her and refused to cuddle in a vain attempt to fight my attraction to her. The shame over my inability to resist the woman I should hate largely fueled my excessive brutality towards her. That knowledge burned like acid in my gut.

Pulling away from those somber thoughts, I cleared my schedule and canceled Grace's training with Romero. Another two hours later, Grace's eyes fluttered open. She squinted at me when I ordered her to remain in bed and brought her breakfast. Per my instructions, the cook prepared her a typical human breakfast she particularly liked; blueberry and walnut pancakes dripping with syrup and a mountain of fresh fruits with Chantilly cream. The pleasure I derived simply watching her devour the food struck me as odd. Once she finished, I carried her to the bathroom for her bath. The baffled look on her face made me chuckle.

"How are you feeling?"

"My head hurts. My neck is stiff and hurts a bit too. I'm feeling a little drowsy."

Even sick and pale, Grace was the most beautiful woman I had ever seen. From her frown and the way she studied my face, she clearly didn't understand my behavior.

"I can bathe myself you know?" Grace said, bewildered.

"I know."

"So… why are you?"

I shrugged. "Because you're sick, and I want to."

Her lips parted as if to question me further, but she frowned and leaned back in the tub. From the way she observed me, I could tell she expected me to grope her while bathing her. Keeping my touches gentle but clinical, I made quick work of washing her. As a selfish treat, I took extra time with her hair. Her confused look was comical.

I wrapped her in a Braxian-sized fluffy towel. It swallowed her slender body like a blanket. She remained stiff in my arms as I carried her to the bedroom. Her eyes drifted to the corner where her cushion used to sit. She stared up at me, blinking. I sat her at the edge of the bed and finished drying her off. Chewing on her bottom lip, Grace raised her arms to help me slip a sheer nightgown over her head. The silken fabric whispered against her skin. I didn't bring her underwear — a man could only change so much.

Using a soft brush, I proceeded to untangle her hair. I loved her long, soft, and lustrous hair. I often wished to be planet-side with her to watch it swirl around her in the wind with the sun glowing through it. Would it bring out the reddish tinge even more?

"Wha… where's my cushion?" Grace asked, bringing me out of my musing.

That wasn't the question she intended to ask. Though she lowered her eyes as she spoke, I didn't miss the glimmer of fear.

She's afraid to say something that will anger me.

Shame and remorse clawed at me from within. It hit me how distant she had remained while I fed her, bathed her and even now as I brushed her hair. Before, every time I showed kindness or took care of her, she blossomed under my touch and looked at me with devotion. Grace always hungered for affection. That vulnerability touched something within me. I understood too well wanting to be loved and cared for. But today, she had a guarded look in her eyes and was closing herself off to me.

"I've removed it. From now on, we will share the bed."

"I see."

My heart sank. I had envisioned a thousand different reactions she might have to this news, but never this cold, indifferent acceptance. Wouldn't sleeping in a proper bed hold some attraction? Something was broken. Grace had every right to be angry with me for yet another unfair punishment she'd received. Is that why she acted so distant? Was it because I didn't care for her after I released her, unlike the first time? Fuck that had been stupid. My damn Braxian pride…

I crouched in front of her so she didn't have to look up to me. "I'm sorry I punished you. You didn't do anything wrong and didn't deserve it. It won't happen again."

Her chin quivered, and she clasped her hands on her lap. "Ok," she said in a small voice.

She's not accepting my apology. I broke her trust.

"I will *never* put you in that cage again."

She nodded and stared at the bathroom door, past my shoulder. "I'm pleased to hear it."

Frowning, I cupped her chin in one hand and gently turned her face towards me.

"You doubt my words."

Her throat worked as she hesitated to answer. "You own me, Anton. You can do what you will to me, as is your right."

Grace shivered and hugged herself. I didn't need to read her mind to know she was thinking back to what happened in my office. My gorge rose at the memory of what I did to her. How could she have looked at me with such affection two nights ago after I'd treated her that way?

I took her hands in mine, unfolding her arms, and locked eyes with her.

"What happened on Jeruna is done and over with. The clan is satisfied, the slate is clean."

Grace's hands tensed in my hands, and her eyes flicked between mine. I took a deep breath before continuing.

"I'm sorry that I raped you."

The sound that escaped her throat wasn't quite a gasp. Her hands tightened further around mine, her nails digging into my flesh. I let the silence hang between us while she regained her bearings.

"A slave is property—"

"To be used at its master's leisure," I interrupted. "Yes, I know the law. That's how I justified following Braxian protocols. But what the contract says and what the law condones do not change the horror of what I did."

Grace shuddered. The haunted look in her eyes told me she was revisiting that moment. I hated that my regrets caused her more distress, but I owed her this apology.

Pleasure barges had very strict rules about rape. After murder, it was the second most serious crime one could commit, and the punishment was extreme. To avoid any misunderstanding, couples who wished to engage in dubious consent role-play had to sign release forms immediately beforehand. Masters only needed a copy of their indentured servant's contract. Legally, a master couldn't be accused of rape since they had the right to use their slave however they pleased, regardless of consent.

"Contract or not, I hurt you in a way no man should ever hurt a woman, and it shames me. I cannot undo what I've done. But on my honor – what's left of it – I swear it will never happen again."

A couple of silent tears rolled down her cheeks. They clawed at my heart. Her anger and contempt, I could cope with. But her sorrow crushed me.

"I do not expect you to forget, but I hope someday you can forgive."

Grace pulled her hands from mine. Although I deserved it, the rejection cut deep. She delicately wiped the tears from her face with the tip of a finger. I had wanted to do it for her but doubted she would welcome my touch.

She nodded and gave me a sad smile.

This felt wrong.

"Why don't you yell at me? Cuss me? Slap me? You should hate me right now."

She lowered her eyes and shook her head.

"Why not?" I knew Grace had dependence issues, but this felt like too much.

She took a deep breath then held my gaze. "You stopped."

I froze.

"When it mattered the most, I asked you not to do it, and you stopped. I don't think I could have ever forgiven you otherwise, even with the Denax. But you stopped."

Except you shouldn't have had to ask, to begin with.

"So what happens now?" she asked, fiddling with the hem of her nightgown.

"Our contract says anything I want." Grace held her breath. "I want many things, Grace, but not your pain."

She exhaled a shuddering breath. A glimmer of hope seemed to flicker in her eyes but vanished so quickly I wondered if I imagined it. Things were definitely broken between us, but I would fix them. I never faltered before a challenge, and none mattered as much as she did.

"You said I never have fun," I said, hoping to lighten the mood. That got her curious. "Well, today I'm taking a day off, and you get to decide what we do. Though you have to stay in bed and rest."

She gave me an 'are you serious?' look.

I smirked. "Stop thinking dirty, you pervert. I said *rest*, not sex. You are still sick. In fact, I have to give you another shot in a few minutes."

Her face heated, and she bit her lip. To be fair, I had somewhat set her up, but still...

"I get to decide?" she asked.

"Yes, you decide."

"Anything I want?"

I couldn't help chuckling. "Yes, anything you want."

The glimmer of mischief in her eyes didn't bode well. I braced for whatever would come my way, already cursing myself for giving her that much power.

"I want us to watch a movie."

That didn't sound too bad.

"Okay," I said slowly. "Which one?"

"Moonlight over Kigamot Sek."

My face fell as her smile broadened. The little minx had chosen the sappiest, most lovey-dovey, tear jerking, sigh-inducing movie ever made. Did I look like I would watch that kind of stuff?

Cringing, I asked, "Really?"

She batted not so innocent eyelashes at me. "You did say anything I wanted."

I sighed, my shoulders sagging. "As you wish."

Grace beamed. I'd sit through a thousand sappy movies to keep that sparkle in her eyes.

"Let's watch it now!"

"I'm afraid not." She frowned at me, probably thinking I was trying to back out. "It's time for your shot. Based on the past three injections, it makes you lethargic for at least a couple of hours. We'll watch it as soon as you come back around."

Pursing her lips in a pretty pout, she lay down while I charged the hypospray.

Grace looked up at me. "So, what did I have? And how did I get sick?"

That knocked the wind out of me. After everything, I didn't want to tell her one of the passionate kisses we exchanged either in my office or at Risqué had put her life in jeopardy.

"You contracted bacterial meningitis. Dr. Farland says you haven't received any of the standard vaccines. That makes you extremely vulnerable to a number of potentially lethal diseases that are considered cured, like the one you got. As soon as you've recovered, we will make sure you get all your other vaccines."

Well, I didn't lie.

"Damn… okay," she said, sweeping her hair out of the way to expose her neck.

Within seconds of the injection, her eyes drooped.

CHAPTER 16
GRACE

Five long days passed since my last training with Romero, reconnecting with Marcus, Anton's punishment, and me catching a potentially deadly illness. I was fine now. Dr. Farland gave me a clean bill of health. He still hounded me about getting a slew of vaccines. I wasn't too keen even though they'd protect me. But my opinion on the matter didn't count for much. Anton made it clear I couldn't skip them.

Making my way to the auditorium to meet Romero, I reflected on the radical changes in Anton's behavior. First, his unexpected apology. He didn't strike me as the type of man who apologized often, if ever. It seemed sincere too and I wanted to embrace it… embrace him. But wasn't that exactly how abusive men operated? They'd hurt you, then apologized saying they'd never do it again. You'd let your guard down and bam, they'd hurt you again. And you'd come up with crazy reasons why they were somehow justified. I'd been down that road with Paul before. However, nothing could ever justify a man, someone, anyone, hurting me because I displeased them. At least, he hadn't accused me of bringing it on myself like Paul used to.

I had a lot of time to think while in that cell. That is, until pain overwhelmed me, and the illness prevented any coherent thoughts.

William had also given me much to mull over. I better understood Anton's obsession with work. Success wasn't merely an ambition for him, it meant his survival. Yet, he already succeeded. What more did he need to prove? Was he just too addicted to his way of life, or did he not know how to be anything else?

I still couldn't get over Anton giving up two full days of work for me. He fed me, bathed me, and watched sappy romantic movies with me – yes movies, plural. You could see the 'time to make you cry' moment coming a parsec away, but I still fell for it. Poor Anton looked distraught as he watched me bawl my eyes out during emotional scenes only to tell him how awesome they'd been. He didn't get it. But for the duration of the movie, my own problems ceased to exist. It's so much easier to be objective about other people's woes. Sure, I shared her painful journey but in the end, I also shared her happy ever after.

I liked the new Anton. He was even better than first-week-Anton, with none of the occasional cold stares that boded ill. When not watching movies, we talked often. Most of the time while cuddling. Our conversations usually revolved around our respective youths as the future felt like too touchy a topic.

I learned a lot about his life on Braxia and his mother's rejection when he tried to connect with her eight years ago. She refused further contact because her husband knew nothing of Anton. When he asked about siblings, she told him she got her tubes tied after birthing him so there would never be another *accident*. What the hell kind of a woman would say something so heartless to her own child, wanted or not? Anton tried to act indifferent, but I could feel his pain. Although he didn't admit it, like me, he longed for a family. Anton worshiped his father and ached to get to know his two younger half-brothers. But they were pureblood. Braxian rules prevented them from mingling or bonding.

Nevertheless, I couldn't relax and enjoy this Anton. How long would this honeymoon last? What would trigger him next? The thought of him putting me back in that cage filled me with dread. His promise not to do that again only made me worry about what he might do instead. How do you prepare mentally for the unknown? My imagination was my worst enemy. Thinking about what Marcus said had been done to Darla and Steffie spooked me even more.

Romero arrived at the same time I did. In my joy at seeing him, I gave him a fierce hug which he returned, laughing. As I released him, it struck me that had Anton witnessed this, he could have taken offense. My heart filled with anguish. Although I kept reminding myself to keep a certain distance with Anton, deep down, I clung to hope. In my mind, I couldn't stop myself from thinking of him as my man.

Before that mess at Risqué, I had convinced myself that once the remaining five months ended, Anton and I would remain a couple. We'd have new rules putting us on an equal footing. However, I no longer believed our relationship could ever be healthy. Giving Romero a hug shouldn't make me fear Anton might lose it. I missed Marcus, yet wouldn't dare suggest spending time with him – not after Risqué. This wasn't the type of relationship I wanted with any man.

"What's wrong?" Romero asked, noticing my sudden change of mood.

"Nothing," I said, not wanting to ruin our session.

Romero placed his hands on his hips. "Tsk, tsk. What did I say about honesty?"

I stuck out my tongue at him. "You said to be honest with my audience. You're not my audience."

"Actually, I said you needed to be honest with your audience *and* in your relationships."

"Nice try, Professor, but we're not in a relationship."

"I beg to differ," he said, sitting cross-legged in one of the small auditorium's front row seats. "I consider us friends. Friendship is a relationship. We also have a mentor-student relationship. That's two relationships meaning you, darling, have to be twice as honest with me."

Despite my somber mood, his grin was contagious. I sat on the stage, my feet dangling over the edge. The small auditorium contained two hundred and fifty seats. Despite the cheerful color of the seating, the room felt dark and barren, like too many failed auditions had sucked the magic out of it.

"We're here for you to train me, Romero, not psycho-analyze me."

"Your emotional state impacts your ability to perform. But I won't pry if you do not wish to discuss it."

I did want to discuss it. The past weeks, I felt more isolated than ever, with no one to share my thoughts with. Aside from Marcus, I could never make real friends. But even that was a special kind of relationship. This industry was cutthroat and most girls I met saw me as either competition, beneath them or tried to use me. Guys… well, if they couldn't get in my panties, they didn't have much use for me.

"I just came to the realization that the man I like can't give me a good relationship. That for the next five months, regardless of our intimate involvement, I must guard my heart so I can walk away."

Romero tilted his head. "What makes you think it can't work?"

"If Anton had seen us hug, I'm not sure how he would have reacted. It was spontaneous and innocent, but he might have gone berserk. No one is more impulsive or spontaneous than me. And yes, you can translate that as I don't think before acting."

Romero smiled, rocking his crossed leg back and forth.

"That shit gets me in trouble all the time. When I fuck up, Marcus gives me an earful or the cold shoulder. But Anton hurts me. He says he won't do it again, but I don't believe it. I don't want to live in constant fear."

Romero nodded slowly, a pensive look on his face. "I agree. You should never accept a relationship where your lover thinks it's ok to hurt you, whatever the reason."

My heart sank. While my head knew this was the right thing to do, it still broke my heart to hear Romero confirm it. Somehow, it made it more final.

"That said, not every crime warrants a life sentence if it's the first offense."

"It wasn't the first time," I said, looking away.

Romero raised a dubious eyebrow. "Had he promised never to hurt you again before and broken his word?"

That's a good point.

I pulled my feet up to the edge of the stage and hugged my legs to my chest. "No. That's the first time," I said before resting my chin on my knees.

"It would be irresponsible of me to tell you that Mr. Myers will keep his word, but Braxians have this thing about honor."

Another good point.

"I think you should give him a chance to see whether he upholds his word. That doesn't mean let your guard down, but don't rule him out yet."

To my everlasting shame, Romero told me exactly what I wanted to hear. Keeping my distance from Anton the past few days had been hard.

"Fair enough," I said, trying to stifle the happiness from leaking into my voice.

"If you play your cards right," Romero said, rising from his chair, "by the time those five months are up, you might be in a position of power to negotiate the kind of relationship you want."

I snorted. "When Anton enters into a deal, he already knows you will play by his rules because you either have no other choice, or it's just too damn good a deal to pass up."

Romero's laughter echoed through the room. "That is quite true. I see someone finally did her homework and learned how her audience thinks." His eyes shone with delight.

It was silly, but that gave me warm fuzzies. I really needed to get over my pathetic need for approval. Romero hoisted himself onto the stage next to me.

"I certainly have been. Did you know that Braxians kill half-breed males?"

"Yes." He smiled at my stunned look. "I did my homework when I first joined the Hive Network. You should have done that before you even came to see Mr. Myers for his help. But I'm glad you are doing it now. What else have you learned?"

Annoyed he pointed out how lazy I was, I elbowed him. He chuckled.

"I've been reading up on their interactions with women. I focused on the place of women in their society, expected behaviors, and protocols."

Romero nodded. "Good. This is key to understanding Mr. Myers."

"I'm not fine with those rules, Romero. They're barbaric and archaic."

"I didn't think you would be," he said, his smile sympathetic. "However, Mr. Myers hasn't asked you to observe those protocols, has he?"

I shook my head.

"You shouldn't follow blindly or lose yourself to please anyone, sweetheart. But understanding the other, their motives and desires is key in any negotiation." Romero brushed my hair aside to look at my collar. "You are not in a position of strength right now. Five months is a long time to be flying blind. Knowledge will be your greatest weapon and shield."

I nodded, my fingers tracing the intricate swirls on my collar.

"Remember when I asked you to figure out what Mr. Myers wanted from you?"

"Yes."

"Have you figured it out yet?"

I chewed on my lip. "Well, had you asked me five days ago, I would have said revenge. But in light of recent events, I think he wants respect and acceptance."

Romero looked at me with such pride that my breath caught in my throat. He brushed his knuckles against my cheek and kissed my forehead. Rising to his feet, he gave me a hand up.

"You know, when I started my career as a vocal coach, one of my most prominent customers was the daughter of the Horvelian Ambassador. Honey, I don't know if you are familiar with that species, but their voices are painfully screechy, and their food is like vomit warmed over."

I made a face at the disgusting visual.

"Imagine my shock when the Ambassador invited me to dinner to thank me for my 'fabulous' work with his daughter. I couldn't refuse without offending him, but there was no way I could stomach that food. So what do you do when the only thing you have to work with sucks big time?"

"You pretend to be sick to avoid going?"

"No, Grace," he said, selecting the track I would be singing to. "That would only postpone the inevitable. I couldn't dodge forever. What do you think I did?"

I shrugged.

"I knew they would serve their traditional food. I looked for things to numb my taste buds. Colvin leaves are your best friends for that. Rub a bit of seedic oil around your nostrils," he said, tapping the tip of his nose, "and you won't smell the stench. So I went, ate what I could handle, and ignored the rest. My host saw me eat from his table and embrace his culture. Not that I only nibbled on two specific dishes and drowned the whole mess with wine. He felt honored."

It dawned on me that this was about Braxian rules regarding women. They were mostly demeaning. However, some of them I could handle. Anton never asked, but how would he react if I did?

"I'm so glad I met you, Romero. Besides Marcus, you're the first person I can call a friend."

"You honor me," he said with a slight bow, visibly embarrassed by my confession. "Come on then, little songbird. Let's train. We have a show in a month."

Over the following week, I enjoyed more of the same sweet Anton – well as sweet as a dominant, no-nonsense man could be. And that did all kinds of inappropriate things to me. Obviously, he knew I was holding back, yet he didn't pressure me. His understanding made it harder to keep my distance. We hadn't had any kind of sex since my punishment. He didn't even request blowjobs. We did plenty of cuddling though and lots of kissing – no tongue.

I didn't know what to make of it.

In a way, it made sense. I couldn't have handled one of Anton's vigorous tumbles after being this sick. Despite that, he spent more time with me. It made me feel cherished instead of his fuck toy. However, twelve days felt like a long time for him to continue apologizing.

Before things went to shit, he would have me suck him off at least two or three times a day, not counting the random times he would bend me over – usually in his office – on the desk, carpet, couch or against the wall. Like all Braxians, Anton could get it up at will, without needing to be aroused. Even after he climaxed, he could choose to stay hard. I was ready to have sex with him again, especially now that I could hope for a cuddle afterwards. Then again, maybe post-coital cuddling wasn't such a good idea if my goal was to keep a wall between us.

This really sucks hairy donkey balls.

However, I had bigger concerns than whether Anton would snuggle with me. Tonight, he would take me to a dance show. It was some tribal ballet from who the hell knew where. Critics hailed it as the biggest thing since faster-than-light travel. Discovering fancy new shows appealed to me, but I was scared shitless that things would go sour again. Aside from the outings on our first week, every other time Anton and I went out turned to shit. First, the Braxian-Jeruna debacle at Sade and two weeks ago, the Marcus mess at Risqué. What would go wrong tonight? And worst, what would Anton do to me once it did?

Anton and I showered together a few minutes ago. Again, he kept his hands to himself. Minutes later, he dressed and left the room. Anton almost always wore black, with a marked preference for leather pants and skin-tight dark shirts. With that crazy body of his, he rocked it like no one's business. Tonight, I wanted us to match.

I put on an open-back, black leather dress with a low v-neck. It didn't show much cleavage but set off my collar nicely. Yes, I still wore the collar. Even caged naked, my collar stayed on. Anton liked my hair down but this time, he would need to suck it up. I couldn't show off my beautiful backless dress with a curtain of hair covering it.

As a concession, I lifted my hair in a low messy bun that could be swiftly undone. I held it up with a vintage jeweled hairpin Anton gave me two days ago. It came in a set including earrings and a bracelet.

The hairpin, made of pure gold, stretched five inches long. At its head, five amber stones, intricately woven with golden coils, fanned out like a peacock's tail. The amber earrings matched my eyes and the gems on my collar. Sky-high black stilettos completed my outfit.

Leaning over the dresser to get a closer look at myself in the mirror, I applied some lipstick. Anton walked back in. He gaped at my appearance, an appreciative look on his face. Our eyes met through the mirror and his smoldered. Something passed between us. Something tender and delicate. He slightly frowned as his gaze lingered on my messy bun before lowering to my bare back. I held my breath, waiting for the verdict. He closed the distance between us. I straightened.

He stopped behind me, staring at my exposed flesh. Taking his time, he placed his hand on the naked small of my back and slid it upwards. His fingers trailed along my skin leaving goosebumps in their wake. I turned around to face him. Anton's eyes roamed over me, full of want. He ran his thumb over my collar, like the first time he put it on me. The look in his eyes told me he was fighting the urge to toss me on the bed and have his way with me.

"Do you have any idea how beautiful you are?" Anton asked.

Without giving me the opportunity to answer, he drew me into his embrace and kissed me. My lips parted, inviting. But Anton pulled away. How could he exercise this much restraint with so much passion burning within?

"Finish up and meet me by the lift." Anton's voice rumbled with desire.

He walked out, leaving me aching with need.

CHAPTER 17
GRACE

It was my first time at the Viaggo. The elegant opera house often featured dance recitals. From where I stood, the reception hall looked like three connecting circular rooms. The décor was reminiscent of the old Earth Renaissance era, with intricately carved darkwood walls, gold leaf work, columns and paintings on the vaulted ceilings. Anton's red empire chair would fit nicely here.

The elite of the elite mingled in small clusters. They were so damn stiff, it was a wonder they didn't break when they sat down. Beautiful bare-chested men in body-hugging black ballet tights served exotic alcoholic beverages and canapés. Tribal tattoos spiraled in knots along their right arm and the right side of their face.

One of them stopped before us, presenting a mouth-watering plate of colorful amuse-bouche. The scent of Firenese Peppers wafted to my nose and I promptly declined. Those things would set your mouth on fire before liquefying your innards. That explained the few patrons turning bright crimson and coughing into their delicate napkins.

Anton's fingers drew circles on my back in a slow, sensuous motion. Since we left the penthouse, his hand seldom left my naked skin. He flaunted me about, introducing me as his companion – not his pet. I was blossoming under the attention; my dress was absurdly sexy and could even make a baboon's ass look yummy. That Anton's deliciously wandering hands attracted more stares further filled me with warm tingles.

However, some stares were less welcome than others, such as the rather persistent ones from a Sarenian man. Humans easily represented a third of the patrons on Venus Hive, mainly due to the large number of nearby human colonies. The others were an eclectic mix of humanoid aliens – though most would skin you alive if you referred to them as such. After all, no human would want to be described as a Sarenoid alien. I liked most species. Many were rather attractive and above all, friendly. Sarenians were gorgeous; tall, lithe, dusty blue skin, silky long hair and small horns shaped like a crown. I could spend hours admiring their beauty. Except they treated women even worse than Braxians.

A large portion of the entertainment provided by pleasure barges such as the Hive Network – more than half of it – was of an erotic nature. Therefore, the patrons, regardless of species, tended to be sexually compatible. The common areas of the station imposed strict rules of conduct. However, specific venues within the station could set their own, less restrictive, custom rules. It was essential due to cultural differences that could engender ugly situations. That said, venues focused on cultural events such as this opera house, museums, and concert halls, catered to a more diverse variety of aliens where anatomic compatibility didn't matter.

We weaved through the patrons, Anton exchanging pleasantries with a few of them while I sipped on a glass of fruity white wine. I almost chose champagne, which I loved, but the bubbles made me sneeze. It wouldn't look very dignified.

To my relief, Caleb and Sheila didn't appear. In fact, I was one of the only performers in attendance. While artists at Sheila's and Seria's level earned substantial wages, Venus Hive was meant for the elite and priced accordingly. Without a 'benefactor' to foot the bill, most people employed on the Hive couldn't afford more than the occasional attendance in the VIP section's events. As a performer for Risqué,

Sheila got to eat there at cost, and as Caleb's squeeze, she got to tag along on some of his fancier outings.

Bored with the droning ramblings of Anton's latest interlocutor, I asked to be excused while I made a quick stop in the ladies' room. Anton nodded. His smirk told me he knew exactly why I was running. My gut told me he would like to do the same. I almost felt guilty abandoning him like that, especially considering I didn't actually need to go. Strutting to the washroom, I took my sweet time examining the patrons and especially the latest fashions from the outer rim.

Thankfully, I didn't find a line at the bathroom. In the Commons, if you wanted to go to the toilet, you might as well make reservations weeks in advance. Here, only a handful of women stood inside. We exchanged polite nods and I 'fixed' my messy bun by messing it up a bit more and retouched my still perfect makeup.

The performance wouldn't start for another fifteen minutes. Running out of excuses to dally, I left the washroom, intending to make a detour to the bar. I wanted to grab a glass of mineral water to wash out the sugary taste the wine left behind. On leaving, I almost crashed into the tall Sarenian man who had been staring at me. The slow smile that stretched his lips made my stomach drop.

"Excuse me," I said, trying to circle around him.

He stepped in front of me, blocking my path. "What's the hurry? I'd like to get to know you."

He was stunning, yet creeped the fuck out of me, far worse than Caleb. His voice was melodic with a purring element to it. The spicy scent of his cologne was enticing.

No, not cologne… pheromone.

I glared at him. "Please step out of my way," I said, my voice clipped. "My companion is waiting for me."

"No one is waiting for you." His voice took on a strange vibration.

Stupid girl! How could you forget?

Sarenians were dangerous, able to ensnare and mesmerize their prey. The males could release pheromones that enticed their victim. They also hypnotized vulnerable targets with a direct stare and the vibration of their voice. I knew better. Marcus warned me against them plenty of times. But I never imagined one would target me in such a public venue.

I opened my mouth to argue, but my mind went blank. Frowning, I tried to remember who I had intended to see after leaving the bathroom. The Sarenian held my gaze, his scent heady. I needed to avert my eyes, but they were glued to his. Through the fog clouding my thoughts, the image of a Braxian half-breed appeared before starting to fade. I clung to it.

"Anton," I whispered.

The Sarenian man hissed. Holding my jaw, his face inches from mine, he said, "Obey. Be silent. Surrender."

His eyes seemed to flash with a light glow, and my body went numb.

He pushed me towards the back corner of the corridor leading to the washrooms, never breaking eye contact until he was certain I was fully under his control. My thoughts remained my own, but my body was his to command. I screamed inside for someone to rescue me. But we were on a pleasure barge. While the opera house expected a certain level of decorum and restraint, no one would frown at a couple giving into their urges in a dark and discreet corner.

"You will never speak of this to anyone. Nod if you understand."

I wanted to claw his face off. Instead, I remained silent and nodded. He slipped his hand under the thigh high side slit of my dress and went straight for my pussy. Finding me without any underwear, his smile broadened, and he made a purring sound again.

"How convenient. You make everything so easy, my sweet beauty. But you're too dry. Get wet for me," he said while freeing his cock from his pants.

My eyes widened at his statement. Get wet for him? How the fuck did he think that would happen? Like I would even want to! Burning bile rose in my throat when I felt moisture pool between my legs. I shook my head in denial, shamed by the betrayal of my own body. My vision blurred as tears poured down my cheeks. This couldn't be happening, not here, not now, not to me.

A cruel laughter rumbled in his chest. "Yes, beautiful, the mind is a wondrous thing."

He crushed my lips with a brutal kiss and painfully squished my breasts. Letting go, he lifted my skirt and placed his hands on my bare ass, lifting me.

"Wrap your arms and legs around me, and hold yourself up while I fuck you," he whispered against my lips.

I watched in horror as my arms wrapped around his shoulders against my will. Suddenly, I fell to the floor, and he slammed into the wall behind him. My heart all but stopped when I saw an enraged Anton holding the Sarenian by the throat. I scrambled to my feet and lowered the skirt of my dress. Tears flowed down my face. Anton took in the state I was in. The look on his face spelled murder. I wilted under his stare, fear choking the breath out of me.

He moved so fast, his fist blurred as he smashed it into the Sarenian's shoulder. The Sarenian's bellow of agony didn't cover the sickening crunch of his bones shattering. I covered my mouth, my gorge rising. This Anton sent deadly chills creeping into my bones, turning my blood to ice. He breathed heavily, veins bulging on his temple and forehead.

"Did he hurt you?" he asked through gritted teeth, while the Sarenian whimpered in pain, struggling against Anton's immovable hold.

I shook my head. The Sarenian's command still bound me to remain silent.

"Did he hurt you?" Anton shouted this time.

Startled, my body jerked in fear. I pressed myself further against the wall, wishing it would swallow me whole and take me away to some place safe. My mouth refused to open. Shaking my head, I tapped the tip of my fingers on my throat, hoping he would understand. His eyes narrowed and his face twisted with blind fury as the message sank in.

"You little vermin," he whispered, his face inches from the Sarenian. "You dare to mesmerize a woman, *my* woman, on *my* station?"

"I didn't know she was your woman," the Sarenian said, groaning with pain. "They said she was your slave. Braxians don't value slaves."

"Does she look like a slave to you?" Anton shouted, spit flying. "How dare you disrespect my woman and me? Release her before I smash your brains against the wall."

A small crowd gathered to observe the scene. Among them, three security guards hurried forward. They didn't interfere but stood at the ready. But right now, one thought haunted me; what would Anton do to me?

"Look at me," the Sarenian man croaked. My head snapped towards him. With a will of their own, my eyes locked with his. "I release you… from all… commands."

The vise squeezing my brain relaxed its choking hold. I looked at Anton.

"Anton, I… I didn't…" Words failed me. I was so scared, I wished oblivion would claim me.

Anton lifted the Sarenian man by the neck and tossed him towards the guards. The crowd parted as he landed with a meaty thud at their feet. He croaked a strangled cry of pain.

"Lock him up. I will deal with him in the morning."

The guards nodded and dragged him roughly out of the Viaggo, not caring about the excruciating pain of his shattered shoulder.

Anton prowled towards me, anger oozing out of him. I shook so violently, my teeth chattered. He towered over me. I placed trembling hands on his chest.

"Anton, please…" I begged. "I didn't want this… I…"

"Shhh," he said, rubbing his thumb over my lips, "You didn't do anything wrong."

A choked sob escaped my throat as relief flooded through me. I collapsed against his chest and into his embrace.

"I am furious right now, but not with you, Grace," Anton said. While his voice was as tense as his body, his hands around me felt gentle. "I just need a moment to get my temper under control."

I nodded against his chest, the soft fabric of his shirt rubbing against my cheek. Behind him, I heard the last fading steps of the crowd scattering. We held each other in silence, regaining our composure.

"How did you know?" I whispered.

"I saw the way he watched you. A pureblood would have challenged him for that alone. I was going to let it slide not to ruin our evening. After you left, I noticed he was gone too and knew he was up to no good. Unfortunately, it took me longer to untangle myself from those fucking leeches." He kissed my forehead. "I'm sorry I wasn't there sooner. He will pay for this. You have my word."

I didn't care about the Sarenian. Relief, sweet, blessed relief soaked me through. My brain was stuck on a joyous loop: I wouldn't be punished. Closing my eyes, I sighed into his chest.

This wasn't an uncommon occurrence where Sarenians were concerned, despite their government's efforts to control its people. It was in their nature and their main method of reproduction. They preyed on compatible females and impregnated them against their will. In case their seed took root, the Sarenians planted a command preventing the woman from terminating the pregnancy or harming the child. The more the female resisted, the more it excited the Sarenians' predatory instincts. They were, therefore, persona non grata in many circles.

In this instance, the Sarenian had not only broken the rule, but he had also targeted the big boss' girl, disrespecting a Braxian in the process. Anton would make an example of him, and I couldn't raise an ounce of pity for the bastard.

A chiming sound indicated the beginning of the show. Anton released me and looked at my face.

"Do you want to stay, or would you prefer to return home?"

I loved him for his solicitude. My instincts pushed me to go home, away from the curious stares of the crowd. However, going home would grant my aggressor another victory. He wouldn't ruin the rest of my evening. Although, leaving could avoid another *incident*. Maybe this was my cue to run while things were still good between Anton and me. But is that what I wanted? Would that be our future? Hiding in the penthouse? Plus, I wanted to see all those sexy tattooed guys in ballet tights do their thing.

Taking a deep breath, I shook my head. "No. This is our night out. I'm not letting that asshole ruin it."

Anton smiled. The approval in his eyes washed over me like sun rays, bathing me in their warmth, and heating me to the core.

Clearing my throat, I said, "Just give me a minute to fix my face. I must look like a clown."

Anton chuckled. "You look beautiful, as always. Go on, I'll wait for you here."

Cupping his face between my hands, I let my eyes speak for me. He smiled, and I rubbed my nose against his before going to the washroom.

~

We returned home with our arms around each other's waist, strolling like two lovers without a care in the world. William greeted us at the Venus Hive Headquarters, no doubt having heard about the incident. Anton gave him a little nod, and William smiled. In turn, he gave me what I could only describe as a fatherly look. He stepped aside to let us through and the whole way to the penthouse, I wondered what had passed between them.

Once we reached our bedroom – yeah, it was *our* bedroom now, not *the* bedroom – Anton helped me out of my dress before quickly discarding his own clothes. Guessing I wanted to wash off the touch of that Sarenian, he took me to the bathroom. Anton was gentle yet thorough as he rubbed every inch of my skin with the washcloth. His touch wasn't clinical but didn't qualify as sensual either. Tender, caring, were the words that came to mind.

He led me by the hand back to the bedroom. When he fetched a nightgown to put on me, I pulled it out of his hand and tossed it aside. I wrapped my arms around him and rested my face in the crook of his neck.

"Be with me tonight," I whispered against his neck.

"Are you sure?"

I nodded, inhaling his scent – male, raw, mine. His hand slid up my back until his fingers combed through my hair, gently pulling it to make me look up at him. Whatever he saw on my face silenced his reservations. He lowered his head and gave me a slow, deep, sensuous kiss. It reminded me of our dance at Risqué. His tongue explored, caressed, and teased, drawing a needy moan out of me.

Breaking the kiss, he lifted me, carrying me to our bed. He laid me down as if I was the most delicate thing in the world. I opened my arms and he settled between my parted legs. The heat of his body took my breath away. Anton supported his weight on his forearms and though I could feel him stiffen against me, he seemed in no hurry to take me.

He traced the curve of my face with his fingertips as if discovering my features for the first time. Continuing their journey downwards, his hand explored my chest, drawing the lines of my clavicles with his fingers. I shivered. Moving down to my breast, Anton rubbed his palm over it. He then cupped it while his thumb circled my nipple. It pebbled under his touch while heat blossomed in the pit of my stomach. His eyes followed the motion of his fluttering caresses. I never felt so cherished in my entire life. It dawned on me that this was our first intimate moment on an actual bed with proper foreplay.

Usually, I would be on my knees sucking him off, or he would bend me over whatever surface was the closest. However mind-blowing those experiences felt, they were fast, hard, and impersonal. This… this was something else.

When his hand finally slipped between my legs, there was no urgency. A deliberate, sensual journey, his eyes locked with mine. My lips parted in a soft gasp when his thumb stroked my nub in a gentle tidal movement. His fingers didn't penetrate, content to fondle my nether lips. A slow fire built in me as my body awakened to his careful touch. The look in his eyes melted my insides. Whatever doubts I held about him and our future, right here, right now, I knew Anton's feelings for me transcended lust or ownership. I probably couldn't call it love, but he cared, deeply.

I sank my fingers in his luxurious raven hair and pulled his face back to mine. His plump, soft lips begged me to nip and devour them. And he tasted good. Every part of Anton tasted good.

"My turn," I whispered into our kiss.

I pushed him on his back, ending the delicious torment of his hand between my legs. Although Anton and I had had sex countless times, I never truly touched him before. Most times, he was fully or partially dressed. The rare times we were both naked I usually bent over, my palms against the shower wall for support while he took me from behind. Tonight, at last, I would savor, taste and discover the magnificent body that had made mine sing for the past two months.

Like him, I explored his face, first with my hands, then with my lips. He cringed as I traced the line of his nose, uncertainty flickering in his eyes. His vulnerable expression told me he feared I wouldn't like what I saw. How wrong he was. I no longer saw his strong brow ridges and prominent forehead as brutish. They denoted his strength, and character.

My fellow humans often compared Braxian noses to that of baboons. I never challenged that notion having barely given the Braxians I've seen before any real attention. But now, looking at his broad, flat nose, I saw no correlation. It was feline in its shape with the elegant nobility of a tiger's. I brushed my lips along the bridge of his nose, and he shuddered, his eyes closing. Nipping at his square jaw, I let my hands roam down his neck, to his broad shoulders.

I rubbed my face against his massive chest, inhaling his fresh, male scent. As far as I knew, Braxians didn't release special pheromones beyond what most species naturally secreted. Yet, Anton's scent soothed me into a sense of safety while arousing me. His skin felt soft, in sharp contrast to the hard muscles beneath. I could spend hours rubbing myself all over him. When my lips latched onto his erect nipple, Anton hissed, his fingers combed through my hair to hold me against his chest.

I smiled. Nearly two months together and I didn't know how sensitive his nipples were. I licked the hard nub, slowly, carefully, sucking on it. My thumb teased the other one and a deep, rumbling moan rose from Anton's chest.

"Grace, stop," Anton pleaded.

I realized then that Anton was one of those men who could climax simply from nipple stimulation. Although I would have liked to continue feasting on that little treat, I caved in. I journeyed down, my tongue exploring the cut lines of his abs. Before I could go any lower, Anton sat up, pulling me to him and flipping me onto my back. I squealed in surprise, disoriented for a second.

He buried his face between my legs. My back arched off the bed as a shout of pleasure tore from me. The intense frenzy with which he licked and tasted me testified to his fading control. Still, he didn't penetrate me with his tongue or fingers. My stomach clenched and my legs shook with frustrated desire. I was so close.

"Anton… I need you."

Mischievous, he continued lapping at me. Then mercifully, he crawled back up to me. I spread my legs wider, wrapping them around him as he settled over me. The scorching heat of his skin against mine stirred the flame burning within. His weight on me was like a cocoon sheltering me. It was like being with him for the very first time.

Eyes locked with mine, Anton pushed himself inside me carefully. Once fully sheathed, he remained still, kissing me deeply. Anton began rocking in and out of me, savoring every moment. He thrust deep before pulling out almost to the tip and back in again. Each stroke fanned the fire burning inside me. My arms tightened around him, my nails digging into his strong, broad back. I couldn't seem to get close enough to him.

Cupping my face, Anton's eyes devoured mine. "Grace…" he whispered. "I missed you. I ached for you."

With each word, the part of me yearned to belong fell even more for him.

I said his name like a prayer. "Anton."

"Tell me you want me, Grace. Tell me you want this with me."

There was an urgency in his plea, a bone-deep need that made my heart throb. The wondrous feel of him filled me, surrounded me. The deep rumbling of his voice sent tingles to my nerve endings. The desperate hunger in his eyes set my body ablaze. How could I not want him?

"I want you with everything that I am."

"Grace… my beautiful Grace. You're all that I want."

I don't know how long our joining lasted. It was gentle, tender, and fervent. Our climax wasn't the devastating tsunami of our usual tumbles. This time, it swept deep, rocking me to the very core of my being. Afterwards, I clung to him, fearing he would push me away. He gathered me into his arms and held me close.

As sleep claimed me, I heard him whisper, "I'm keeping you, Grace."

I smiled.

CHAPTER 18
ANTON

The last three weeks with Grace opened my eyes to how cold and empty my life had been. Things were good, *really* good between us. The way she looked at me, touched me... She made me feel attractive, desirable, wanted. Not the type of adjectives non-Braxian women attributed to our kind.

With my wealth and status, I'd had more than my fair share of beautiful women. Human females loved my body and what my money could do for them. But I had no illusion that they cared for me or my face. It was a mutually beneficial agreement; they got red carpet treatment to VIP venues and events, most of them seeking to advance their entertainment careers, and I got to fuck gorgeous women and flaunt sexy arm candy when socializing. Braxians, including half-breeds like me, had a voracious sexual appetite. While we could get hard at will, we couldn't soften on a whim, and rarely without release.

Since Grace, my orderly, predictable, cold world turned upside-down. I liked the man I became around her; more relaxed, less concerned with protocols and image. Grace still thought I worked too much but my schedule significantly lightened. It was ironic to think that for years, I'd run the largest entertainment network in the Eastern Quadrant of our galaxy yet hardly ever enjoyed any of it.

Usually, I sat through a performance studying the customers' reactions to see what to improve or leverage in other shows. But Grace had the most delicious way of distracting me from work. By her scent, 'distracting' me excited her. It was a blessing her sexual drive kept pace with mine. I wasn't an exhibitionist myself. However, I knew Grace was dying to visit Sade and for us to put on a bit of a show there. For her, I would do it – once I found an outfit that covered her enough throughout the action.

The way things were going between us, I felt confident Grace would stay with me of her own free will at the end of our contract. After my outburst at the opera house, it became clear to everyone that Grace wasn't some temporary squeeze; she was my woman. In my heart, Grace was my mate. The patrons and staff also treated her as such now. She blossomed under the attention and deference they lavished upon her.

We didn't discuss our relationship. With a little over three months left on her contract, we had time to decide. My clan remained the problem. They wouldn't accept Grace as my mate. However, as long as we didn't have children, she could be my concubine. They would demand she behaved like a Braxian consort when Braxian delegations visited. I couldn't see her agreeing to that. My people didn't treat women kindly. I didn't want Grace acting like a Braxian woman, a concubine, or a slave. While I didn't mind some of the greeting rituals, the rest was just too demeaning.

As expected, Gerwin's clan raised a stink about their banishment. But since I had them by the balls, Clan Leader Caldes soon tempered his tone and agreed to apologize for the slight. However, my father made it clear Gerwin offended me. Therefore, he must formally apologize to me.

I could have kissed my father.

My own clan cringed at my father's verdict. Gerwin refused. Pride forbade him to beg forgiveness from a half-breed. He chose banishment from his clan instead. On the heels of that announcement, the Magnar himself requested to meet with me in person.

That meeting was tonight.

I delayed as much as possible before telling Grace. As my consort, she needed to be by my side. This is where things would get tricky. By Braxian law, female slaves were free for all. Any man who wanted a slave, even while a guest at another Braxian's home, could expect her to submit. Consorts were off-limits. That said, common courtesy required the host to offer his consort to guests of similar or higher rank.

Most Braxians groped the concubine as a sign of appreciation for the gesture, then released her. Not fucking her showed your esteem for the host. However, not all Braxians observed that unspoken rule, especially if the woman was particularly attractive. Only a mate couldn't be touched under any circumstances, nor would she be offered.

I didn't know Magnar Ravik. From all accounts, he was progressive, which wasn't well-received by some of the elders. Times had changed but Braxia lagged behind, groveling for scraps. I hoped Ravik was progressive enough to treat me with esteem despite my half-breed blood and not demand too much from Grace.

Him granting me an audience was a huge honor. That he came here rather than summoning me to Braxia gave me hope. However, Clan Caldes had been highly influential under the reign of Magnar Sigmer, Ravik's father. Under Sigmer's rule, half-breed hunting became a sport. Rumors claimed he had owned a trophy room covered in skulls of half-breed he personally killed.

Sigmer had brought Braxia to the verge of bankruptcy by not adapting to the changing times. His unexpected death stirred a sigh of relief from the embattled younger generation who saw very few prospects for their future. Things noticeably improved under Ravik, but it would take more than two decades working with a reluctant council to fix nearly a century of mismanagement.

Every time things were getting better with Grace, Braxia came and fucked with us.

I stood outside our bedroom, trying to work up the courage to break the news to Grace. With a heavy sigh, I pushed the door open. She sat on our bed, a bunch of holocards scattered before her. They were the portfolios of musicians, backup vocalists, and dancers she was considering for her new show.

There was something strange in the look she gave me. Grace gathered the holocards and placed them on the nightstand. She patted the mattress beside her for me to sit. I complied.

"I guess you're finally ready to tell me what's been troubling you all day?" she asked softly.

"Was it that obvious?"

She gave me a sad smile. "I'm starting to know you, Anton. I'm also guessing that it will upset me. Let's just get it out of the way."

I shifted, cracking my neck to release a painful knot. "The Magnar is coming for a visit tonight. It is a great honor for my clan and me."

She exhaled and clasped her hands on her lap. While her face remained neutral, her knuckles whitened.

"Is he coming alone?" she asked.

"Yes."

"How nice do I have to be to him?"

I felt a sour taste in my mouth as I struggled to find the words. This whole situation infuriated me, but worse, it shamed me. What the hell kind of a man couldn't protect his woman?

"You're my consort, Grace. He's not supposed to do more than cop a feel."

She opened her mouth to say something, then closed it. I could guess her thoughts; 'not supposed to' didn't mean 'would not.'

Grace may never forgive me if things got rough. I would protect her of course, but the Magnar wasn't Gerwin – he would squash me like an insect.

"When does he arrive?" she asked, looking away.

It wasn't in defeat. The stiffness of her back and the hard line of her jaw spoke of repressed anger. She didn't want me to see how she felt, on her face, in her eyes.

"He will be here in an hour or so."

She nodded. "I should go get ready then." She rose gracefully and walked to the bathroom.

"I'm sorry, Grace."

She paused in the doorway. "I know," she said without turning to look at me, then closed the door behind her.

William commed me to let me know the Magnar had arrived. I went to get Grace as she needed to be by my side when I greeted him. To my utter shock, she walked out of the room wearing a diaphanous, thigh-length white dress. It was sheer enough to tease about her delicious curves but opaque enough to hide any indecent details. Barefoot, no underwear, her long reddish-brown hair cascaded down her back. She looked good enough to eat. It was also a perfect traditional Braxian concubine outfit.

Where the fuck did she get that?

Despite my curiosity, I escorted her to the lift in silence. The Magnar would arrive any minute and we couldn't dally.

Right on cue, the lift chimed as we took position in front of it, Grace standing two steps behind me. My stomach lurched at the sight of the behemoth revealed by the doors opening. Magnar Ravik was almost eight feet tall, his head only inches from the lift's ceiling. He easily weighed over four hundred pounds. The stretchy dark fabric of his clothes seemed about to tear with each movement of his rippling muscles. Like me, raven black hair fell to his shoulders. As the purest bloodline on Braxia, the Magnar's features were as brutish as they came. His strong brow line and broad forehead gave his hard face a permanent, terrifying scowl.

However, his eyes held my attention. They shone with keen intelligence and wisdom, in sharp contrast with his fearsome appearance.

The Magnar stepped into the room. He gestured for his two guards to stay in the lift with William who took them back down.

"Magnar Ravik," I said with a deferential bow, "your presence honors me. Welcome to my home."

"Anton Myers of Clan Aldriss, we meet at last." His voice rumbled like a waking volcano. "I accept your hospitality and thank you."

His obsidian eyes drifted to Grace. Heart pounding, I schooled my features and introduced her.

"This is my consort, Grace," I said, gesturing towards her. "My concubine and my house are yours."

The words scorched my lips and twisted my innards. To both the Magnar's and my surprise, Grace approached the Magnar then kneeled at his feet. Sitting back on her haunches, she rested her palms on her knees and bowed her head.

"Welcome, Magnar Ravik. Health, wealth, and strength to your clan," Grace said. Her voice sounded steady, respectful, and beautifully raspy.

I didn't know when she learned the Braxian greeting protocols observed by concubines, but it honored me, my clan, and the Magnar. My chest hurt realizing that despite me hurting her repeatedly over my culture and clan honor, she still embraced them to please me.

I don't deserve her.

A strange look settled on the Magnar's face. He stared at her bowed head for a moment before facing me. In the traditional gesture of acceptance, he placed his hand on her head.

Magnar Ravik said, "Thank you, little Grace. You may rise."

Grace stood, head bowed, her hands clasped in front of her. The Magnar held her by the shoulders, giving her an appreciative once over. "I heard of your consort's beauty, Anton. It by far exceeds even the most outrageous tale." He gently lifted her chin with a finger, and she submitted to his examination. "Submissive and respectful, too. She brings great honor to your house."

His words should have filled me with pride and joy. Deep down, the part of me that longed for the acceptance of my people reveled in receiving such high praise from the Magnar himself. However, it drowned in the sickening feeling in my stomach as he placed a possessive hand on the back of her neck.

I swallowed hard and gestured for him – them – to follow me into the living area. The tension in Grace's shoulders belied the impassive expression on her face. I spent nearly two decades building my empire so I wouldn't be at another's mercy again. Yet, here I stood, feeling more helpless than ever before.

Ravik sat on the loveseat, his massive frame filling two-thirds of it. He pulled Grace onto his lap. He made her sit sideways, pulling her bare feet onto the cushion. Sitting across from them in the plush chair, I forced my eyes not to stare at his big hand resting on her knee – under her flimsy dress – or the slow movement of his thumb on her naked flesh.

"Food? Drinks?" I offered, my voice barely hiding my tension.

A discreet smirk stretched the corner of the Magnar's lips, indicating he wasn't fooled by my attempt at detachment. "No, thank you. I won't be staying long."

Thank fuck for that.

"The Caldes banishment stirred quite a commotion. It is all the talk on Braxia."

"As such things are wont to be," I said.

Is he here to challenge the banishment on their behalf?

"I understand he insulted you and physically attacked you after accepting your hospitality?"

Through my peripheral vision, I saw Ravik's hand moved up and down Grace's thigh.

I forced my eyes to remain on his face. "Correct. Elder Pattel and two others witnessed his attack. Gerwin brought it upon himself."

"No need to be defensive, young Anton. The idiot had it coming. Leader Caldes should be thanking you for ridding him of that poor excuse of a firstborn. Gerwin couldn't have managed the clan after his sire. Good riddance."

I inhaled sharply. Such blunt honesty with a mutt threw me.

"Forgive me, Magnar. It is a sensitive topic for me."

"I can see why it would be," he said, his tone conciliatory. "You have done incredibly well for yourself, Anton Myers. Impressive, especially for a half-breed."

Grace stiffened at his comment. That drew his attention. He narrowed his eyes at her.

"Does it bother you that I call your consort a half-breed?" Ravik asked Grace.

I felt my blood draining, fearing he might take offense to her response. Grace chewed on her bottom lip, clearly hesitating. To my surprise, the Magnar gently caressed her cheek.

"Do not be afraid, little one. Speak freely. On my honor, no harm will ever come to you from me."

Grace licked her lips, then said, "Yes, it does. I don't understand why people make such a big deal of his genetics. It shouldn't matter. Only his accomplishments should."

Ravik smiled. "You like him, don't you?"

I held my breath as she nodded shyly at him.

"Yes, Magnar. I like him a lot."

He took her hand and raised it to his face. Leaning his cheek into her palm, he closed his eyes.

"Say my name," he whispered.

"Mag—"

"No. Just my name," he said, interrupting her.

"Ravik," Grace said softly.

His brow creased, and he pressed her hand against his cheek with an almost pained sigh. I wasn't sure what I was witnessing, and why the Magnar would allow me to see this. Grace stared at him, stunned at first. Then her lips parted as if sudden understanding dawned on her. She raised her other hand to his cheek, cupping his face. He opened his eyes, their gazes locked in a silent communication. It made me uneasy. Yet, my gut told me this needed to play out.

Grace combed her fingers through his long hair. He closed his eyes again and exhaled a shuddering breath when she whispered his name in his ear. Wrapping his arms around her, he held her in a tight embrace. She kissed his cheek. My fingers dug into the chair until I felt the material begin to tear. The look he gave her was tender. Magnar Ravik handled her with more care than I could have hoped for. But her reaction baffled me. Scared me. Releasing his embrace, he brushed her hair aside then gently kissed her lips.

"Thank you for your warm hospitality, little Grace. Both the

Magnar and the man will not forget. You may go. Your consort and I have much to discuss and little time to do so."

Grace got off his lap and kneeled before him. The weight crushing my shoulders and constricting my lungs lifted. After Ravik caressed the top of her head, she rose to her feet and glanced at me. I smiled and we both watched her leave.

The Magnar's tender expression evaporated the minute Grace faded from view.

"For such a smart man, you're quite an idiot." His voice was icy.

"Magnar—"

"Don't Magnar me," he snapped. "Why the fuck would you let me or any other man touch your woman?"

That threw me. "It is tradition. You are the Magnar. Doing otherwise would have been—"

"The right thing to do," he said, interrupting me. "It isn't tradition, it's Braxian garbage. I guess you're as big a fool as the rest of them."

I sagged in my chair, dumbstruck. His words dripped with treason. Was that why he left his guards with William? Was he baiting me to speak up against Braxia only to have me jailed? I opened my mouth. Closed it. Opened it again.

"What if I decided to fuck her?"

My teeth clenched. "You're a fully mature Braxian. You'd never fit without killing her."

"Your father sired you, and your mother lived to tell the tale." His eyes were hard, unflinching. "Nothing a bit of patience and plenty of Denax wouldn't take care of."

My blood ran cold. Ravik wasn't that much bigger than my father. Denax was an extremely effective lubricant and dilator. I used it on Grace the night I almost took her ass. I had only intended to give her enough to prevent tearing or significant harm. With proper time and preparation, she could have enjoyed it.

Ravik smiled at my expression. Magnar or not, I wouldn't let him fuck Grace. Though from his earlier comment, it didn't sound like he planned to.

"Let me tell you a tale, young Anton," Ravik said, leaning back in his seat. The couch creaked under his massive weight.

I nodded, grateful for the conversation to steer away from fucking Grace.

"Thirty-three years ago, for my twelfth birthday, my father gave me a human slave. She was a beautiful wisp of a girl, a fourteen-year-old named Lissy. I became sexually active a few months prior, and Father considered it a rite of passage to deflower a human female."

It was more than a rite of passage. Virgins were hard to come by. Beautiful human virgins even harder. Wealthy clans paid high prices to get willing young females for their sons to bed. It became a sign of status. Between the ages of eleven and fourteen, a Braxian male's girth was still small enough for a human woman to handle with reasonable ease. By fifteen, coupling with a human usually resulted in serious tearing without Denax. However, frequent and excessive use of the dilator endangered the woman's health.

"Within a year, I committed the unforgivable. Not content to fall in love with a slave, I also impregnated her with a male." He snorted at my stunned expression. "But that wasn't the worst part. I allowed my son to live and kept him a secret for fifteen months. Can you guess what happened next?"

"Your father discovered his existence."

"Yes."

I couldn't imagine what that must have been like. Magnar Sigmer had been a zealot and a bigot. For his own son to taint their bloodline, with a slave no less…

"A human snitched on us. The Narinda colony's ambassador came to discuss possible trade agreements." His lips stretched in a sneer. His hatred for the human still burned bright. "He knew Braxian protocols. When Lissy refused him, he complained to my father who had guards escort him to her quarters. If she refused him again, they would hold her down for him and then punish her. Apparently, she was breastfeeding our son when they barged in."

I shifted in my seat, imagining the young girl watching in horror as the guards dragged her child away. By then, she would have been sixteen or seventeen.

"When I returned early from the training camp, I naively thought my father summoned me as a reward for the distinctions I earned during combat training." Ravik emitted a sad chuckle. "The guards said he awaited me in the courtyard. When I saw over a dozen juveniles from elder clans gathered there, I thought they came to celebrate me."

I knew where this tale headed. Yet, I listened with morbid fascination.

"When they saw me, their smirks told me something was wrong. That's when I saw my Lissy, naked and shackled on an altar. Near her, my son wailed in a cage like an animal. My father made me watch as the juveniles took turns – fifteen in total, one for each month I'd kept my son's life a secret. He chose them because their age made them the perfect size to fuck a human without killing her in minutes."

I couldn't begin to imagine the horror he must have felt. And his son... He had been old enough to understand they were hurting his mother while his father didn't help her.

"By the fifth one, Lissy stopped calling out for me. When the last was done, my father held the cage up for me. Then she understood. She begged and pleaded. I broke our son's neck and placed his dead body on her chest. And so they remained until the next morning. She took her own life the following day. From the doctor's account, she would have died anyway from internal injuries."

As horrible as that was, Ravik showed mercy to Lissy and their son. The altar usually had a wall behind it. The sire was expected to bash the child's head on it so the blood and gore rained down on the mother's face. Then he would place the corpse on her chest.

"I could have saved her. I could have saved them both by simply renouncing my clan. Instead, I spent the next thirty years with their deaths on my conscience. Six of those juveniles now sit on my council. Every day, I eat and drink with them, work with them, socialize with them. And all I see, are those bastards rutting over my woman while she begs me to save her. There's a special kind of hell for men like me."

I would have killed them.

"You were just a boy, Magnar."

"I was old enough to put a child in a woman's womb," he said, curling his lips. "I should have protected them. At that age, despite all the odds stacked against half-breeds, you not only lived but also became your clan's main provider. What does that say?"

"That we had different priorities. Your father groomed you to rule Braxia after him, according to his beliefs. I strived to make myself invaluable to my clan for the right to live."

Ravik smiled and crossed his leg. "Your Grace loves you."

My heart thumped. "I believe she has affection for me."

"Foolish boy. She loves you. I know that look." His face took on a faraway expression. After a moment, his eyes refocused on me and took on a determined look. "I want you to renounce your clan."

My breath hitched. "Excuse me?"

"Renounce your clan, mate your woman, and have children."

He had no right to make such a demand. One could renounce of their free will or be banished for a grievous offense, but not coerced into renouncing.

"Is that an order, Magnar?"

Ravik snorted. "To save you, your father showed the courage I lacked. Krygor Aldriss faced a lot of challenges and criticism for sparing you. Do you think he did all this so that you can spend a lifetime of Braxia bullying you?"

There was something more to this. "Why do you care?"

"Had my son lived, he could have been you. I'll never know. What I do know is that Braxia is a cesspool of ignorance, bigotry, and stupidity. Our people must change and adapt to the times or face oblivion. Do you really think my father's death happened by accident?"

Why the fuck was he revealing all this to me? Several rumors whispered of foul play but why confess to me of all people?

"Magnar Sigmer wasn't always popular," I said, cautiously. "We all expected someone to challenge him sooner rather than later."

"He was a fanatic and should have been put down long ago," Ravik bit back. "Bottom line, Braxia must change. I can only lay the groundwork and raise my sons to continue after me."

I nodded. "You have set a number of progressive ideas in motion that will help Braxia."

"But it's not enough. Half of my time is devoted to pacifying foreign governments because yet another clan took excessive revenge over a slight. That can't go on."

I'd always wondered about that. Darla and Steffie had been nobodies, with no powerful protectors or family to seek justice on their behalf.

"The purge of half-breeds needs to stop. I've been watching your progress for a long time. Since you reversed the fate of your clan – sixteen years ago was it..?"

"Yes."

"An increasing number of lesser clans are sparing their half-breeds," he continued. "Most of them still don't make it to puberty, but it's a start. You've set the bar for what half-breeds can be… and above all, what half-breeds will or won't accept."

My breath rushed out as a light finally went off in my head.

"You set me up," I whispered. "This whole consultation deal, you knew that sooner or later, Gerwin would provoke me."

Ravik lifted his chin. "Yes. I knew they would eventually challenge you. Why do you think I sent those three idiots with Pattel?"

I shook my head in disbelief.

"For what it's worth, the consultations are genuine. Had you not fought back, I ordered Pattel to keep you safe. However, I didn't think you would take it lying down, and you didn't disappoint."

His comment touched me. Ravik was only a few years younger than my father. I was a sucker for paternal approval.

"How does renouncing my clan benefit you if your goal is to show they shouldn't kill half-breeds?"

Ravik's grin broadened and he spread his arm on the backseat of the couch, staking claim. "By giving the Empire a big fuck you. By showing all Braxians you don't need them; they need you. By reminding them, just like you reminded Clan Caldes, that a half-breed owns them."

I narrowed my eyes and he chuckled. I thought my trails better covered.

"Without the protection of my clan, the others might come after Grace or me. Worse still, they could come after any child we have."

"And face my wrath. Renounce, and I will make you Friend of the Empire."

That knocked the wind out of me. As long as Ravik remained in power, that title effectively made me untouchable. Anyone who attacked a Friend of the Empire not only forfeited his life, he also brought down the banishment of his entire clan.

"You have given me much to think about."

"I thought you'd feel that way," Ravik said as he rose from his seat. "The hour is late. I must depart. Although, I would see your mate one last time."

"Naturally," I said, pretending he hadn't called Grace my mate.

This time, she came enthusiastically. It bothered me a little. Somehow, Grace guessed the nature of his loss and gave him what he needed. Comfort.

Grace's hands looked tiny when she placed them in Ravik's. She held his gaze, a gentle smile on her lips.

"You take good care of your mate, little Grace."

Her eyes widened, but she didn't challenge his choice of words. "Yes, Magnar."

"Ravik," he corrected. "When we meet in private, I would have you call me Ravik."

"Yes, Ravik."

He smiled and placed a gentle kiss on her forehead.

"Anton," he said, with a farewell nod.

I bowed. "Magnar Ravik."

He snorted. "That was meant for you as well, silly man."

My throat tightened at the tremendous honor. "My apologies, Ravik."

"Until we meet again," he smiled, entering the lift.

CHAPTER 19
GRACE

Two months passed since the Magnar's first visit. He came twice more after that. At first, he terrified me. Seeing how roughly Gerwin handled me at Sade, I didn't know what to expect. His careful, almost tender touch baffled me. But when he asked me to say his name, and his reaction finally made it clear – I reminded him of someone he had deeply cared about. Romero would be proud how I applied his teachings. Between playing the part of a Braxian concubine, and assessing what my audience – the Magnar – wanted, my performance deserved a standing ovation.

To be fair, I didn't need much acting to deal with the Magnar. After he promised never to hurt me, I realized he was a nice man carrying a lot of pain deep within. It pleased me to soothe some of it. I was growing quite fond of him, especially since he seemed to bear some kind of fatherly affection for Anton. But men, Braxians worst of all, were every shade of awkward when it came to conveying their feelings. Anton and the Magnar seemed to have this big conspiracy thing going on and curiosity chewed away at me.

However, things were going too well between Anton and me to jeopardize them with curiosity. We never spoke of the contract anymore, even though it hung over our heads like a thunder cloud.

That didn't stop us from having wild, raunchy sex over every surface of his office at random times of the day.

Last month, Anton gave me the greatest surprise. We were leisurely strolling down the walkway, trying to decide which bar to go to when we ran into Marcus. Even though Anton admitted his mistake after punishing me, I didn't know how he would react. I missed Marcus but couldn't seem to find an appropriate way to broach the topic. In a way, it felt cowardly not to address that issue now with Marcus nearby, but I was picking my battles.

When he noticed us, Marcus hesitated, giving us a polite nod from a distance. To his shock and mine, Anton sauntered towards him. After a friendly greeting, we talked about interesting clubs on the main walkway. Marcus suggested a couple he particularly enjoyed. Midway through the conversation, Anton asked Marcus to address him by his first name. He then told him to come visit any time because I missed him. Staring at Anton, I blinked away the tears welling up. I pressed myself against him and he held me close. My lips against his neck, I whispered a soft thank you. He kissed the top of my head before releasing me.

When I glanced back at Marcus, the look on his face spoke of his happiness for me. He wanted this for me. Since then, Marcus and I met at least once a week. Sometimes at the penthouse, sometimes at a restaurant. Anton didn't question me or hover around us during those visits.

I was falling in love with Anton, and it scared me. Part of me couldn't dismiss his violence, even after two and a half months of peace. That didn't mean it wouldn't happen again with the right trigger. I felt torn between protecting myself and seizing the moment – giving what was blossoming between us a chance to grow.

Only seven weeks remained on our contract and Anton showed every sign of wanting to continue. But more importantly, I was three weeks away from my first show. It wouldn't be a full show. I would do the first part of Seria's – two songs; one at the beginning of the show, the other right after the intermission. Romero and I discussed what my debut performance should be like. We agreed that a tiny set to whet appetites was better than a full-length program. It would also be a test for us to see what to adjust.

That show scared the fuck out of me. It had been years since I'd felt any kind of nerves before going on stage. I had never worked so hard for anything and that made it more precious. If my show – if I – wasn't well received, it would crush me. To perform in a VIP venue on Venus Hive, to be admired and lauded by the elite had been my greatest dream. Yet, as I walked towards the backstage of the rehearsal auditorium, I realized the elite's opinions didn't matter the most. I wanted this to be a success for my three men, Anton, Marcus, and Romero. They had believed in me, invested in me and supported me, each in their own special way. This would be my thank you for giving me the confidence and means to chase after my dream.

My dancer trio should already be on stage awaiting me. Romero would join us in thirty minutes, after our warm-up. We were still writing the choreography for the second song. I would perform the first song solo, to showcase my voice. The second song would display my showmanship; sexy, classy, with plenty of flash and dazzle.

As I approached the curtains, a horrible sense of déja vu swept over me as the voices of gossiping dancers reached me. I stopped.

"I wonder how she can still walk after banging Mr. Ant, let alone dance. Did you see the size of his thing?"

That was Marlina's voice. A pretty strawberry blonde, with a to-die-for hourglass figure. An overly prominent nose and a bitchy attitude kept her from being beautiful. She was a talented dancer, but her mouth prevented her from landing long term gigs.

"How would you know what size Ant's cock is?" Sacha's voice asked. "There is no way in hell he got naked for you."

"Unlike certain wannabes in this room," Marlina said, "I performed at Sade's grand opening. I was in the front row seat when Ant whipped it out and Miss Gracie polished his knob like no one's business. Fuck, she can deep-throat with the best of them. Watching her go down on his hammer, I wished I had a cock of my own to get head like that."

I gripped the curtain. In my anger, I could feel my nails digging into my palms through the thickness of the fabric. Yeah, I could give mean head and took pride in it. But Marlina made it sound cheap and dirty.

"I don't think we should talk about that," Carrie said, her annoying nasal voice echoing through the room. "Grace probably wouldn't like it."

"Oh stop being such a tight cunt," Marlina said. "Everyone on the fucking station wonders about them. You should have seen her outfit that night with that crazy fluffy tail up her ass. It was epic. For sure they've done anal. Her asshole must be the size of a fucking wormhole to—"

"That's enough, Marlina," Sacha snapped. "Look, you may be better than the rest of us 'wannabes' but we've got a pretty damn good gig here. Grace is super nice with us. And I'm not getting fired because you're talking shit about the boss' girlfriend."

My face heated with humiliation. That fucking outfit had been such a source of embarrassment. I couldn't believe the little bitch was talking so much shit, knowing I was on my way here.

"Sacha kind of has a point," Carrie said.

"Whatever, you bunch of pussies." Marlina's voice dripped with contempt. "But she's not his girlfriend. She's his cum bucket. We all know he bought her ass."

"He's walking around with her like she's his wife, not his whore," Sacha said. "You do know that he castrated that Sarenian that tried to rape her at the Viaggo, right?"

Anton had made a brutal example of that Sarenian. Not only did he castrate him, but he also burned his retinas and slashed his vocal cords. That man would never rape another woman or mesmerize anyone again. After getting maimed, the Sarenian was put on display in a cage at the main junction between the Commons and the VIP sections so patrons would know what would befall them if they broke the laws of the station. Although, people said it was what would happen if you messed with the boss' woman.

"Either way," Sacha said, "that's none of our business. We're here to dance."

"I'm not talking shit, just stating facts," Marlina argued. "Then again, she's a hot squeeze and plays him like a pro. If you stop being such an uptight pussy, Carrie, I might take you along to Sade. I bet you'd love to see how she swallows a monster cock."

"You could get me in?" Carrie asked, sounding excited.

"No, she can't," Sacha said. "She got her ass fired. Why the hell would you even want to do that, Carrie?"

"I didn't get fired. My contract ended," Marlina said.

That was a lie. Marissa, the owner, fired her for her stinky attitude.

"Come on, Sacha, everyone wants to go to Sade," Carrie said. "It's impossible for people like us to get in."

"Forget her, Carrie," Marlina said. "I'll get you in and you'll see why Mr. Ant's ugly ass is burning so much money on her. She must have been a teen hooker or something to be able to fake it so good while that ape is riding her."

My pulse raced and my skin tingled with the first tremors of anxiety at the thought of a confrontation. But I've had enough. I was tired of people walking all over me, talking down to me, and taking advantage of me. Eyes closed, I fisted my hands to control their trembling and took three deep breaths to center myself. Silencing the insecurities that threatened to rob me of my will, I pushed my shoulders back and stepped onto the stage.

I found the three girls standing by the warm-up barre.

"That's quite enough out of you, Marlina," I said, relieved my voice didn't shake.

Carrie and Sacha paled. Marlina stiffened, a hint of fear in her eyes. Then pride kicked in, and she lifted her chin. At that moment, she bore an eerie resemblance to Darla on Jeruna. History knows what that cockiness and attitude earned her.

Crossing her arms over her chest, Marlina said, "Some people can't handle the truth."

"You don't know jack shit," I said, pointing a threatening finger at her. "My man is paying your fucking wages. My man also happens to be Braxian. You would do well to inform yourself about what happens to stupid little girls who disrespect Braxians."

She rolled her eyes. "Yeah, ok. Whatever."

I fought the urge to slap her. Then it dawned on me.

"You know what," I said, "you have a lot of growing up to do. I hope for your sake that it won't be the hard way. But here's another truth for you: we don't need to put up with your shit. Get the fuck off my stage. You're fired."

Sacha bit her bottom lip, her eyes widening. Carrie's throat worked as she took a couple of steps closer to Sacha, putting more distance between her and Marlina.

Marlina's nostrils flared. "You can't fire me! I have a contract."

"Wrong, stupid girl." Oh, how the tables turned. "Your contract is with *me*, not Anton. Second, you obviously didn't read the contract. If you had, you would know that I can fire you at any time, for any reason, at my own discretion with no compensation whatsoever. So you can walk out with whatever dignity you've got left, or I can have you dragged out."

Marlina opened and closed her mouth, like a fish out of water. She looked to the other dancers for support but both Sacha and Carrie averted their eyes.

"This isn't over," Marlina hissed, leveling me with a venomous glare.

She stormed off the stage, shoving the backdrop curtains aside. My blood boiled, and I could feel myself tremble within. However, it was righteous anger that fueled the fire, and... pride? I turned back to face my remaining dancers.

"Grace," Sacha pleaded, "we didn't..."

"Relax, Sacha," I interrupted. "I've been here long enough to know what you did and didn't say." She swallowed hard and exchanged a worried look with Carrie. "You have a good head on your shoulders and a proper sense of priorities."

Sacha sagged against the barre, a relieved smile on her lips. "Thank you, Grace. You're a cool boss."

After returning her smile, I let the warmth melt from my voice when my eyes turned to Carrie.

"Let me give you one piece of advice, Carrie," I said. "Girls like Marlina are poison. You stay the fuck away from them or be ready to go down with them. Your gut told you what she was doing was wrong, didn't it?"

Carrie hugged her midsection and nodded.

"Then you should have shut her down. Instead, you let her suck you in with a promise to take you to 'cool' places. But at what cost?" I walked towards her, my heels clicking. "When I was a couple of years younger than you, I let myself get ensnared by two girls like Marlina. I wanted to be part of the in-crowd. That almost cost me my career, if not my life. Today, one of them is dead, the other is a ruin."

Carrie flinched, fear seeping into her eyes. Good... Fear was good. It would keep her away from naïve choices she didn't fully understand the consequences of. I wished someone opened my eyes back then, not a boyfriend who I thought was simply trying to control me.

"Listen to your gut. You're here to dance. Do you know how many girls would kill to be performing on Venus Hive at your young age? Focus on your career and stay out of the drama. Understood?"

Carrie nodded emphatically.

"Good. Now, we've wasted enough time. Let's get to work."

The girls agreed, happy to move on from the unpleasantness. I couldn't quite define what it was, but during the confrontation, something changed. Not only within me but also how they looked at me. Obviously, there was some fear; losing their job with Anton's girlfriend could get them blacklisted. But I could see more. I didn't want to call it respect, yet... Whatever it was, I liked it. More importantly, it felt good not to let myself get pushed around.

I turned to start the music and froze. Romero stood by the curtain. My breath hitched at the look in his eyes.

He winked before marching towards the girls. "Alright, enough slacking around. We've got a show to prepare!"

Tonight, Anton's behavior baffled me. It swung between curiosity and concern. It's like he couldn't decide if he felt worried or excited. He told me to dress in a sarong eerily similar to the one I wore on the first day. He wore similar black leather pants and dark t-shirt as he did that day. The chef prepared us a fine meal, with most of my favorite dishes. We talked about simple, light things. However, multiple times throughout the evening, I caught Anton looking at me as if trying to read my mind.

After dinner, we slow-danced in the living area, quietly, for what felt like hours. We rarely danced at home. That and his strange behavior confirmed he deliberately sought privacy for whatever he wanted to do.

What further worried me was that Anton hadn't become aroused. Whenever we danced, within minutes of close proximity, I would feel him strain against me. His hands would become more adventurous, his embrace fiercer and his lips more demanding. But not tonight.

What the hell is going on?

Without warning, Anton stopped the music and led me to the plush couch. He sat down and pulled me onto his lap. I faced him, my knees on each side of him. He rested his forehead against mine. I wrapped my arms around his neck and waited.

After a moment, he pulled back and looked at me with an unreadable expression. My stomach knotted with apprehension.

Anton sighed, then said, "I'm releasing you from your contract."

My brain went numb. I stared at him trying to comprehend what he had just said. The words refused to sink in.

I wanted to ask him why. Did he want me to leave? Did I owe him the difference for the remaining seven weeks? Did I upset him somehow? But those were not the words that came out of my mouth. My arms dropped from around his neck.

"You don't want me anymore?" I whispered, my broken voice baring the blistering hurt that was shredding my heart.

"I didn't say that."

"Have you met someone else?"

Please, not Sheila!

"No, there's no one else."

Then what?

"You want me to leave?"

"No, Grace. I want you to stay," Anton said. It both soothed my heart while adding to my confusion.

"As your consort?"

"Yes."

I wrung my hands, trying to understand. My thoughts seemed to drown in a pit of quicksand. "So why release me? Why not keep me?"

Anton cradled my face. "I don't want to own you anymore."

What?

"Why not?" I asked, nonplussed, my eyes flicking between his.

"Because I want what we've had for the past three months to be real," Anton said with a vulnerability I had never seen from him before. "I don't want you merely obeying the clauses of our contract."

I took a moment to gather my thoughts.

"So… what does that mean, you releasing me? I can leave, debt free?"

He stiffened at my question. His hands dropped from my face. This wasn't the response he wanted. But I needed to know exactly what I was getting myself into before I committed one way or another. How ironic he taught me so well.

"Yes," he said, his tone slightly clipped. "The debt is repaid. If you wish to leave, you may go. You can keep all the clothes, jewelry, and accessories I bought you. Romero's one-year contract is paid in full. Same with your dancers and all other costs related to your debut show."

That was ridiculously generous. But upon further reflection, it made sense. He introduced me to a whole new world, light-years away from my previous life in the Commons. This debut show and my training with Romero gave me access to a future I couldn't have achieved before. Losing those tremendous benefits would be reason enough for a woman to stay with him. With this offer, he eliminated that argument.

Being Anton's consort provided many other privileges: VIP entrance everywhere; people falling all over themselves to please me — well to please Anton by pleasing me; the fabulous penthouse; him splurging money on me for clothes, jewelry, etc. Yeah, it would be hard for him to know if someone stuck around for him or for all those benefits.

That said, Marcus had the twelve million credits Anton had refused to take as repayment of the debt. Marcus told me if things went south with Anton, he would split the amount fifty-fifty with me. So I could leave Anton, keep Romero and my show while enjoying the life of luxury I had grown accustomed to.

The nervous ticking along Anton's temple revealed his inner turmoil. He could see me analyzing the situation. Was it doubt or fear in his eyes? At that moment, I realized I wielded power over him. His whole life, everyone rejected him. He built his empire to no longer be at the mercy of other people's whims. Yet, here he was, putting all that power in my hands. If I left, it could crush him. He would keep his head high and proud because that's who he is. But he would never make himself vulnerable again.

"That is very generous of you," I said, shifting on his lap. He responded with a stiff nod. "And if I chose to stay, what would it mean?"

He blinked, the flash of hope in his eyes quickly hidden. "Then we continue as we have these past three months, just you and me."

"No other women?"

"I don't cheat," Anton said. "Besides, I don't want anyone else."

I silenced the happy warmth spreading through me at his words.

"But what about your Braxian friends? What will happen the next time they visit?"

Anton's face hardened. "Nothing."

The question angered him but I could feel his anger wasn't with me. There couldn't be any misunderstanding as far as that went.

"What do you mean nothing?"

"They will not touch you," Anton said. "No other man will ever touch you again. And I will never again ask you to do something you don't want."

"Braxian protocols—"

"Fuck Braxian protocols," he interrupted. I repressed a smile. "We're not on Braxia. This is our home. They follow *our* rules."

Home… our home. I wanted to kiss him, sing, dance, and shout my joy aloud. The way he looked at me, it was clear he was regaining hope that I would stay. There was no question I wanted to. But we still had a big issue to sort out – the deal-breaker.

"I like you a lot, Anton," I said. "I mean, I'm falling in love with you."

My voice caught in my throat as a raw emotion crossed his face. His hands tightened around my waist. It suddenly dawned on me that no one ever spoke these words to him. At least, I had Marcus who loved me, though he wasn't in love with me.

"For months now, I've hoped you would want to keep me because I too want to keep you. But you've hurt me, Anton. You've hurt me badly. That's not ok. I don't want to live in fear of the man I care about."

His face crumpled in shame. He lowered his gaze.

"Yes, Grace, I have," he said. "There's nothing I can do or say to apologize enough for it. It will never happen again."

"How can I be sure?" I asked, voicing the fear that had plagued me since the last time he punished me.

"I haven't harmed you in over three months, and I won't." Anton cradled my face in his hands again. "Remember what I told you back then? I want many things, Grace, but not your pain. I can't give you any other proof than the past three months."

"But nothing happened in the past three months to give you grounds to punish me," I argued. "That night at the opera, when that Sarenian attacked me, I was more terrified imagining what you would do to me than him trying to rape me. What would have happened had you arrived minutes later, after he'd had his way with me?"

He flinched at my words, visibly hurt.

"Every time we go out, I dread something will trigger your anger. I can't live like that."

The pain in his eyes as his hope faded clawed at my heart.

"What are you saying?" Anton whispered.

"That I refuse to be hurt, physically or mentally by my partner, beaten, brutalized, or caged because I did something to offend him.

Under the contract, I had no choice but to accept whatever you did. Without it, I can choose. I want to be with you, Anton. You've made me happy these past few months. But if you ever hurt me again, whatever the reason, as much as it would break my heart, I will walk away."

"On my honor, my life, I swear to you, I will never hurt you again. I'll sign a contract if you wish."

I finally allowed my happy smile to shine through. "Then I guess you're stuck with me, Mr. Myers."

The same raw emotion crossed his face. "So, you choose me, Grace? You want to stay with me?" His voice faltered on the last words.

"Yes, Anton. I choose you."

His kiss felt gentle, careful, like the fluttering of a butterfly's wing. "Grace... My Grace," he whispered against my lips. "My beautiful Grace. You're my everything."

CHAPTER 20
GRACE

Once again, I was a free woman, no longer bound to a contract that put me at the mercy of another's whim.

Anton changed me. It wasn't just in the way I dressed, but the way I perceived myself. People could never stare enough at me. However, before, I would settle for any attention, even the demeaning, disrespectful kind. Not anymore. Today, I wanted respect. I deserved respect.

Since Anton released me from our contract two weeks ago, things changed in subtle, yet wonderful ways. Anton made even more time for me, involving me in his business. It made me feel valued. He openly displayed his affection, whether in public or private. Although he hadn't said he loved me, I knew Anton felt deeply for me. Words weren't all that important to me – actions were. That he'd defy Braxian protocols for me said it all.

Anton offered to deposit a spending allowance in my account to do with as I pleased until I started making my own money. I declined. I wanted him to know we were together because my feelings for him were genuine. Also, there was never any real reasons for me to spend. Anytime we went out, the venue would put it on Anton's tab. He opened an unlimited line of credit for me in every clothing, jewelry, shoes, and accessory store on Venus Hive. Ok, those I didn't decline. However, I didn't abuse his generosity.

Really? How about all those shoes?

Alright, I did tend to go overboard on shoes, but as an artist, I'd get plenty of opportunities to wear them all at least once. And we cut short our rehearsal because of that shoe obsession. We now rehearsed in full costumes. My heels were so high, I might as well be a ballerina walking on pointe. I was the queen of 'fuck-me' shoes. However, it was one thing to strut around in them, quite another to perform a perfectly timed choreography. Result? Twisted ankle.

A healing cream would fix it in no time, but Romero was being extra cautious. I couldn't blame him. Anton would lose it if Romero allowed anything bad to happen to me during rehearsal. So here I sat in Dr. Farland's office, getting the usual third degree about my health, habits, addictions or lack thereof. Why they kept asking those stupid questions was a mystery since the routine blood analysis provided all the answers.

Farland pricked my finger with a stylus before sticking it in the analyzer, then reclined in his metal chair while he waited for the results. Seeing how bony Farland was, that chair had to be painful to sit in. But then everything about that man and his office felt hard, cold, and clinical. The room's whiteness blinded me. The sparse furniture consisted of a metal desk, an examination table, and a metal shelf with various scanners and devices. Aside from a large vidscreen, the walls were completely barren.

While he waited for the results, he continued to question me. What the fuck did my temperature, lack of dizzy spells or absence of nausea have to do with a twisted ankle?

"Why are you asking me this, Doctor?" I asked, confused. "Is something wrong with the vaccines you gave me? I mean, I'm just here to check on my ankle before my show."

He cast a glance at the analyzer. "Your blood test indicates that you're pregnant."

I gripped the armrests of my chair, feeling as if my world tilted. Although he was a brilliant physician, Dr. Farland's reputation of being a jerk with terrible bedside manners finally proved accurate. This was not how you told someone they were pregnant.

I shook my head. "That's impossible. I have a three-year contraceptive implant with a little over one year left. There's no way I can be pregnant."

Farland rolled his eyes. "What is it with human women? Did you all skip your sex education classes? Do your teachers not warn you that human contraceptives *may not work* with an alien partner? Do they not tell you to consult a physician and see if your contraceptive needs adjusting?"

I gaped at him. I hadn't attended any sex education classes. My 'education' had been hands on by Mr. Carston, the orphanage's caretaker, who felt I was old enough at twelve to learn how to please a man. Marcus had taught him better – permanently.

"But Anton is half-human…"

Farland looked at me like I was stupid.

Apparently, half alien is all it takes. But how?

"My implant prevents me from ovulating. I haven't had periods in years. How can I possibly get pregnant?"

"A Braxian's seminal plasma – the fluid his seed swims in," Farland said, miming semen swimming, "is made not only to protect the sperm from getting destroyed or damaged by a woman's natural spermicide, but it also helps regulate the progesterone level of the woman to increase the chances of implantation. The more you're exposed to his semen, including orally," he added with a meaningful look, "the more it overrides the effects of your contraceptive. So unless you were using condoms, it was only a matter of time."

Right. With Anton and me fucking like rabbits, it's almost a miracle it didn't happen sooner. And that's not even talking about how many times I swallowed.

Family.

The thought spread a warm feeling in my stomach. I didn't mind getting pregnant. In truth, I wanted a family – a big one. In my mind's eye, I pictured tiny hands reaching for Anton's face, pulling his lips with that crazy strength babies seem to have.

They would be half-breeds.

Cold coils of fear shattered the pleasant image. Braxians didn't allow half-breeds to have children. Would Anton follow that rule? Did he even want children? Would his clan come after our baby? After me?

When Anton released me from our contract two weeks ago, he promised not to follow Braxian protocols. Did that include our children? Was I even ready to have children with him? What if he became violent again? Then it wouldn't be just me being hurt, but my child. My parents hadn't wanted me, but my children would be loved.

"How far along am I?"

Farland pursed his lips and had another look at the analyzer.

"I'd need a different test to give you a more accurate date, but based on these readings, I would say three months.

THREE MONTHS?

I placed a hand over my flat belly. Three months ago, Anton and I made love in his bed for the first time. Noticing my gesture, Farland smirked, glancing down at my belly meaningfully.

"You'll be showing soon enough. Thinner women like you often don't show until the fourth month, so you'll be ok for your debut performance. But Braxian babies tend to be big. You'll grow as fat as a whale."

Could he be more of an ass?

"Alright, thank you, Dr. Farland," I said, my tone frosty. "Now, if you wouldn't mind, can you patch up my ankle? I want to go home."

He waved at the examination table, with a mocking expression. I limped over and sat down, my legs resting on the table. Farland began rubbing the healing cream over my ankle. Even though he was a jerk, his ministrations were gentle and efficient.

"Now, in terms of termination options—"

I glared at him. "Excuse me?"

He held my gaze, his stare stern and unwavering. "You're bearing a mix-breed, fathered by a clanned Braxian half-breed. Their rules are very clear regarding such pregnancies."

"Fuck their rules. This is my child. Nobody will harm him."

"Myers needs to know. He will have a say in this," Farland said.

I pointed a threatening finger at him. "How I handle my pregnancy is my fucking business. You stay the hell out of it."

"He has the right to know," Farland insisted. "There will be serious repercussions for him if you keep this a secret."

I pulled my foot out from his mending hands and slipped my shoe on. "I will handle Anton and my pregnancy. Don't forget your oath."

"You're welcome to sue me if you wish, but you have one week, Ms. Hopper. If you do not inform Mr. Myers by then, I will."

Without another word, I stormed out of his office.

I roamed aimlessly along the walkway, unable to form anything that even remotely resembled coherent thoughts. Part of me believed Anton would want our child. He often expressed gratitude for his father sparing his life. It would only make sense for him to want to do the same for his own child. But what of his clan?

He swore he would never hurt me again.

Hurting my child would hurt me. However, I couldn't gamble on my child's life.

I blinked, realizing my steps unconsciously led me to Marcus' hotel. The lift took me to his suite.

The sound of muted music wafted through his door. Marcus was throwing another 'party.' Sure enough, when he opened the door, the smell of sex, drugs, and alcohol greeted me. A towel wrapped around Marcus' waist tented in front of him. I averted my eyes, strangely uncomfortable. Sweat glistened on his naked skin and his chest rose and fell from recent exertion.

"Gracie, this is kind of an awkward moment for a visit," he said with a slightly embarrassed grin.

He knew I didn't approve of this lifestyle. Marcus was a smart, handsome man with a heart of gold. This was such a waste… But right now, I had bigger issues than Marcus' philandering.

"I'm pregnant."

That sobered him.

"Come in," he said, pulling me inside.

A full-blown orgy raged within the apartment. At least two dozen people rutted all over the living room in every kind of pairing possible.

A few of them catcalled as we came in. Marcus waved them off and led me to my former bedroom. I was glad he didn't allow people in here.

"Give me a minute to go fix myself up and I'll be right back, ok?"

I nodded. Taking off my shoes, I sat cross-legged on the bed. That didn't last long. While the cream did wonders, sitting in that position put too much strain on my ankle. Crawling up the bed, I rested my back against the headboard, my legs stretched in front of me.

Marcus returned barefoot, wearing a white t-shirt and light gray slacks. He sat next to me on the edge of the bed. His hair was still damp from the quick shower he had taken. I was grateful for the fresh, clean scent that emanated from him.

"So, you've got a little bun in there," he said, nudging me.

I'm not sure why, but that burst the dam open. With deep, gut-wrenching sobs, I bawled my eyes out. Marcus pulled me into his arms and let me cry onto his chest. He didn't say a word, just stroked my hair. Eventually, I pulled myself together and wiped my face with the back of my hand.

"Do you want to keep it?" Marcus asked.

I nodded my head, still wiping my tears.

"Does he know?"

I shook my head.

"Are you afraid he's not going to want it?"

"I–I don't know," I said, sniffling. "I'm pretty sure he will want it, but what happens if he doesn't?"

"What do you want to do?"

"I want to tell him, but I'm scared for my baby's life. What if he doesn't want it, Mar, and forces me to kill it? He owns this place. Maybe I should be off station when I tell him. Then, I can just come back if he's ok with it. But if he's not, I can go to Haven or one of the other sanctuary colonies that protect half-breeds."

Marcus recoiled. "I don't think leaving is a good idea. How far along are you?"

"Three months," I said, tears trickling down my cheeks.

Marcus took my hands in his and rubbed his thumb over my knuckles, soothing me. "Do you know what it is?"

"I didn't ask about the gender. But Dr. Farland talked about termination. Males are the only half-breeds Braxians terminate, so…"

"Look Grace, let's not make any hasty decisions. You're not showing yet," Marcus said, glancing at my belly. "Give me a few days to think about this. No one will harm you or the baby."

"One week, Mar… I only have one week."

"Why?"

"Dr. Farland will tell Anton if I don't tell him before the week is up."

Marcus cursed under his breath.

"The fucker wants to cover his ass. Ok. We'll figure it out. For now, go home and relax. Stress can't be good for the baby."

"But what about Anton? I don't want to leave him, Mar. He took a big leap of faith when he released me from our contract. I owe him the same. But it's not only about me anymore."

"Don't say anything yet. Just act like business as usual. Anton cares a hell of a lot about you, Gracie. We'll figure out the best way to tell him, alright?"

I nodded, hope surging back in my heart.

"Whatever would I do without you?" I said, hugging him.

He returned the embrace and shrugged. "Probably get into even more trouble."

I chuckled. "Probably." We held each other. "Well, I better fix my face and go home before Anton starts wondering where I am. And your guests are probably starting to complain there's one less cock in the fray."

Marcus burst out laughing. "Not one less cock, sweetheart. The *best* cock is missing."

I shook my head and rustled his hair. "You're hopeless."

The next six days proved trying. Contrary to rumors about me being good at faking it, I sucked at it. Despite knowing my pregnancy wasn't showing yet, I tensed every time Anton's hands or mouth roamed over my stomach. He could feel something was troubling me and finally called me out on it. I brushed it off, saying it was just nerves at my upcoming debut. Thankfully, he bought it.

Tonight, Risqué was packed. Many patrons got turned away unless they had reservations. While I wanted to believe people came to see me, I knew most only wanted to suck up to the big boss or to feed the gossip mill.

However, right this instant, gossips and brownnosers were the least of my concerns. After many backs and forths, Marcus and I agreed I would tell Anton tonight right after the show. Hopefully, it would be an extra cause for celebration. If not, I would use a stun dart on him to make my getaway. No one would question our absence for a few hours.

With my face so well-known, sneaking out might become tricky. Marcus prepared a disguise for me. This weekend was one of the busiest of the year. It celebrated the creation of the Galactic Council, representing the Eastern and Western Quadrants of the known universe.

With the celebrations, citizens from most of the planets in the sector gathered on Venus Hive for the countless events. Among them was a large delegation of Inugians. Inugi's atmospheric pressure was much higher than most civilized planets. Although they also breathed oxygen, our lower atmospheric pressure would cause them to die from oxygen poisoning. So when they traveled off-world, they wore atmospheric suits which partially veiled their features.

Marcus obtained a replica for me, as well as fake IDs, copied off those of one of his Inugian acquaintances whose family owed him a favor. She had arrived with the Inugian delegation a couple of days ago, so security wouldn't question seeing her name on the departure list.

Our region, the Eastern Quadrant, had mostly abandoned religion, in sharp contrast to the Western Quadrant who all worshiped the Goddess. However, right now, I wished I believed in some higher being that would help things work out with Anton. I really didn't want to have to use any part of plan B.

The first show would start in less than forty-five minutes. I needed to stop daydreaming and get ready. As I began undressing, a soft knock resonated on the door.

"Come in," I said.

Zenia, one of the ushers at Risqué, poked her head in. "Sorry to disturb you, Ms. Hopper. There's a man out back saying he needs to speak with you. It's quite urgent. You would know what it's about."

I frowned. The Inugian disguise was only supposed to be delivered after my first set to avoid the wrong eyes stumbling on it. Why did it arrive so early?

"Be right there," I said, adjusting my dress and putting my stilettos back on.

I rushed to the back entrance which lay empty and silent. We planned to exit from here if plan B went into effect. Employees occasionally came back here to chat during their break. But with the show about to start and the patrons arriving, all hands stayed busy. I reached a hand to open the back door when the door to the utility room swung open, revealing a man I had never seen before.

"Over here Ms. Hopper," he whispered, gesturing for me to come join him in the utility room. I hesitated. "Hurry!" His urgency prompted me to comply.

I stepped in. He closed the door behind me and shoved a pile of clothes at me.

"Put this on, quickly," he said.

It looked like slave clothes found on some flesh markets, veil and leash included.

"What is that?" I said, cold tendrils of dread spreading along my spine. "Where's Marcus."

"Marcus is otherwise occupied," the man said. His thin mouth twisted into an ugly sneer, revealing a row of crooked teeth. "Put it on now, you cunt, before I blow your fucking head off."

He shoved a blaster in my face. I squealed, recoiling in fear.

What the hell is going on?

He slapped me hard. I fell back against a rack of pristine tablecloths. It groaned under my weight. I pressed my palm against my throbbing cheek.

"Make another fucking sound and I'll beat you bloody," he growled. "Now put the fucking clothes on."

Shaking, I obeyed. I pulled the sheer, short beige dress over my head. The dress was opaque enough that it couldn't be called nude, but transparent enough to show the curves of my body and nipples. With it, a dark veil hid my face. Technically, it was to protect the identity of indentured sex slaves since they might not want people to know they whored themselves out for a period of time.

I stole a glance at the man. He didn't strike me as someone Marcus would hire to look after me. A strand of greasy brown hair fell over dark brown eyes. His beaked nose looked like it had been broken once or twice before. Broad and stocky, he stood only a couple of inches taller than me.

"Take off that collar and put this one on instead."

I didn't want to take the collar off. After Anton released me from our contract, I joked about not having to wear the collar anymore. It deeply disturbed him even though he tried to hide it. The collar meant a great deal to him. He had it made especially for me, with the gems a perfect match to my amber eyes.

"Make me repeat," the man said, "and I'll punch your fucking teeth out. I don't need you pretty."

I obeyed, choking back my tears. No sooner did I detach it from around my neck that he ripped the collar out of my hands. He stared, running short fingers with dirty fingernails over the gems. With trembling hands, I attached the new collar. The leash dangled to the floor.

"Hand over the earrings."

Sniffling, I eyed his blaster still trained on me. I gave him the beautiful earrings part of the bracelet and hairpin set Anton had given me. He closed a rapacious hand around them before tossing the veil at me.

"Now put this on."

Relieved that he hadn't noticed the long, bejeweled hairpin made of gold in my hair, I swiftly complied. As soon as I was done, he tugged on the leash, drawing me to him. His face was only inches from mine and his breath stank of cheap whiskey. I held my breath, fighting the urge to gag.

"You're going to follow me quietly, like a good little slave."

I felt a sting in the side of my neck. Startled, I saw his right hand lower, holding a glinting injector. My own hand flew to my neck. I could feel a tiny bump under my skin.

"What did you do?" I asked, terrified.

"Just gave you an incentive to obey. You make a sound, try to signal anyone for help, I'll detonate the implant. And I promise you, sweetheart, if this shit goes off, you will beg for death. Now move. There's someone waiting to get better acquainted with that tight cunt of yours."

CHAPTER 21
ANTON

My Grace… In all the terrible years growing up on Braxia, I never imagined I could be happy one day. Keeping myself safe from harm had been my focus. After leaving Braxia, I deluded myself into thinking humans might welcome me. It didn't take long to realize I didn't belong there either. I had made peace with the knowledge mine would be a lonely life. At least, humans didn't try to kill me just because I breathed. Plus, my wealth and power ensured my bed would never be cold. I was content with that life. Until Grace…

I didn't deserve her – not after what I did to her. And yet, I could never let her go. The way she looked at me, touched me, snuggled against me. Grace meant it when she claimed to be falling in love with me. It shone in her eyes, in the way she gave herself to me. I never dared to hope anyone would have such feelings towards me.

From the first time I laid eyes on her, I knew she was the one. To think it was all almost ruined beyond repair over a teenage prank and my barbaric beliefs. Once again, I owed William. This time for forcing me to come to terms with my inner conflict. Braxia enslaved me my whole life. I almost allowed it to destroy my one chance at happiness. And I was happy, truly happy.

I took a huge gamble releasing Grace from her contract. One I feared I lost when she confronted me about harming her. Had she walked away, it would have destroyed me. However, her display of strength, determination, and self-preservation had been impressive. Grace was coming into her own and showing the spine that had lain dormant. I took that bet because like she had with me, I was falling in love with her. No, I already loved her. If what we had was an illusion, it was better to end it now. She had no idea the extreme changes I was making so that we could have a future together. The Magnar's interference simply forced me to move faster.

Tonight would be Grace's consecration. The first time I heard her sing on Jeruna, I knew she could be a star. Romero gave her the polish she needed. Grace hadn't let me attend her rehearsals, feeling too self-conscious. It was odd considering she always hummed around the house. To my shame, I snuck in anyway and listened backstage. The sound of her sultry voice put me in a trance. It fell over me like a gentle caress with the warmth and sensuality of a lover's embrace. Tonight, all of Venus Hive would fall at her feet.

My woman...

Dr. Farland strolled up to my private booth, interrupting my thoughts. He was as thin and dry as his personality. Although only in his mid-forties, the doctor already showed quite a bit of gray in his short ginger hair.

"Dr. Farland," I said.

"Mr. Myers." He gestured at the room crawling with patrons. "Successfully crowded night, isn't it? Your consort's debut show has the whole station buzzing."

"It does," I said, puffing my chest with pride. "She will blow them away."

Farland didn't usually make small talk. He wanted something and I wanted to muse about my mate. Clearing his throat, he cast a not-so-subtle glance at the couch of my semi-circular booth. I swallowed down my irritation and gestured for him to take a seat.

"I trust Miss Grace's ankle has fully recovered from Sunday's sprain?" Farland asked, in an unassuming tone.

My eyes narrowed. He was fishing, but for what?

"I wasn't aware she sprained her ankle. She's been walking around with no limp. Clearly, it was either nothing serious or so well-treated she felt it unnecessary to bring it up."

"Ah yes," he said with a toothy grin. "It was nothing some healing cream couldn't handle. Thankfully, she didn't need to postpone her show over a twisted ankle. Especially now, seeing how little time she has left to perform before her condition forces her to stop."

I froze.

He's not fishing. He's here to tell on her.

"Her condition?" I asked, playing along.

"Well... hmm... You are aware that she's pregnant, right?" he said, smiling.

"Yes."

His smile faltered.

He hoped to shock me.

"Oh... Well, that's good news. Since she hadn't mentioned her twisted ankle, I wondered if she revealed finding out about her pregnancy that day."

I crossed my legs before leveling him with a cold stare. Grace's pregnancy came as no surprise to me. I suspected for a while. Her breasts were fuller and far more sensitive to my touch. However, the night after we ran into Marcus on the walkway, my suspicions were confirmed. A woman's scent changed once she became pregnant. At the beginning of the second month, her scent took on an earthy, woodsy aroma. That's when I knew she was bearing our son. A daughter would have given her a richer, spicier scent.

Now I knew why she seemed edgy all week. Why the distress though? Did she not want it? Did she fear I may not want it?

"And so, Dr. Farland," I said, my voice oozing with contempt, "you decided to take it upon yourself to rectify that possible oversight?"

He stiffened at my tone. "Miss Grace implied she would keep her pregnancy a secret from you," Farland protested in self-righteous outrage. "You had the right to know. Especially considering it's a male. Since she's already three months in, if certain decisions have to be made, you need to act now to respect Intergalactic Law. So I told her she had a week to come clean or I would inform you myself."

Farland didn't realize how the table between us saved his life. Had he been within my grasp, I would have crushed his skull.

"Let me see if I've got this straight," I said, my voice dangerously low. "First, you threaten my mate to rat her out."

Beads of sweat pebbled on Farland's brow. "Mr. Myers, it's—"

"I'm not finished," I hissed over the table. "Second, not only do you break your professional oath by revealing her condition without her consent, you do so one day before *your* deadline."

The doctor, squirmed in his seat, visibly eager to get away. I stood up and leaned forward. My hands twitched with the need to break his scrawny bones.

"Third, you dare imply that my son, my child, my flesh and blood, should be terminated – put down like a rabid beast? Is this what you think my father should have done with me?"

Farland blanched. His jaw worked but he couldn't form coherent words.

"You have twenty-four hours to get your skinny ass off my space station. You are banished from any of my Hives. Now get the fuck out of my face."

Farland scurried around the table. He rushed to the door, almost toppling into a patron. People stared but I didn't give two shits. My blood boiled.

How dare he even suggest killing my son?

No one would touch my child. NO ONE! He would not live in the fear I had, constantly looking over his shoulder, hoping he'd get to survive another day. Never would he wonder if he was loved or wanted. I sat back down.

Grace… She wants him. She wants our child.

Why else would she keep it secret from me? Deep down, I had hoped it would be the case. Marcus mentioned she wanted a family. Question was, did she want one with me? I wasn't a pretty man and she was so beautiful. Although she had gotten over my face, would she want my features on her children?

This was supposed to be her special day. That fucker ruined what should have been the most exciting week of her life with his threat. And why the hell did he come here to drop his little news? Why didn't he wait until tomorrow and let her have this night? Did someone put him up to it?

I looked through the crowded room, noticing Caleb. He was entertaining a few patrons. Marissa, a gorgeous woman with deep brown skin, shoulder-length dark curly hair, held onto Caleb's arm. She owned Sade and was a very sought-after Domme. I couldn't help wonder if she was Caleb's latest squeeze or if he was hers. Caleb parted with Sheila nearly two months ago. Without him bringing her into the inner circles and her declining popularity, Sheila would soon find herself on the ever-growing list of has-beens.

She is desperate and ruthless enough.

But that wasn't proof. I eventually found her by herself near the bar. Her eyes were drilling into me. I looked away. Yes, she might have fucked good old doc for this. The bastard probably never imagined dipping in her pussy would get him banished. Either way, her time here was at an end. Her performance had grown stale. I doubted she still enjoyed performing. That shone through and turned off the audience.

And once my Grace blew them all away tonight, Sheila would be history. Speaking of Grace, I needed to reassure her about the baby. But when? I didn't want her spending the rest of the evening stressing. However, if she didn't want him, now wasn't the right time to discuss the matter either. I rubbed my hands over my face in frustration. Why couldn't everyone just leave us the fuck alone?

Checking the time, there were still twenty-two minutes before the beginning of the show. I gestured at one of the waitresses nearby. She set a glass of brandy in front of me. I lifted it to my lips just as my personal com chimed.

"Myers," I said.

"Anton, William here. Is Grace with you?"

I stilled. "She's backstage, preparing for her show. Why?"

"Can you confirm that she is indeed backstage?"

"What's going on?" I asked, rising from my seat.

I wove through the crowd towards the changing rooms, a sense of unease gripping me.

"It may be nothing, but Brandon tagged a Samuel Trent boarding his shuttle with a veiled indentured sex slave. It wouldn't be a big deal but she was wearing Mystique. According to him, her body height, size and hair color all matched."

Whispers of fear coursed through me. Mystique was an extremely expensive perfume, averaging a few hundred credits per ounce. I bought Grace a bottle and she loved it so much, that's all she wore anymore. No slaver would use something that fancy on a sex slave.

"What about her collar?"

I heard him repeat the question to someone else, Brandon I assumed.

"Standard leash," William answered.

"Don't let them take off," I said.

I rushed through the throng. One of the patron's yelp of protest died in his throat when he saw who had bumped into him.

I didn't care.

As I neared the corridor leading to the changing rooms, Sheila cut me off with her usual fake smile.

"Mr. Myers, I haven't seen you in a while."

She traced her hand along my arm.

"I don't have time right now," I said, trying to go around her.

She stepped into my path, blocking my way again.

"Oh come on," she said, taking a seductive pose. "Surely you—"

"You listen *real* good," I grounded through my teeth. "Block my path again and I'll toss you on your ass. I have no interest in whatever the fuck you're peddling. Now I'm on my way to check up on the woman I intend to marry. You stay the fuck away from her. Should I ever find out that you tried to mess with her again, in any way, you will discover what happens to those who cross a Braxian."

She paled. Shoving her aside, I hurried to Grace's dressing room. I barrelled through the door. The room lay empty, her sequin dress hanging on the hook. There was no sound of water from the shower.

"Grace?" I called out, knowing she wouldn't answer. "She's not here," I said in the still open com. "Don't you let that fucking ship off the station."

"You got it," William's voice replied, the com crackling with static.

I went to the dancers' dressing room. Muffled voices seeped through the door, partially drowned by the music and chatter from the dining room. Hoping against hope, I knocked and opened it without waiting. The girls froze mid-sentence. Romero stood in the corner, without Grace.

"Where's she?"

Their surprise turned into worry upon hearing the tension in my voice.

Carrie answered, "She should be in her dressing room, cha—"

"No," Sacha interrupted. "She isn't. Or at least she wasn't when I checked before. Zenia said some man wanted to talk to her in the back."

Cold dread washed over me. I rushed through the empty hallways. My footsteps on the tiled floor sounded unnaturally loud to my ears. I reached the back to find it deserted, as was the back alley. Coming back in, I noticed the closed utility room door. I opened it. Grace's silk sarong scarf lay crumpled on the floor.

"It's her. I'm on my way," I said in the com. "Is Marcus on that ship?"

"I'll find out."

Romero and the girls rushed to find me holding Grace's dress in my hand. I terminated the com, hating the thought that this may not be a kidnapping but an escape. She might have resorted to this if she wanted to keep our child and feared I would kill it. Ignoring them, I headed for the docking bay.

CHAPTER 22
GRACE

The man loaded me into a hovercab so we could reach the docking bay quickly. During the short ride, he forced me to put my thumb on his datapad's signature box. I didn't need to read it to know he coerced me into becoming an indentured sex slave.

As expected, the docking bay overflowed with visitors. William increased security at the gates and I recognized a number of familiar faces. I didn't know the guard who checked my abductor's identifications. However, I recognized Brandon a few feet away in his riot gear. Brandon often ensured security at the headquarters and knew me well. The chances of him recognizing me in this outfit were slim though.

My abductor answered routine questions, including his name: Samuel Trent. The guard ignored me. Brandon headed our way to hand the guard a datapad. They exchanged a couple of words then, as Brandon was about to leave, his nostrils flared. He turned towards us and frowned looking at me. My pulse raced.

Recognize me. Please recognize me!

He eyed my hair and veiled face. Stepping closer to me, he leaned forward and inhaled discretely. Why would he...

He recognizes my perfume!

"Samuel Trent," Brandon said, looking over his identifications on the datapad, "what is your business on Venus Hive?"

"Entertainment, naturally," Samuel answered. "With all due respect, sir, I've just gone through all that with your colleague. Is there a problem?"

"And you're about to go through it with me," Brandon deadpanned.

Yes!

"You arrived this morning. Why are you leaving so soon?"

"I came to pick her up. As you can see, she's a nice piece and I have some customers eager to get to know her better, if you know what I mean."

We all knew too well what he meant. What I both wanted and dreaded to know was who those customers were. Samuel targeted me specifically. This felt well planned. Surely whoever they were knew not to fuck with Anton.

"Do you have the contract?"

"Naturally. Right here," Samuel said, tapping a couple of instructions on the datapad.

Of course, there was no name for me. Should it be contested, the fingerprint was proof enough. Brandon gave it a cursory glance before looking at me.

"I'd like to see her face."

My stomach dropped.

"Well now, you know that's not possible. She's veiled for a reason," Samuel said. "You must respect her wish for anonymity."

Brandon pinched his lips but couldn't argue – it was the law. From the look on his face, it was obvious Brandon didn't want to let it go. Samuel slipped a hand in his pocket, no doubt reaching for the remote detonator in case Brandon pressed the issue. Fear coiled in my belly.

"Is that correct, Madam?" Brandon asked. "Do you wish to retain your anonymity?"

No! Like hell I do!

I swallowed, then nodded. Brandon narrowed his eyes but didn't challenge my statement.

"You may proceed," he told Samuel, handing him back his datapad.

Samuel tugged on my leash for me to follow. Despite the fear that twisted my insides, a sliver of hope blossomed in my heart. Brandon sensed something wasn't right. I knew he would communicate his suspicions to William. I needed to hang on until they came for me.

It felt like a long walk to the ship. People jostled around us, calling to each other. Every delay gave me another reason to hope. Unfortunately, we reached the dingy rust bucket Samuel called his ship far too soon for my liking. The small star cruiser had known better days. Judging by its size and make, it looked ideal for a two-man crew. It could even be one-manned with a solid enough AI integrated onboard.

The ramp lowered and Samuel pulled roughly on my leash. If he kept this up, he would break my neck. To my surprise, the inside of the ship didn't look as bad as the outside. The light gray wall paneling bore many scrapes and scratches, but it was clean. It was at odds with Samuel who didn't seem to be too big on personal hygiene. The stale air inside the ship made me realize this may not be Samuel's ship. If someone paid him to abduct me, he might have bought this tub from a refurbishing shipyard.

"Who are you? And why are you doing this?"

"Quiet bitch," Samuel said, giving the leash another tug. "Your new master will tell you what he wants if and when he wants to."

I bit my lower lip as we followed the narrow corridor past the bridge to a closed room in the back. The door swished open at Samuel's approach. The smell of oiled leather assaulted my nose. Dangling from the ceiling, sturdy chains with shackles at the end swayed quietly. I swallowed as a bondage bench sitting beside a range of canes, whips, and floggers entered my line of sight. My skin prickled as my imagination ran wild, picturing them biting my flesh. I didn't even want to think what the metal chest of drawers and large shipping crate beside it might contain. As I stepped into the room, my eyes fell on the huge bed, and more importantly, the massive man standing in front of it.

"Gerwin…" I breathed, feeling faint.

"As promised, here's your new pet," Samuel said, unhooking the leash from my collar and removing my veil.

"Hello, little human," Gerwin said, a cruel smile stretching his thick lips. "Looks like we're finally going to get properly acquainted."

Terror choked me. Gerwin had forced his fingers brutally inside me at Sade. Without Anton's intervention, he could have seriously hurt me. Now wasn't the moment to give in to panic, though. Gerwin was a bigot with an irrational hatred for half-breeds. If he ever found out about my baby, he would kill us both. I needed to buy myself time. But how?

He wants respect and submission.

And then I knew.

"Yes, Master," I said.

I bowed my head and walked towards him.

"Hey!" Samuel called out, reaching for me.

Gerwin lifted a hand, indicating for Samuel to stop. From the corner of my eye, I saw him watching my movements intently. In accordance with the Braxian house slave greeting protocol, I knelt before him. Forcing myself to ignore the grime on his shoes, I kissed his feet then rested my forehead between them. Above me, I heard Gerwin's slow chuckle.

"The mutt actually trained you well," Gerwin said. He gently tapped my cheek with the side of his foot, indicating I had permission to rise. "Trent, get us the fuck off this station before they notice she's missing."

Samuel grunted and walked out of the room. The door slid closed. Cold sweat ran down my back as Gerwin circled around me. His huge hand caressed my skin, squeezing my breasts and ass along the way. His touch was rough, but thankfully not as brutal as that first time at Sade.

"Take off your dress."

Hands shaking, I did as he commanded. The cheap material scraped my hands like sandpaper. I balled the dress and held it against my stomach, like a shield. Gerwin ripped it away then tossed it to the ground.

"You know," he said, circling me again as his calloused hands roamed over my skin, "my original plan was to fuck you bloody, tear that tight cunt of yours to shreds – your ass too if you lived past round one. Then I would have shoved your corpse in this nice little crate," he said pointing at it, "and sent you back to the mutt, with my regards."

Goosebumps rose over my skin. "Please—"

"Quiet, slave," he said in a tone that brooked no argument. "I said 'my original plan' which your proper show of respect made me revisit."

A single tear of relief silently slid down my cheek.

"As it seems you know your place, I might keep you around. Why waste such a nice pussy when I can fuck you every day, anytime I want, and any way I want?"

Those were almost Anton's exact words when Gerwin asked why he hadn't fucked me to death as punishment for Jeruna.

"I intend to have my cock inside you within the hour, so let's get some Denax in you. Then you get to suck me off until that pussy of yours is ready for a real man. You better make it good if you don't want to end up in that crate. Get on the bed," he said, shoving me back.

My knees hit the bed's edge and I stumbled onto the stiff mattress. Turning on my back, I watched Gerwin as he retrieved a large bottle of Denax from the chest of drawers. He stalked back to me and I instinctively started crawling back up the bed. He caught my ankle and dragged me towards him and the edge of the bed.

"Spread them," he ordered, flicking open the lid of the bottle.

My legs shook as I willed them to part. I didn't see the size of Gerwin's cock at Sade, but I knew he would be bigger than Anton. It would take more than one application of Denax to loosen me enough to receive him without tearing. Gerwin drizzled some of the dilator over my pussy before starting to massage it in and around my opening.

Blocking out the feel of his unwanted touch, I focused on how to delay the moment he would take me. If my instinct was right, Brandon raised his suspicions already. William didn't leave things to chance and would investigate. I just needed to hang on.

Repulsive as it sounded, I would suck Gerwin off 'and make it good.' I didn't want him hurting my baby. I would take my sweet time and make it last. My biggest problem was the damn implant. It needed to come out before security showed up.

If they show up.

Never mind that. The question was where to find a blade sharp enough to cut the damn thing out without butchering myself.

"Such a pretty little thing," Gerwin mumbled to himself.

The citrusy scent of Denax permeated the room as he poured more of it between my legs. His fingers worked the lotion in and out of me. Gerwin became aroused and his motions got more forceful.

"Do you have any idea how badly I want to ram my cock inside you right now?"

He flicked down the lid of the Denax bottle then tossed it to the ground, his other hand continuing to stretch me. My eyes widened in fear when he leaned over me, supporting his weight on his forearm. He crushed my lips with a brutal kiss, and the taste of iron exploded in my mouth. I whimpered but stayed still. His mouth trailed down my neck to my breast, sucking on it with such greed it felt as if my nipple would tear off. They had become more sensitive of late, so I felt his brutality more acutely.

"Please," I pleaded, tears pooling in my eyes. "You're hurting me."

At first, I thought he would ignore me, but then he stilled. Even the motion of his hands stopped. His mouth released my nipple, which smarted from the recent abuse. Breathing heavily, I watched in confusion as he wrinkled his nose, nostrils flaring. He sniffed at me as if trying to identify a smell. He recoiled. A look of great disgust etched on his face. He launched off the bed, away from me.

His horrified expression threw me for a loop.

What the hell just happened?

Sitting up, I sniffed at myself, trying to understand what triggered such a violent reaction. I could only detect the refined aroma of my expensive perfume.

"What—what's wrong?" I asked, frightened.

"What's wrong?" he growled. "WHAT'S WRONG? That mutt fucking ruined you! He stuck an abomination in your womb!"

Pure dread washed over me.

My baby... He knows about the baby.

"What?" I repeated, numbly.

"The half-breed impregnated you with his tainted seed. I can smell it on you."

My hands flew to my stomach, in protection.

"Smell?" I said with a shuddering voice. "You can smell pregnancy?"

"Didn't the mutt tell you? We can smell pregnancy. By the stench, you're carrying a male."

He stepped towards me. I tried to crawl back on the bed, but he grabbed a handful of my hair, pulling me savagely to him. Crying out, I feared my scalp would tear right off. As he held me in front of him, I stood on shaky legs. Gerwin yanked my hair back, holding it down, exposing my neck. My hands gripped his shirt for support. Something sharp pricked my skull.

My hairpin.

Gerwin took another long sniff at me and once more, his face contorted with disgust.

"You reek! Your bastard is at least two or three months in. That fucking mutt thinks he gets to further taint a Braxian bloodline?" Gerwin brought his face inches from mine, hatred burning in his eyes. "He took everything from me. Now I'm going to destroy everything he ever cared about. You and your abomination are going in that crate."

Anton knew. This whole time he knew.

For three months he said nothing, allowing it to live. He wanted our child. Why didn't he say anything? Did he fear I would reject it like I feared he would?

I didn't see the blow coming. Gerwin's fist crashed into my stomach. My breath rushed out of me, and I doubled over. Except, I couldn't quite fold down with his hand still holding me up by the hair. I gasped but no air came in.

The second blow knocked my feet out from under me. He hit my ribs. I heard a crack. The agony spreading throughout my chest felt like the fallout of lightning striking my side. For a moment, I dangled like a broken doll, too winded to react. A fistful of hair tore from my scalp, unable to sustain the weight of my body. It felt as though a sharp knife sliced off the back of my head. I wheezed a silent scream.

I collapsed, my head thudding on the hard metal floor. Warmth trickled down the back of my head and along my neck. Gasping for air, I curled up in a ball. I braced for the blows that would rain down on me.

None came.

Gerwin grabbed my wrist and dragged me to the middle of the room.

"Descend," he ordered.

The chains clinked above my head in response to his command. Pulling my arm up, Gerwin clasped a handcuff around my wrist. He grabbed my second wrist, yanking it up savagely. My scream came out as a throaty groan. I couldn't breathe with the shackles stretching my arms up. At this rate, my broken rib would pierce my lungs and I'd drown in my own blood.

Kneeling to relieve the pressure, I heard Gerwin's footsteps recede behind me. A drawer opened and he rummaged in it. His footsteps approached again. My heart tried to pound its way out of my chest, and I shuddered at what he might do. Each tremor stirred a lancing pain in my side. I didn't even want to think about my baby right now.

Please, don't beat me. Please, don't beat me.

The canes, floggers, and whips loomed in my mind. My imagination swelled with the different horrible ways he could kill my unborn child. Gerwin yanked my head back by the hair. My strangled cry died in my throat when I came face to face with his crotch. His cock stood erect in front of me like a bat.

It will never fit.

Before I could protest, Gerwin shoved an open mouth gag with teeth guard between my lips. My eyes bulged as I tried to spit it out. Gerwin clamped his hand over my mouth to keep it in. At the corner of my eyes, I noticed a remote in his other hand. He thumbed the interface, and I felt the gag stretch my jaw wider.

However, Gerwin's palm on my mouth also covered my nose.

Already starved for air, I pulled on my restraints. He chuckled at my vain struggle. I tried to get up, but Gerwin kicked my feet from under me. I fell back on my knees with a loud thud. The violent pull of the chains tore at my wrists anew. It was as if the broken bones of my ribs were trying to pierce through my skin. Each breath, each movement was sheer agony. My struggles faltered as, lungs burning, dark dots appeared before me.

Gerwin's hand mercifully moved off my face, only to grip the blood-soaked hair at the back of my head. I didn't care about the pain as I greedily gulped in as much air as my lungs would allow. Without giving me sufficient time to catch my breath, Gerwin tried to shove his turgid shaft into my mouth. However, even though the gag already stretched my mouth to a barely tolerable level, the opening only allowed the tip of his cock to fit in.

When he thumbed the controls again to stretch it further, I gurgled for him to stop, pulling urgently at my shackles. My face was about to split in half.

"I don't care if I have to break your jaw," Gerwin said, "I will have my cock down your throat, and then up your cunt. By the time I'm done with you, how pretty you still look won't matter."

With a grinding sound followed by searing pain in front of my ears, my jaw unhinged. The room spun and my vision blurred. Gerwin once again tried to fit through the gag's opening. His thick cock invaded my mouth, the blunt tip hitting the back of my throat.

A blessed veil of darkness enshrouded me.

I came to, feeling the metal plating scraping against my skin as Gerwin dragged me to the bed. The back of my throat felt like a battering ram assaulted it. A sharp pain stabbed at it in sync with my erratic heartbeat. Gerwin tossed me on the bed, and I landed heavily on my broken ribs. I cried out, then coughed blood. Rolling onto my back, the blood and saliva pooling at the back of my mouth nearly choked me. My throat was too bruised to swallow, but the gag keeping my jaw open made my mouth water. I tilted my head to the side so the drool could seep out.

Anton, where are you?

Whether or not Anton was coming, he wouldn't be here in time to save us. Gerwin parted my legs, preparing to enter me. Even with the Denax he used, I wouldn't survive him pounding into me. If I was to live through this, I had to save myself. But how? He was too strong, and I was too weak and battered.

Gerwin tried to slam his cock home but met with too much resistance. The tip of his cock entering me felt like a fist. I screamed, my back arching off the bed. A sharp sting at the back of my head forced me to turn to the side.

My hairpin.

My fucking hairpin! Why hadn't that registered the first time? I raised a hand to my hair, fumbling through it, trying to get the pin out. My fingers brushed over the bald spot, and I felt my gorge rose. Gerwin leaned over me, lifting my leg to open me wider. He tried to ram himself in again. I screamed, causing my dislocated jaw to flare with agony. Tears and snot ran down my face. My blood coated fingers struggled with the pin latched in my hair. When Gerwin tried to pound in a third time, I felt my core begin to tear. I'm not sure if he gained an inch, but when he lifted my other leg over his shoulders, I knew the next time would kill me.

With all my remaining strength, I ripped the hairpin loose, pulling some of my hair with it. I closed my fist around its jeweled end and wielded the five-inch hairpin like a dagger. Blinded by rage, I stabbed at Gerwin's eye. I overshot and struck his forehead instead. He roared, pulling his head back. The movement caused the hairpin to tear a long gash down to the middle of his cheek. He slapped a hand over his wounded eye.

The sight of blood pouring down his face and the sound of his pain awakened the most primal part of me. I didn't want to flee anymore; I wanted blood, to maim, to kill.

I stabbed at him in a frenzy. The first swing missed, but the second one sank into the meaty cheek just below his other eye. The bone prevented it from digging deeper. I slashed down, splitting his cheek open. Blood sprayed my face. The satisfying wet sound of his flesh ripping fueled my bloodlust. Gerwin stumbled back, his good eye looking at me with both pain and shock. With a growl-like cry, I lunged for his face again, but he took a step back. The pin landed in his jugular notch. Before I could move away, Gerwin grabbed me by the upper arm and tossed me across the room.

I crashed against the chest of drawers and thumped to the floor, the wind knocked out of me. Shock snapped me out of my haze. The agony radiating from my broken ribs and the excruciating throbbing of my dislocated jaw came back to the forefront, even more acute than before. Struggling to remain conscious, I glanced at Gerwin who kneeled hunched over on the floor. Blood trickled from the wound, indicating I had missed the aorta. But the wheezing sound coming from him confirmed I punctured his airway.

Leaning on the chest for support, I hauled myself up. Each movement fueled the torment from my injuries. My eyes zeroed in on the remote resting atop the chest. I grabbed it and stumbled around the bondage bench to the bathroom.

Gerwin's angry growl behind me spurred me on.

"I'm going to fucking kill you," Gerwin hissed after me.

Throwing myself inside the bathroom, I slammed the door close behind me. I activated the manual lock. Seconds later, I heard Gerwin ram his massive frame against the door. It shook but showed no sign of caving in. I thanked my lucky stars that the ship was an older model with thick armored steel doors.

He continued banging on the door, no doubt thinking his Braxian strength would suffice – but the door held. I could hear him cursing me. Tuning him out, I took stock of my injuries. I didn't know the bruised and harried creature that looked back at me in the mirror. The gag holding my mouth open exposed the damage to my throat. With my red eyes and bloated face covered in blood, I looked like a creature from the depths of hell.

Although I knew it couldn't stay on, the thought of removing the gag terrified me. The pressure on my jaw was horrendous, but how much worse would it hurt removing it? As I lifted the remote control to shrink the gag, my entire body began to shake so violently I had to stop and get my fears under control. The substantial pressure would cause irreparable damage in the long run – it needed to come off. I repeated this like a mantra to work up my courage. After the third false start, I began resizing it, pausing from time to time when the pain became unbearable.

A sizzling sound soon followed by the scent of burnt metal drew my attention. A dark spot appeared on the door before turning red as a laser torch worked through it. I stared in horror at the slowly expanding cut.

The door is thick. It will take a long time to cut through.

Once more, I felt grateful this was an older ship. I placed a protective hand over my stomach, refusing to believe Gerwin had killed my son. His parents were survivors. He must be as well.

"You hang on too, you hear me? Don't you dare give up."

Forcing my eyes away from the door, I looked back into the mirror. I braced myself and finished resizing the gag in one go. My knees buckled under the searing pain from my face, battered throat, and broken ribs. Panting, I leaned on the sink for support, fighting the need to pass out.

The gag fell in the sink with a clinking sound. The throbbing in my face was excruciating, especially in front of my ears. My chin and lower lip were numb. Drool and blood mingled on my chin. I couldn't close my mouth properly. I had to hold it shut with my hand, except to spit in the sink so I didn't choke. For a moment, I considered trying to set my jaw. Maybe it wouldn't hurt so much then. But I couldn't handle any more pain.

A quick glance at the door showed me Gerwin had already cut through one-quarter of the left side of the door. This was too fast. I watched with morbid fascination as he chipped away at my last defenses.

The sizzling stopped. The muffled sound of Gerwin's voice talking seeped in. I wanted to curl up in a corner and give myself over to terror, but I willed myself forward. Taking support on the wall, I lurched to the door and placed my ear against it. The cold metal surface soothed my throbbing face.

"…you mean they want to board us?" Gerwin's voice asked. "Why the fuck are we still docked?"

Anton! They found us!

Tears of joy, relief, and hope flooded my eyes. I couldn't hear Samuel's response. Brandon came through for me. I both laughed and cried as my hand found its way to my stomach again.

"Daddy's coming, honey. Daddy's coming for us. We're going to be ok," I whispered.

"You tell them we'll kill the bitch if they come anywhere near the ship," Gerwin said, then paused for a while, listening to Samuel's answer. "Listen to me, you stupid human," Gerwin wheezed, "they're not coming onboard for a routine check. They're here for the girl." Silence again. "Fine. Do it your way! But if Myers gets onboard with the security guards, kill the girl."

The implant… Fuck!

Anton would be with them, I'd bet my life on it… literally. The damn implant needed to come out now. Heart pounding, I stumbled back to the sink and rummaged through the cupboard. A toothbrush toppled into the sink. There was nothing of use, not even an antiseptic. A quick look around the bare bathroom confirmed my fears – no blade. I banged my hand against the mirror, but it was glassless. The sizzling sound resumed as Gerwin went back to work on the door.

Bracing against the sink, I realized my fist still clenched around the hairpin. Blood and gore covered the long golden pin. Turning on the hot water, I rinsed it. I eyed its blunted tip with dread. It wasn't sharp enough, but that's all I could use. Trent would detonate the implant without remorse. I remembered the coldness in his eyes. This thing would come out, even if I had to maim myself getting it done. My baby deserved to live. Blocking out the sound of the laser torch, I caressed my tummy.

We've come too far to fail now. Mommy's going to be strong.

Taking as deep a breath as my broken ribs allowed, my fingers explored the location of the implant. I stabbed the hairpin into my flesh. My throat too raw to scream, I squealed in pain. Blinding tears blurred my eyes. The pin's rounded tip forced me to stab with more strength than wisdom dictated. My hands were shaking, and blood made the pin skid off my skin. I prayed I wouldn't hit an artery.

The stench of blood mixed with burnt metal was nauseating. I felt lightheaded. The shallow breaths I took to spare my ribs weren't enough to help me stay conscious. I slid down the wall and sat on the cold, hard floor. Sitting on the toilet was too risky. If I passed out, which I believed would happen soon, the fall might do even more damage. Blindly, I kept tearing the skin at the base of my neck and pressing it between my thumbs to try to push the implant out.

The door glowed red as the cut lengthened. Some heat emanated from it, warming my naked flesh. But it couldn't fight the insidious cold from the floor. I vaguely realized the sizzling from the door was getting drowned by a rushing sound in my ears. It grew louder while a tingling feeling spread throughout my body.

I'm going to faint.

Not now... please not now. I continued plucking at my neck until nothing but darkness remained.

CHAPTER 23
ANTON

As I raced to the hovercar William dispatched for me, I saw Marcus approaching Risqué. He carried a gift box. A pretty, if somewhat slutty-looking, strawberry-blonde walked by his side. Relief and fear warred within me. His presence meant Grace wasn't running away with our baby. But that also meant whoever took her truly had evil intentions.

Maybe this is his alibi, and he'll join her later.

I made a beeline for him.

"Where is Trent taking her? Where are you taking Grace?"

Marcus recoiled, confused. It seemed genuine.

"Trent who?" Marcus asked. "What are you talking about?

"You're going to tell me the man who took Grace to the spaceport isn't yours?" I asked, ignoring the blonde's stare.

Marcus blanched. Whatever suspicions I held evaporated. He turned to look in the general direction of the docking bay.

"Grace…" he whispered. "We need to get her back."

He shoved the gift box at his companion. She gasped, almost dropping it in surprise.

"This way," I said, rushing to the hovercar.

"Marcus!" the blonde called after him.

"Sorry. We'll talk later," he shouted over his shoulder.

We got in the vehicle, and the security guard raced us to the docking bay.

"How? How did he take her?" Marcus asked.

I quickly summarized what happened.

"I've heard of Samuel Trent. He's a shady fuck," Marcus said. "This is a job. But who hired him? No one is trying to get to me through her. Anyone on your end?"

If they knew she was pregnant, my clan might come after her; but not like this. They would demand I terminate the pregnancy first. There was only one person I could think who hated me this much with nothing left to lose.

"Gerwin," I whispered, a sense of foreboding coursing through me. "He's going to kill my son."

Marcus stiffened. "You know."

I glared at him. "I've known for months."

Tapping my com, I hailed Elder Montag and Clan Leader Curbis, both of whom were currently visiting the station. I requested their immediate presence at the docking bay. If my instinct proved right, I would need witnesses to kill the fucker without risk of retaliation.

"She wants to keep it," Marcus said, as soon as I ended the com.

The tension in his voice confirmed my suspicions. They thought I might want to kill the baby. I turned to face him.

"So do I," I said. Marcus sighed, his shoulders sagging. "She was going to leave me, wasn't she?" I asked. When he didn't respond, I repeated, "Wasn't she?"

Marcus held on to the front seat to avoid bumping into me as the driver made a sharp turn.

"She loves you, Anton," Marcus said.

Even though I knew it, that hit me in the gut. I still couldn't believe a woman like her could love me.

"She wanted to tell you tonight," he continued. "Grace is going to be a mother. Her duty is to the baby first. She would have left you if you intended to harm her baby."

That made sense. It hurt me that she doubted I would want our child. Yet, pride and gratitude soared in my heart at her protective motherly instincts.

Our son will truly be loved.

"I love her too," I said.

Marcus smiled.

The hovercar pulled up by the docking bay where William, Brandon and another security guard met us. I tapped my foot as I waited for the Elders to arrive. In the meantime, I got William up to speed on my suspicions. Moments later, Dr. Laura Enders showed up with her medical assistants and a portable medical unit. While grateful for William's foresight, fear at what Gerwin might already be subjecting Grace to gnawed at me. I could only hope he would delay 'playing' with her until they set off so he wouldn't detect her condition.

I was about to give up on the Elders when I saw them turn around a bend. Fenton, Magnar Ravik's closest friend, tagged along. I gave them the most basic greeting then hurried them through the crowd to Samuel's spaceship. William hailed the ship, warning them to prepare to be boarded. I hoped this would delay any harm potentially coming to Grace. William and his guards cleared the path ahead for us.

Naturally, Trent argued with William on our way there. He questioned the request for a 'routine inspection' and complained this would mess up his schedule. Once we reached the ship, a short period of radio silence sent a shiver up my spine. William was about to inform Samuel we would override the ship's access when the hatch opened, and the ramp lowered.

As much as I wanted to rush in and search for Grace, I wasn't trained for these kinds of situations. I trusted William implicitly. He loved Grace like a daughter and would see her safely returned to me. William entered with two guards. Marcus and I followed with the three Braxians behind us.

Trent greeted us outside the airlock. The look of self-righteous outrage on his face quickly faded when he noticed the three Elders and me. A series of emotions crossed his face before settling on a calculating look.

"Let's cut to the chase," Trent said before William could state his demands. "You're not here for any kind of routine inspection."

"Correct," William said. "We want to see the girl, right now. Our scanners reveal the presence of an undisclosed passenger whom we believe is in violation of a banishment order. We want to see them both."

Trent sneered, pure malice shining in his eyes. The small hair at the back of my head stood on end.

"See, I can't do that," he drawled, pulling a small controller from his pocket. "This contract says the bitch goes to my client and I take my client back to a safe location. But I've got to give it to you guys for finding out so quickly. Here's what's going to happen. You're going to get the hell off my ship, release the damn grapplers, and let us off the station, without pursuit."

"Over my dead body," I said.

"And mine," Marcus said, stepping forward.

"Then you two boys might as well keel over now," Trent said. He waved the controller in front of us. William's expression darkened. "See this little trinket here? If you don't get the fuck off my ship in the next thirty seconds, I'm going to activate it. And when I do, that little cunt out back isn't going to be so pretty anymore and not so alive either."

I took a couple of steps forward. Trent raised the remote and waved it again.

"Eh! That's close enough, pal."

"You've said your piece, now let *me* tell you what is going to happen," I said. "You're not getting off this station with her. And you're not going to kill her. If you do, not only will you have no leverage left, but I will destroy you in the slowest, most painful way. Now take me to her and I might show you mercy."

Trent held my stare. Reading my unwavering determination, his face hardened.

"You're not going to leave this ship, are you?" He chuckled sadly. "Mercy, my ass. You Braxians, mutts included, don't know the meaning of that word. You're going to kill me no matter what."

He was right. I would kill him. How painfully depended on the state I found Grace in.

"Give me my woman, Trent."

"Fuck you, Myers, and fuck that cunt. You're never getting her back."

As if in slow-motion, I saw myself lunging at him. Even as I grabbed him, his thumb activated the detonator. I slammed him against the wall. Trent screeched as his spine shattered against the hard surface. Boneless, he collapsed on the floor. The remote flew out of his grasp. I watched it bounce on the metal plating, knowing the implant had gone off. The sound of my blood rushing through my veins deafened me. Marcus cried out Grace's name and scrambled for the remote.

My fingers felt frozen, the numbing cold spreading through my body. Dazed, I ignored William's voice calling out to me. I stumbled towards the back room and slapped my hand on the opening mechanism. I needed to see her with my own eyes. The door slid open. The room reeked of Denax, blood and burnt metal. The BDSM paraphernalia barely registered in my brain. All I saw was Gerwin standing before a bathroom door with a laser torch in hand.

She locked herself inside.

Gerwin's bleeding, ravaged face told me Grace fought for her life. She must have sat there, hoping, praying for me to rescue her. And I failed.

I'm so sorry, my love.

Gerwin turned at the sound of my footsteps. He took a defiant step towards me, while the others gathered behind me.

"I demand a Trial by Combat," Gerwin wheezed, his lip lopsided.

"You get to demand nothing, Gerwin the anCaldes," Elder Montag said. "You violated your banishment."

"Have you not brought enough shame to Clan Caldes?" Elder Curbis said, stepping beside me.

"He's a mutt!" Gerwin roared. "He impregnated the human!"

"I'm going to kill you, Gerwin," I said, my voice strangely flat. "I'm going to kill you for ever touching my woman."

"Touching her, mutt?" Gerwin chuckled. "I didn't just touch her. I fucked her face real good." He gestured holding a head and thrusting his hips forward. "Broke her jaw too. She won't be singing any time soon. Might have also ripped her pussy." Even bleeding and wheezing, he smirked, looking satisfied. "That is, after I beat that abomination you put in her belly to a pulp."

He was taunting me, hoping I would lose it. With Trial by Combat, his fault would be forgiven if he won. Gerwin banked on his superior size and strength. However, the damage Grace inflicted on him could give me an edge.

It was odd that I hadn't attacked him already. But losing Grace killed something inside me.

My will... I have no more will to live.

Then I saw a bloodied clump of hair – Grace's hair – torn from her scalp. It lay on the floor, discarded. Something snapped inside me. My neck tensed, my temperature rose. A red curtain fell before my eyes as a deep, feral growl erupted from my throat.

Gerwin's eyes widened, and I heard the Elders intake a sharp breath behind me.

"He's going into battle rage," Fenton whispered in awe.

"Impossible," Elder Curbis said. "He's a half-breed."

Usually, only the most elite fighters in warrior clans achieved this state of pure battle focus where speed, accuracy, and strength were all multiplied.

It was like having an out-of-body experience as I watched myself lunge at Gerwin. He punched me and missed. While I knew he moved normally, to me, it looked as though he moved through water. I easily ducked under his fist and slammed my elbow into his punctured jugular. His clavicle gave way. Blood exploded out of his mouth as he doubled over, gasping for breath.

More...

I wanted his blood all over my hands and for the room to drown in his screams. Grabbing him by the back of his shirt, I tossed him across the room. He crashed into the chest of drawers, landing badly. His shoulder dislocated with a popping sound. Gerwin groaned, coughing blood.

More...

He scrambled to his feet. The bone of his dislocated shoulder protruded under the skin, while his arm hung at an odd angle. I marched up to him, aching to hear the sound of his bones shattering. Standing behind him, I grabbed a handful of his hair. Gerwin slammed his elbow backward into my face. My teeth rattled in my head and blood filled my mouth. But I didn't feel the pain. Pulling his head back, I smashed his face against the chest of drawers. The sound of flesh meeting metal fueled my rage further. His good arm tried to elbow me again, but I easily avoided the blow. I rammed his face once more against the hard surface.

This is a pureblood? This is what I feared?

Gerwin bellowed in pain and anger and tried to push off the chest. He back-kicked me. It grazed my calf, missing its target. The third time I bashed his face down, bones crunched. Gerwin slumped to his knees.

I'm going to skin you alive and bathe in your blood.

I grabbed a handful of hair in both hands and put my foot between his shoulder blades. An animalistic roar erupted from my throat as I pulled with all my strength. Hair and skin tore off his skull.

"Anton, enough!" a booming voice shouted behind me.

No.

My bloodlust wasn't sated. Gerwin's scalp bled down my arms. I tossed the clumps to the floor and reached for him again. Three pairs of hands restrained me. I hollered and tried to shake them off, but they took me to the floor. Their joint strength and weight forced me into submission.

"Enough, young warrior. Enough," one of the voices said. "You have won your battle and avenged your honor. Calm."

My roars echoed through the room until my eyes landed on Marcus. Standing in front of the bathroom door, he used Gerwin's laser torch to carve it open. The red haze fell from my eyes and my shouts of fury turned into keening. Marcus' lips were moving. As my rage abated, I was able to make sense out of his words.

"We're coming, Gracie. Hang on, you hear me girl? You hang on. We're almost there."

My Grace… My love.

"Let me up," I whispered, my voice broken.

After a slight hesitation, the Elders released me. With heavy steps, I lurched towards the door. As I circled around the bondage bench, I noticed William kneeling next to Marcus. Using his own laser torch, he cut down the lower part while Marcus worked the upper one. I stood behind them, watching the torch carve a slow path to my beloved. The two men's lines met in the middle. William slapped a magnetic handle on the cut-up face before pulling.

Marcus bellowed Grace's name at the sight revealed before us. He fell to his knees, convulsing with body-shaking sobs. William sagged against the doorframe, his face twisted with sorrow. Numb, I walked into the bathroom and removed my shirt. Grace lay naked on the floor, blood pooling by her face. The skin at the base of her neck was shredded, savaged by the implant exploding. The odd angle of her jaw confirmed Gerwin hadn't lied. Angry bruises rose along her ribs.

Kneeling beside Grace, I knew I couldn't go back to the emptiness, the coldness, the hopelessness of my life before her.

Gerwin should have won. I should have died with her… with them. My wife… My son…

I slipped a hand behind her back, lifting her to wrap my shirt around her. She stirred.

"Grace?" I whispered, not daring to hope.

Her eyes fluttered, and she took another gasping breath.

"Oh Grace, I'm here, my love. Keep breathing! It's over, you're safe now." I looked up at William and Marcus who stared at me. "Get the doctor in here now!"

I kissed her forehead before leaning mine against hers, thanking whatever power spared her life.

CHAPTER 24
ANTON

That Grace survived was the greatest blessing I could have ever hoped for. That our son lived was a miracle. Dr. Enders couldn't swear he would make it to term, but she sounded optimistic. The baby's vitals were stable and strong, Gerwin's blow having missed him. But the trauma Grace sustained might be too much for her body to also handle a pregnancy. Two weeks into her recovery, both of them thrived. We agreed to take it one day at a time.

The plastic surgeon managed to repair most of Grace's shredded neck. I could barely see the faint lines where Grace carved out the implant. To think I almost didn't gift her that pin because I loved her hair free-flowing. Grace didn't recall digging out the implant, only trying to do so. We found the implant's mangled casing a foot from her face.

Despite nanotechnology and the revolutionary medical advances, healing Grace's jaw and ribs could take two months. Dr. Enders couldn't get over how Grace's jaw hadn't broken right off. Her eardrums also sustained some damage, as had her throat during Gerwin's assault. Knowing I had hurt her in a similar fashion would haunt me for the rest of my days. Whatever our respective motives, my actions made me a monster same as him. I would devote every hour of my life making it up to her.

Thankfully, the doctor felt fairly confident that Grace would make a near-full recovery. All damage to her scalp had been mended and her hair was growing back. For the time being though, singing was out of the question.

Grace hated how Gerwin derailed her debut show. She felt especially bad for her dancers, Sacha and Carrie. She begged me to intercede with the owner of Sade to give them a shot while she recovered. Marissa didn't need any additional dancers but, as a favor to me, she gave them a small gig.

After she recovered enough, Grace and I talked about our family. With my history, why she doubted I would protect my son baffled me. I knew she waited for me to take her as my mate. But I needed to do this right, and make sure her life and that of our son and future children wouldn't be at risk again. Then I'd marry her in the human tradition.

In my eagerness to get Grace medical attention, Gerwin slipped my mind. It turned out Fenton informed the Magnar of what was transpiring on his way to the docking bay. Ravik ordered him to bring Gerwin to him alive. With Elder Montag and Elder Curbis helping, they hauled him back to Braxia to face the Magnar's justice.

At first, I felt cheated – Gerwin was mine to kill, regardless of the Magnar's agenda. Although he apologized for the ruthlessness of his actions, Ravik didn't reconsider his position. According to him, the grievous injuries Grace and I inflicted upon Gerwin were sufficient personal vindication. The public trial was too important for the half-breed cause for him to pass up. In the end, I didn't really give a shit as long as Gerwin died.

The clans were torn by the Magnar's interference on my behalf. Yes, Gerwin violated banishment, but I remained a mutt. However, two respected Elders and the Magnar's own confidante witnessing me enter battle rage caused the real uproar. Few warriors on Braxia achieved battle rage. Those who did, called Berserkers, were revered by their clans. It was a rare genetic trait passed on within the main warrior clans. On the field of battle, once a Berserker entered battle rage, he could enhance the strength, speed, and endurance of his clan mates, turning them into Furies.

The trial proved the potential worth of a half-breed. It dealt a devastating blow against Clan Caldes. As I refused to leave Grace's side to attend the trial on Braxia, my father stood in my stead. When the guilty verdict was announced, as per custom, the sentence could either be carried out by the offended clan or by the clan of the condemned, in a gesture of peace.

Gerwin had received financial assistance, likely from someone within his former clan. Those credits allowed him to hire Samuel Trent. Fearing I would permanently sever all business deals with them, Clan Leader Caldes begged for the privilege of carrying out the sentence on his son, Gerwin. My father declined. He would carry out the sentence personally and all of Clan Caldes was to bear witness.

Three days later, Gerwin the anCaldes, firstborn son of Clan Leader Raylor Caldes, was flayed alive by my father. He was then tied to a pole at the entrance of the clan's compound to die a slow death. He would hang there for thirty days as a warning to respect the banishment laws. At the end of the proceedings, the Magnar publicly declared me Friend of the Empire.

While unable to visit Grace himself, Magnar Ravik sent his personal physician to Dr. Enders. He promised to come as soon as he could.

Over the past couple of weeks, we spent an outrageous amount of time in bed, talking and watching sappy romantic movies. I was developing some kind of immunity to their overly sweet gushiness as I no longer ached with the need to airlock myself whenever watching them.

We cuddled a lot during that time with the occasional kiss. Greater intimacy wasn't an option. Knowing the extent of my sexual drive and appetite, Grace worried. She didn't bring it up, but I felt her tense every time we went for a short stroll and women passed by. Eventually, she offered to suck me off.

That angered me.

Yes, like all Braxians I was constantly horny, but that didn't make me a sex-starved rutting beast. As much as I loved her lips around my cock, her jaw was in no condition for that kind of action. Moreover, I believed she was in denial of the extent of the psychological trauma Gerwin inflicted upon her during his assault. Once her body fully healed, I expected it would take more time before we became intimate again. Even though I ached for her, I would wait however long she needed. I loved her. No other woman even felt attractive to me anymore.

The doctor said we could have sex again, as long as we were careful. It was my choice not to. First, I didn't trust myself to remain gentle in the throes of passion. Second, I knew Grace wouldn't tell me if it hurt her. Third, I wanted her to know that it wasn't sex that made me want a lifetime with her. And when the pressure got too much, well, I had two very capable hands.

As sappy movie five-hundred-and-so-damn-many-I-lost-count ended, I couldn't withhold a deep sigh. Grace rubbed a soothing hand along my back.

"Worried about your father?" she asked.

I nodded, frowning.

Tonight, my father and our clan Elder Baras were coming to see me here, at the penthouse. It had been four years since my father last visited the Hive. It coincided with the repayment of the loan. I wasn't sure what to expect. They had an announcement to make, and I believed it had to do with Grace's pregnancy. I had an announcement of my own to make. No matter how well I prepared for it, fear gnawed at me.

"Is he…?"

"No, Grace, he won't ask me to kill my son," I said, knowing that thought kept her up at night. "He wouldn't demand from me what others couldn't force him to do. But I don't know what the council wants and that scares me. My father and Elder Baras wouldn't make the long trip here to speak to me unless it was something very important."

Grace nodded, then leaned forward to kiss my lips. It was gentle, soft, and comforting.

"Do you think he'll want to see me?"

"Yes. I'm pretty sure he will."

She shivered and I rubbed my hand reassuringly along her back.

"Will he ask… anything of me?" she asked, her tone hesitant.

I knew where this headed. "He may ask to examine you. If he does, I would like you to allow him." As expected, Grace stiffened at those words. "Do not worry, love. It will not be sexual. You only have to stand in front of him while he looks at you. If he touches you at all, it might be your stomach. However, I suspect he will only inhale your scent, to confirm you are indeed with child and that it belongs to his bloodline."

She exhaled a shuddering breath, but said, "Okay."

When Clan Leader Krygor Aldriss, walked into the penthouse, the room seemed to shrink to half its size. I instinctively lowered my head and dropped my shoulders, feeling like an eight-year-old boy again. My father was an impressive specimen of strength, power and lethal poise. He was only slightly smaller than the Magnar. His facial features, so like mine, were more pronounced. The thickness of his prominent brow gave his fearsome face a more intimidating edge. His pitch-black eyes rested on me as I bowed my head in respect.

"Clan Leader Aldriss, Elder Baras, welcome to my home."

"Anton," my father said, with a slight nod.

Elder Baras nodded and I waved them into the living area. My father strolled in with his usual measured gait and sat down on the three-seat couch. I couldn't help the sense of pride every time I laid eyes upon my sire. He embodied everything I always aspired to be: strong, determined, and invincible. At fifty-one, he looked more like my older brother than my father. Baras took a seat next to him. The elder councilman was a few years older than my father, and one of the more moderate in the clan. He never approved of my father letting me live and made no secret of it. However, unlike many others, he never mistreated me. His clan leader spoke and he followed.

I placed three glasses on the coffee table in front of them and filled them with the finest Braxian brandy. We saluted each other and drank. My father refilled our glasses and I sat across from them.

Formalities out of the way, in a show of respect for his seniority, I waited for my father to initiate the conversation. Originally, I requested to talk to him, but he informed me that the clan had an announcement to make. As they would be coming to the Hive to discuss it, I could say my piece then. I wondered if he suspected what it was.

"Recent events have caused quite the stir on Braxia," my father said, his expression unreadable.

"I merely responded to an attack against me and mine."

"I wasn't chastising you," he deadpanned.

My face heated. Damn if he couldn't systematically make me feel like a petulant boy.

"You took the proper actions and Gerwin got the retribution he deserved."

I nodded. "Thank you, Clan Leader, for standing in my stead and carrying out the sentence on my behalf."

"Do not thank me, Anton. The pleasure was all mine."

His feral grin made me shudder. Even Elder Baras gave him an uneasy look. From all accounts, my father took a sadistic pleasure at skinning Gerwin alive. I wanted to believe his viciousness had been revenge for the years I suffered on Braxia, but I would never know.

"You are always full of surprises, aren't you?" my father asked. "Friend of the Empire? I didn't realize you were so well acquainted with the Magnar."

My face heated again, this time with pleasure.

"Magnar Ravik and I have indeed become friends."

"So, the rumors that he comes to visit you are true?" Elder Baras asked, incredulous.

I couldn't resist the urge to gloat. "The Magnar shares my table at least once every month."

Baras' eyes widened before sliding over to my father, spying his reaction.

My father leaned back on the couch. The subtle smile on his lips was hard to define, but the pride in his eyes was undeniable. My chest constricted at the unspoken approval.

"And now, like both my pureblood sons, you, my firstborn, are a proven Berserker, duly blooded before witnesses, and unequivocally victorious."

My lips parted in shock. Baras frowned but didn't say a word. I had two younger half-brothers; Dheran and Gorav. As the firstborn, I should have become my father's heir. But mutts didn't qualify. Therefore, as firstborn pureblood, Dheran would become his heir. It was the first time, as far as I could recall, that my father referred to my brothers and myself on an equal footing.

"Between this, your elevated status with the Magnar, and your lifelong accomplishments that have benefitted the clan as a whole," my father said, gesturing at the luxurious interior of the penthouse, "the Council of Elders has convened to discuss your status within our clan."

My brain froze. This couldn't be headed where I was thinking. I examined my father's face. The earlier pride faded, replaced by a strange and intense look I had never seen before. He seemed... tense.

"It was the unanimous council's conclusion that, in spite of being a half-breed, you will be granted full clansman status. From this day forth, you will be known as Anton Aldriss."

My breath caught in my throat. It was like two tons of unrefined duralium dropped on my chest. I shot out of my seat and paced back and forth, my thoughts firing in a million different directions.

I paused and looked, bewildered, at my father's impassive face.

Anton Aldriss. I could finally bear my father's name.

All my life, I had wanted nothing more than to be fully acknowledged and accepted. There was no greater honor than to bear the name of my sire.

"Full status and your name?" I whispered, disbelieving.

"Yes, my son," my father repeated.

I ran a nervous hand through my hair.

After all these years, why now?

"Although," Baras added cautiously, "clan leadership would still fall to Dheran who has been groomed since birth for the role."

I nodded absently. "Of course."

The last thing I wanted was to lead the damn clan. Anyway, I would get challenged the minute I rose to power. Berserker or not, I couldn't defeat purebloods in single combat.

I refilled my glass and downed it in one go, the burn going down helping me to gather my thoughts. My father's strange detachment confused me. After all the challenges, the clan accepting me, at last, should be a victory for him. Did he not want me bearing his name?

"You do not want me to be called Aldriss, do you?" I asked, trying to hide the hurt in my voice.

My father's eyes narrowed, a strange emotion flickering through them. "First, if I didn't want you bearing my name, you wouldn't have lived long enough to be able to."

Good point.

"Second, I am the leader of this clan. The council is there to advise me, not command me. You wouldn't get this offer if I didn't agree."

I took back my seat, my hands clasped on my lap.

"For as long as I can remember, I've never wanted anything more than to be a full member of this clan, to be accepted as your son, and have the great honor of bearing your name."

My father's face remained unreadable while Baras' took on the bored expression of someone about to sit through a speech they didn't particularly care to listen to.

"There are no words to express the joy this offer brings me. However, with the utmost respect, I must decline."

"What?" Baras hissed, a look of outrage on his face. "You dare?"

"Silence," my father said to Baras, though he continued staring at me. A strange glimmer lit his dark eyes. "So, Anton, you refuse full clanship, and you refuse my name?"

I closed my eyes and exhaled a shuddering breath before looking back at my father.

"I want to bear your name, Clan Leader. I honor you above all others. But I am and will always remain a half-breed."

My father nodded, whether in acknowledgment of my honoring him or to my being a half-breed, only he knew.

"I have a mate now, and she's bearing me a son. The Fates willing, she will bear me many more offspring. I will *not* renounce them, for anything, or anyone."

My father's eyes narrowed. "The Council already agreed that allowances would be made for your son."

I snorted. "What allowances? That you clan him without full privileges unless he also achieves battle rage? That the clan won't harm him but will turn a blind eye whenever every other clan hunts him for sport?"

Baras had the decency to look embarrassed, for he had been among those who hadn't intervened on my behalf.

"What of my daughters? Are they to become sex slaves for the enjoyment of the clansmen? And my mate? I will not have Braxians come into my home and expect Grace to crawl before them like some common whore."

"It is our way," Baras growled.

"It is *your* way," I bit back. "*I* am not Braxian. And I will *not* have my family subjected to your barbaric Braxian laws."

Baras gasped and turned to my father. My father remained impassive, the same strange glimmer flickering in his eyes.

"What are you saying, Anton?" he asked.

I took in a deep breath. "What I am saying is that I, Anton Myers, firstborn son of Krygor Aldriss, solemnly declare to you, Clan Leader Aldriss, and as witnessed by Clan Elder Baras, that I officially renounce my clan, effective immediately."

The pounding of my heart was deafening. My father refilled his glass. The sound of the liquid pouring down disturbed the eerie silence. Leaning back in his chair, my father swirled the amber liquid in his glass. He didn't drink… yet.

"And so, Anton Myers, firstborn son of Krygor Aldriss, it will have taken you twenty-eight years to complete Ghabrak. It was about time."

What?

"Clan Leader!" Baras said, turning to my father.

"Silence, Baras."

"But you can't…"

"I said silence!" my father shouted. "Do you dare pretend to tell me what I can or cannot do with my own blood?" His eyes leveled Baras with a menacing glare. "Anton has renounced the clan. Your duty is done. Now remove yourself, and leave me with my son."

Shaken, Elder Baras bowed and swiftly entered the lift. I looked at my father, bewildered.

Ghabrak? I achieved Ghabrak?

This rite of passage allowed young Braxians to become men. Most completed it between the ages of sixteen and twenty-one. It was the sire who set the conditions the son must meet to prove himself worthy to bear his father's name. Those conditions normally revolved around the vocation of the clan. Warrior clans would have combat achievements, while farmer clans focused on agricultural, production, or transformation knowledge. However, the father didn't communicate the conditions to the child. Attaining it without guidance was proof you had reached the necessary maturity to earn manhood. Half-breeds didn't receive Ghabrak.

"You wanted me to leave the clan," I whispered, hurt.

"Yes," my father said before downing his drink, "but merely as a consequence of completing Ghabrak." I frowned in confusion, making him chuckle. "I wanted you to stop being a victim, Anton. Braxia made you a victim. You defied every odd, survived the impossible, rose far beyond anything I could have ever dreamt for you. And still, you bowed to Braxian law while it whipped you like a dog."

I felt gutted. Braxia indeed made me a victim, and I allowed it.

"I was trying to make you proud," I said.

"Whatever made you think I wasn't already?"

He put the glass down.

"I was always proud of you, Anton. Do you think I would have faced so many challenges for allowing you to live if I didn't want you? If I wasn't proud of you? You are my firstborn and my greatest achievement. Until your woman walked back into your life, I despaired you would die a slave to Braxia."

I drowned in a maelstrom of emotions. My eyes burned and my

vision blurred. I struggled to swallow down my tears. A man didn't cry. I wouldn't shame myself this way before my father.

"But on Jeruna, you were so angry…"

"I was beyond angry," my father grounded out. "I was livid. But it was never with you. That should have been your moment of glory. You achieved at such a young age what no other Braxian achieved before. And they robbed you of it."

So many misunderstandings.

I had been convinced my father wanted to banish me, like every other clansman. That the only reason he hadn't was because of my Hive project.

"I never doubted you would succeed, Anton. You always succeed."

"Thank you, Clan Leader. I—"

"Father," he interrupted. "You can call me Father."

Once more, I blinked away the tears before they emerged. "Thank you, Father."

He smiled. I couldn't remember the last time he smiled at me. I cleared my throat.

"I want you to know that although I've renounced the clan, all business agreements with Clan Aldriss remain in effect. I see no reason to tamper with our mutually beneficial arrangements."

Though he tried to hide it, I saw the flicker of relief in my father's eyes. Most of their revenues were tied to their involvement in my ventures.

"However," I said, "I do have a parting gift for you." My father raised a surprised eyebrow. "I don't know what the future of my relationship with the clan will be. Should we ever have a fallout, I don't want you beholden to me."

"You owe me nothing. What I did was a father's duty."

"Say that to all the half-breeds whose brains their fathers bashed onto a wall."

My father nodded in concession.

I handed him a data key containing all the information about the business I set up for him and quickly explained what it entailed. My father owned vast agricultural lands unsuitable for growing local produce. However, they were perfect to grow neflium, the main food source of the Berulians, a primitive people on Sargaros. They signed an exclusive trade agreement with my father as their sole supplier in exchange for rare minerals and gems that happened to be abundant on their planet. In a couple of years, my father's wealth would be substantial.

"Thank you, son." The humble expression on his face touched me far deeper than any words he could have said. "The hour draws late. I would meet your mate before I depart."

"Of course," I said, and commed Grace to join us.

She looked breathtaking in a black and amber sarong dress that made her eyes sparkle. I rose to my feet as she entered. Back straight, chin up, she looked regal walking up to me. She slipped her small hand into mine and nodded at my father.

"So there you are, my Anton's Grace," he said.

"Hello, Mr. Aldriss."

My father extended a beckoning hand towards her. "Come, child. Let me have a look at you."

She gave me a worried glance before complying. Her steps hesitant, she approached my father still sitting on the couch. He quietly examined her, never touching her.

"You are very beautiful," my father said.

"Thank you, sir."

"May I?" he asked, gesturing towards her stomach.

Her fingers gripped the hem of her dress. She nodded and gave me another tense look. Without touching her, my father leaned forward, closed his eyes and inhaled. Straightening, he stood up, forcing her to take a couple of steps back. He looked at me and gave me an odd smile.

"Your son smells just like you did. The blood is strong within him. He will be as fierce as you are."

Grace smiled, putting a protective hand over her belly. She came back to stand next to me and pressed herself against my side.

"Do you love my son, Grace?"

"Yes, sir," she said. "With all my heart."

Her soft hair tickled my lips as I kissed the top of her head. My arm wrapped around her as she leaned deeper into me. My father nodded, a pleased expression on his face.

"I can see now why you would renounce your clan for her."

Grace jerked her head back, a stunned look on her face. "Anton?" she whispered.

"As long as I was clanned, I couldn't marry you. So I renounced."

She squealed with joy and launched herself at me. Pearls of tears trickled down her cheeks as a blinding smile brightened her face. Grace kissed me, her fingers digging into my back. My father's presence should have embarrassed me, but it didn't. I allowed myself to revel in her affection.

However, his amused chuckle eventually brought us back to order.

"I would have you call me father, and I would call you daughter, if you consent."

I don't know which of us felt the most shocked. Her lips quivering, Grace nodded her agreement. Sweeping emotions no doubt numbed her ability to speak. She craved belonging, especially to a family. Her parents' abandonment still pained her.

"As for you Anton, your name in the Hall of Records was always Anton Aldriss." My father smiled. How many more bombs would he drop on me? "It would please me if you would consider using it."

My stomach fluttered at the thought. I frowned.

"But, the rules say you can't," I said, fearing to hope.

"The rules also said I shouldn't have let you live."

"But... I have renounced. That would make me Anton the anAldriss."

"That's a Braxian rule. You're not Braxian," he said with a smirk.

I laughed. This rebellious side of my father had never been so plainly displayed before. It was... nice. I should have realized sooner that my renouncing freed him of the rules that shackled both of us.

"Think about it," he said, walking towards the lobby. "I must take my leave." He called the lift and faced me while waiting for it to arrive. "Your brothers wish to get to know you. It would please me if you did."

Dheran had been six years old when I left Braxia. He would be twenty-one now. Gorav would be eighteen. I always dreamt of a relationship with them but never imagined it possible.

"It would please me as well, Father."

He smiled and the lift chimed.

Nodding to each of us in turn, he said, "Son. Daughter," then entered the lift. Its doors closed before him as we called out our farewell.

EPILOGUE
GRACE

Sitting in the amazing Atrium Anton built for our children, one would think we were in a luxurious Dantorian garden. Large trees, soft grass, beautiful waterfalls, holographic sky and even real birds nesting in the trees gave the illusion that we were on a planet's surface instead of out in space. Since our wedding, Anton realized Venus Hive didn't cater to the families that worked here. Although other patrons weren't barred access, the entirety of the Atrium was to remain family friendly. This meant, no sex or lewd behavior.

Sitting at a picnic table, I pored over the rehearsal schedules for my next show, while keeping a distracted eye on the children. Naya, our youngest, and Cullen, our second-born, played some kind of ball game with Marcus. Gavin, our firstborn, sat beside me, drawing.

Though my debut show had been delayed by three months, it eventually occurred and had been a resounding success. I regularly performed sold out shows. Carrie hadn't worked out. I guess a one-time 'beware of the in-crowd' speech wasn't enough to get a young, foolish girl back on the right track. However, Sacha and I became friends, and she held a permanent spot on my show. She was a talented, hard-working dancer. It was my first time having a true female friend, or any kind of friend to be honest – excluding Marcus. She and Brandon also hit it off and made a very cute couple.

As part of his reward for saving my life, Brandon was offered a promotion, which he declined. He didn't want a desk job. Instead, Anton gave him a fancy three-bedroom suite in the residential sector, fully paid and furnished, plus a large performance bonus. Brandon had been saving every credit to pay passage for his mother and sister who were stranded in a poor human colony on some backwater planet. Needless to say, Anton booked them first class cabins on a luxury cruiser.

Marcus now did freelance work for Anton. He was still too much of a free spirit to be bogged down with an official job. It felt too 'settled down' for him. He mainly scouted new talents for which he received finder's fee. He also handled some contract negotiations for Anton who was delegating more and more of his duties to have more time with our family. While Marcus continued some of his wheeling and dealing, he no longer involved himself in shady transactions.

Sheila left Venus Hive a few months after I gave birth to Gavin. She no longer seemed able to book a contract that didn't require some kind of horizontal performance as well. But even those eventually dried up. Apparently, she found a modicum of popularity on Lilith Hive. It was a step back. However, it beat landing on a ghetto-like pleasure barge such as Callan Fall.

I heard Anton's approach before he stepped into my field of view.

"Working again," Anton smiled, lessening the scolding that was nonetheless present in his tone.

"Maybe?" I said, scrunching my face, feeling guilty.

It became somewhat of a running joke between us. When we first met, Anton's life revolved around work. Now, our family was the center of his universe. He was a wonderful father and made sure our children knew how much he loved them.

Naya had him wrapped around her pinky. It was time we gave her a sister so she didn't become an insufferable spoiled brat. Anton, her uncles Dheran, Gorav and Marcus, even her Grappa Krygor doted on her. She also had William, Romero, and Brandon jumping through hoops. Well, ok, who was I kidding? I was a sucker for her too.

Despite only being one-quarter Braxian, my children's heritage shone through their prominent foreheads and flat, broad noses. Nevertheless, my own genetic contribution was quite visible with their features being softer, less pronounced than Anton's. I didn't know how the rest of the world saw my children, but I didn't care. They were the most beautiful things in the world to their father and me. I couldn't stop feasting my eyes on their little faces, on the happiness in their expressions, and their boisterous laughter.

Anton sat on the other side of Gavin. He rustled our son's hair, as black as his.

"Who's that you're drawing, little man?" Anton asked.

"That's Zhara," Gavin said, his voice strangely wistful.

"Who is Zhara?" I asked, confused by the strange looking girl in the drawing.

She had gray skin and large light yellow eyes. Chevron-shaped ridges ran up her forehead, and cheetah-like spots covered her shoulders.

"Her real name is Zharina," Gavin said, looking at me with amber eyes identical to mine. "She lives very far away. And I'm going to marry her."

"Marry her?" Anton asked, amused. "You're not even five yet. That's a little young to get married, don't you think?"

"I'm not going to marry her now, silly Papa," Gavin said, with the most adorable frown and pout. "Zhara is still a baby anyway; she just turned three. She says I will become a great warrior like Grappa, and we will meet for real during a rescue mission. And then we'll get married."

"How do you meet her now?" I asked.

"In my dreams."

He said it so matter-of-fact I had to repress the urge to smile. Gavin had an incredibly creative mind. I would have to read up on how to handle my child's imaginary friend.

"Gaveeee!" Naya's little voice shouted. "Come play, Gavee!"

"Ok," Gavin shouted back, before hopping off the bench.

Anton pulled me closer to him. I rested my back against his broad chest and he wrapped his arm around me.

"That daughter of yours is so entitled," I said.

I felt his rumbling laughter against my back. "She certainly is." Anton's voice was filled with pride.

"We need to give her a little sister soon to keep her in check."

"Baby-making?" Anton asked, his voice deepening. "Sign me up. When and where?"

"The brat-pack in good hands," I said seductively. "Now seems like a good time."

"Lead the way Mrs. Aldriss."

THE END

THE ANT AND THE GRASSHOPPER*

Jean de La Fontaine

A grasshopper gay
Sang the summer away,
And found herself poor
By the winter's first roar.
Of meat or of bread,
Not a morsel she had!
So a begging she went,
To her neighbour the ant,
For the loan of some wheat,
Which would serve her to eat,
Till the season came round.
"I will pay you," she saith,
"On an animal's faith,
Double weight in the pound
Ere the harvest be bound."
The ant is a friend
(And here she might mend)
Little given to lend.
"How spent you the summer?"
Quoth she, looking shame
At the borrowing dame.
"Night and day to each comer
I sang, if you please."
"You sang! I'm at ease;
For 'tis plain at a glance,
Now, ma'am, you must dance."

* This classic fable by Jean de Lafontaine was the inspiration behind
Anton's Grace.

ALSO BY REGINE ABEL

THE VEREDIAN CHRONICLES
Escaping Fate
Blind Fate
Raising Amalia
Twist of Fate
Hands of Fate
Defying Fate

BRAXIANS
Anton's Grace
Ravik's Mercy
Krygor's Hope

XIAN WARRIORS
Doom
Legion
Raven
Bane
Chaos
Varnog
Reaper
Wrath
Xenon
Nevrik
Rogue

PRIME MATING AGENCY
I Married A Lizardman
I Married A Naga
I Married A Birdman
I Married A Minotaur
I Married Wonjin

I Married A Merman
I Married A Dragon
I Married A Beast
I Married A Dryad

THE MIST
The Mistwalker
The Nightmare

DARK TALES
Bluebeard's Curse
The Hunchback

BLOOD MAIDENS OF KARTHIA
Claiming Thalia

VALOS OF SONHADRA
Unfrozen
Iced

EMPATHS OF LYRIA
An Alien For Christmas

THE SHADOW REALMS
Dark Swan

OTHER
True As Steel
Alien Awakening
Heart of Stone

ABOUT REGINE

USA Today bestselling author Regine Abel is a fantasy, paranormal and sci-fi junkie. Anything with a bit of magic, a touch of the unusual, and a lot of romance will have her jumping for joy. Hot alien warriors meeting no-nonsense, kick-ass heroines give her warm fuzzies.

Before devoting herself as a full-time writer, Regine had surrendered to the other passion in her life: video games! As a professional Game Designer and Creative Director, her previous career had led her from her home in Canada to the US and various countries in Europe and Asia.

Facebook
https://www.facebook.com/regine.abel.author/

Website
https://regineabel.com

Regine's Rebels Reader Group
https://www.facebook.com/groups/ReginesRebels/

Newsletter

http://smarturl.it/RA_Newsletter

Goodreads

http://smarturl.it/RA_Goodreads

Bookbub

https://www.bookbub.com/profile/regine-abel

Amazon

http://smarturl.it/AuthorAMS